A SECRET GIFT

Tonya Penrose

www.BOROUGHSPUBLISHINGGROUP.com

A SECRET GIFT
Copyright © 2020 Tonya Penrose

ISBN: 978-1-951055-97-4

To my writing chairs for their continued support

ACKNOWLEDGMENTS

I owe an enormous debt of gratitude to the talented and award-winning author and playwright, Phillip DePoy. You've guided my writing journey and declared the stories worthy of being bound. If not for you…

Thank you gifted Lindsay for always pointing my creative compass toward True North. To Tom who listens to me read humor scenes again and again, and always finds a chuckle. Don't lose that laughter meter.

For my two Musketeer writing friends who pushed and prodded. It worked. Maybe now you'll let me choose the coffee house for meetings? You have lousy taste.

Big thanks to Boroughs Publishing Group for allowing me to break a few rules along the way.

A SECRET GIFT

Chapter 1

Halley was known for her punctuality. Ten o'clock sharp found her seated in an attorney's office. An appointment that, as of a half hour ago, she'd no idea about. The mysterious early morning phone call from Sam Langdale requesting her immediate presence had been a surprise. It'd also piqued her interest.

"I have a *what?*" Halley's expression no doubt reflected the shock she felt at she'd heard. Sitting behind his desk, the portly attorney regarded her with sympathy, his kind manner doing nothing to alleviate her confusion.

He offered a kind smile. "You have a benefactor. And might I say, an extremely kind and generous one." Mr. Langdale leaned forward, glancing at the open file resting on his imposing antique mahogany desk. The trappings Halley saw in the office said: successful law practice. "A benefactor offering a most unusual gift. Let me endeavor to assuage any fears. This endowment is legal and without question serious and most considerable. You have my word on this, Ms. Bowen." Sam Langdale rubbed his chin. "Yes, I'd say you're indeed a most fortunate woman."

Halley stared off into space, willing her mind to absorb what he'd said. She took a deep breath. "Okay, for the moment, I'm going to humor both of us and ask for more details. I'm keeping my skepticism, but I'll accept your word on the legitimacy of this gift." She felt as if the leather wingback chair embraced her growing anxiety. She smoothed the token corporate black pencil skirt and tilted her chin toward the man behind the desk. "Please proceed, Mr. Langdale."

"Well, to put this succinctly, you have a benefactor that wishes to help you experience your ideal life. I think you call this flight of fancy your 'dream life.' Quite the uncustomary gift, I must say." Langdale cleared his throat.

"Excuse me, but how does this benefactor know anything about what I refer to as my 'dream life'?" Halley had never felt more baffled yet intrigued.

"Please allow me to continue, and I will endeavor to answer what questions I can afterward." Langdale didn't pause for Halley to agree. "Your benefactor overheard your wish and wants to offer you a chance to experience what the benefactor refers to as your joy and heart's desire, but of course, with a few straightforward stipulations."

Halley found a modicum of composure, swallowed an oath, and leaned back into the chair's protection. "Ah, the stipulations. Still, I'm fascinated. Go on." She pulled a pen and a small notebook from her leather satchel.

Reading from the file, Langdale began, "As I understand this aspiration, you long to live in a Port Royal bayfront cottage, where you will pen an impassioned romance novel. Connect with your spirit. Leave the stress of the corporate world which you've grown weary with and exit our Queen City of Charlotte's lifestyle to live happily ever after a few hours away." Langdale's face split into a grin as he pushed tortoise-framed glasses atop his head. "I think those are the high points. I'm presuming this will be your first attempt at authoring a book?"

Halley was confused. Port Royal, her absolute dream place? Who would know about that? She found a few words to gather a response. "Yes, it would be my first book, but I wrote for our local town newspaper to help pay for college, and I have this plot idea for a romance—never mind. What else?"

Langdale nodded, his expression mirroring amusement. "Yes, well, your benefactor believes you are worthy of developing this prospect, but, as I said, with some stipulations."

"Okay, give me a second here." Halley released a breath. She stood and paced across the room, turning her attention back to Langdale. Yep, he was real, no hallucination. Her mind offered no logical explanations. Why her? The tooth fairy never came to see her, and Santa lacked dependability when she was a child. Her spirit trumped her thoughts, prodding her to trust this benefactor indeed existed, and right now, she craved to hear more about this surreal gift. "Excuse me, but could I have some water?"

Langdale smiled. "Of course." He poured a glass of water from the nearby carafe. "Please, won't you return to the chair? Allow me to continue detailing this for you. Forgive my haste, but I must be in court soon, and then I'm on a flight to London."

Halley settled and nodded as disbelief washed over her once more. A benefactor. Simply nuts. She picked up her notebook and turned to a blank page. Pen in hand, Halley waited.

"The stipulations are as follows: You will move to Port Royal within a month and locate a suitable cottage to call home. There you will devote yourself to the writing life. This next requirement might give you pause." Langdale coughed, which added to the growing flush of his cheeks. "Ms. Bowen, you are to find, and more, experience a grand passion with a man of your choosing to enhance your writing knowledge of enduring love firsthand."

"What? You can't be serious. *Me* find a guy and have some grand passion? Honestly, I can't even fathom—"

"Please, I'd like to finish," Langdale said, holding up his hand. He flipped to the next page, continuing. "You have one year to satisfy these conditions. Further, you need to understand and agree that an evaluation of your progress and success will be done by your benefactor and myself at regular intervals in that stated year. Ms. Bowen, are you following me?"

Halley massaged her temples, daring a migraine to intrude on this lunacy. "Yes, I suppose so, but this great romance part—"

Langdale eyed her warily.

Halley moved the empty glass his way. "I'm going to need a refill before you share more, and maybe an aspirin to chase it."

The attorney tilted the carafe, emptying the contents into Halley's glass while opening his desk drawer. He placed the aspirin bottle next to the glass. "Understandable reaction." He waited for her to take the aspirin and chase it down with water. "Forgive me, but you and I need to wrap this up."

"Yes, I know. It's so much to try and absorb. Please go on." Halley twirled the pen nervously.

Langdale's voice shifted into a lawyer's tone. "A determined amount of money shall be deposited in your name at Port Royal's bank to cover the purchasing of a cottage. Additionally, you'll be provided a stipend to cover living expenses, but you'll need to take a part-time job for incidentals. Your benefactor believes that employment offers you the occasion to know the seaside town while still giving ample time for writing and socializing. If you successfully meet the terms of the agreement at the end of said year, your benefactor will deed you the cottage and a generous sum stated in the agreement I have before me. Understand from that day forward, you are free to live life as you see fit, but with no further financial assistance." Sam glanced at Halley, one eyebrow raised in question.

"I'm with you." Halley waited in anxious anticipation for the "but."

"On the other hand, if you fail to meet the terms of this agreement, you will be left to your own devices. You must vacate the cottage. However, no repayment of any monies given to you is required. Of course, the cottage won't get deeded to you, nor will you receive the last monetary disbursement. Naturally, you retain your personal belongings, and any work done on your novel goes with you. The document is straightforward without complexities. I'd like to ask now if this most substantial gift proposal is to your liking, Ms. Bowen?" Langdale looked at his diamond-encrusted Swiss watch.

"Seriously? Do you think I have that answer after what I've heard? Mr. Langdale, I only have questions. Scads of them. Starting with this absurd 'grand passion' part. Might you elaborate?" Halley knew her past love life could be described as dismal, and that was her being kind to herself. Why in Hades would she want to bother her 'dream life' with some cliché romance? And if honest, her dating life never reached the level deemed romantic. It was more like lukewarm affection—once. She unclenched her teeth, accepting that truth before every tooth gave way. "Look, Mr. Langdale, love and marriage aren't in my plans."

Langdale covered a grin with his hand before replying. "I must confess that I'm no expert on romance and grand passion, but I trust you will come to understand."

Halley sat thoughtfully. Her changing expressions mirrored her bewilderment. "Let me see if I've grasped this proposition. I have an opportunity to live my ideal life in a setting that I adore. I'm to find a cottage on the bay that speaks to me, priced within reason, of course, write my great romance novel, and receive an allowance to help with necessary living expenses. Oh, I'm to secure a part-time job to help offset other non-essential costs."

"And to allow you to meet people and become a part of the town's day-to-day doings," Langdale confirmed.

"Yes, yes, the doings. And then we're back to the part where I'm to find a man that I fancy so that I gain the firsthand experience with being in love?" Halley's exasperation grew with her thoughts. "Mr. Langdale, my head is overwhelmed by what you've offered, and I feel enormous gratitude to this benefactor. Sincere gratitude. Truly. The generosity of this person is extraordinary, and I suspect—she?"

"You are correct. I'm free to say your benefactor is indeed a woman, a most refined woman of means," Langdale responded. "I admit feeling quite fond of her, and besides, she's a cherished longtime client of our firm. You need to harbor no concerns about her character or sincerity."

"So, I can't help being curious about how she knows me, and there's no way I can cajole you into telling—?"

Langdale shook his head. "Sorry. Confidentiality."

Halley released a whoosh of air. "Okay, I need some time to ponder this gift and its many entangled strings." She thought about leaving a job that never fed her spirit but only her bank account. Could she afford to make this life-altering shift? She didn't have a husband or kids. This chance might never come her way again. Imagining living in Port Royal brought an immediate release of the work stress that had stalked her daily for the last few years. Happiness found her spirit. Halley looked across the desk at Langdale, her face glowing. "May I give you my answer, say, in a week?"

Langdale's look gentled on Halley. "I'm sorry, but you must state your decision before leaving this office. Your benefactor doesn't want time to allow your mind to override your heart. She believes in you and your dream, and sincerely hopes you will allow her to open this door for you." Langdale paused. "Look, I'm going to step out for a few moments and attend to some other matters. Please look over the simple-worded agreement. You'll see the benefactor has no desire to interfere in the way you conduct your life. When I return, I expect your answer." Langdale stood, but his expression remained sympathetic.

Halley managed a nod while accepting the papers. "Wait, Mr. Langdale. Can you maybe spare me thirty minutes? Before I can make this huge life-altering decision, I need to make two phone calls. I can't give my answer until I speak with my sister and employer. I trust their responses will provide the clarity and practicality I need to move forward one way or another."

"Of course. I do grasp the weightiness of this moment and quite understand why you're feeling overwhelmed. Please, by all means, take that time. The offer does indeed bring a significant life change, but also an enormous lifetime opportunity. Why not start by asking yourself if you possess the courage and belief in your writing to at least try on that yearned-for 'dream life,' Ms. Bowen?"

Chapter 2

It was almost a perfect morning. It would have been perfect if Halley's super-skeptical younger sister, Beth, hadn't shown up at her condo for the trillionth time that week with another fret about Halley accepting her benefactor's unusual gift. Beth's worry gene had activated the day after she'd encouraged her to make the move. Halley had omitted enlightening her sister about the stipulation for finding romance. She'd done her best to sweep that particular fret out of her conscious mind.

Halley reflected on the two life-changing calls made from Langdale's office less than two weeks ago. The surprise of Beth blessing the move and promising to keep silent about the benefactor's offer hadn't left Halley. The call to her boss felt equally surprising. He'd encouraged her to chase the writing aspiration and even assured her a position with the company would always be waiting if she ever wished to return. All obstacles had evaporated like a puddle on a scorching summer day.

Since walking out of Sam Langdale's office, the whirlwind preparations to close down one life and start anew had lessened. Her escalating excitement on embarking on this new path remained. Halley hadn't paused to process all she'd agreed to, which was probably wise, or she'd surely have checked herself into a nunnery with a note pinned to her shirt.

The grand adventure would be underway in less than an hour. The movers had placed her few belongings in storage until she found a cottage. Halley's gaze swept the rented, furnished uptown condo once more to ensure the place looked tidy. The anxious face of her Persian calico cat, Éclair, waited in her carrier for the trip.

"You've tuned me out again," declared Beth.

"Not me." Halley parked the broom in the closet. "I heard each fret—all of them—for the last ten days. The one now was an encore. Aren't I worried about being lonely and bored in Port Royal after

Chapter 3

The dining room at Buttercup was drenched in candlelight and greeted Halley's early arrival. Walls colored in a muted shade of yellow set an inviting mood. The large oak trestle table allowed four diners to sit along each side with Irene and Joe anchoring the ends. Ferns in large silver metal urns stood as sentinels at the double glass doors leading out to a breakfast veranda. A grouping of oil paintings hung above the massive wood-carved buffet and represented all manner of vintage boats anchored at Port Royal Bay. Halley appreciated the room's eclectic feel, which made an ideal backdrop for Irene's delectable dishes. Her mouth watered, anticipating tonight's fare.

Meals were served family-style, making conversations easy among the guests, but Halley knew it was the relaxed vacation vibe that guests found the most charming. The dining room had fostered many lively but respectful exchanges in the past. She never knew what topics of conversation would blossom from one meal to another, but always left the table smarter than before she sat down. Mick flashed in her mind.

"Ugh," she groaned. He'd no doubt claim a seat next to her. She turned, hearing voices.

Two couples near the same age entered, bringing big smiles. "Hello there. We're the Chesters, and this other delightful couple is our friends, the Nelsons." Mr. Chester extended his hand to Halley.

"I'm Halley Bowen, and it's nice to meet you all. Choose your seats anywhere." Halley sat down and watched the four select chairs on the opposite side.

Mrs. Nelson unfolded the navy-striped linen napkin, admiring the centerpiece of hydrangeas. Her grey curls drooped down her forehead, creating a face reminiscent of a flapper. Her focus landed on Halley. "Do you happen to know what's being served this evening? I do so have a taste for—"

"Evening, folks. I hope you all brought a hunger for shrimp. They're fresh off my boat and in Irene's kitchen getting dressed up. Name's Captain Mick." The burly man wore a flash of red mixing with grey hair and a seafarer's weathered face. He kept his chuckle going and nodded to each person until he saw Halley. "Ahh lassie, you've come back to us, and so soon," Mick's Scottish brogue slipped out as he rounded the side where Halley sat.

Halley smiled and accepted Mick's squeeze that always emptied her of breath. "Yep, I'm back. I can't get enough of your shrimp." Halley moved her chair to allow Mick's frame to arrange itself next to her. She waited for the inevitable.

"So, is everyone enjoying their visit to our little seaside village? Of course, you are. You know, our Halley here has a debt I'm thinking needs claiming soon. Right, my gal?" Mick's hearty laugh caused the table's candles to flicker.

Halley gulped the glass of water. She smiled at both couples.

"Go on, lass. Tell our friends here."

Halley released an exasperated sigh. "Okay, fine. Mick has this ridiculous rule that anyone single under thirty-five must spend a day on his boat if they dine on his celebrated shrimp Irene serves at the Buttercup. And believe me, if I knew of this decree, I'd have passed on the shrimp the first time." Halley stole a glance at the captain.

The Chesters and Nelsons joined in the merriment. Mr. Nelson spoke first. "Sounds like a win-win to me."

Halley chirped next. "Oh, it's hardly a win for me. The scoundrel makes you work the whole day, pulling nets and sorting shrimp. I keep telling Mick the labor might ruin my enjoyment of all shrimp—"

"And, I tell this clever gal that's an excuse I'll not accept. Mayhap I collect on the debt this visit while the wind's still balmy." Mick patted Halley's shoulder and sent a wink to the others.

"How invigorating to experience a day at sea. I do hope we'll be around to hear about your excursion, Halley," Mrs. Nelson said.

Joe entered the room carrying two platters, sparing Halley anymore of Mick's good-natured taunting. "Here we are with the most delicious shrimp scampi you'll taste on the east coast, compliments of Captain Mick's shrimping skills." Joe placed the dishes in the center of the table and left.

"Yes, I say our Mick is the shrimp whisperer. His catch always pleases the palate," said Irene arriving with a tray. She sat bowls of steaming rice and corn on the cob down and disappeared back to the kitchen.

Irene and Joe returned, bringing the remainder of the meal—arugula peach salad and praline cheesecake left on the buffet for later. The bowls and platters moved around the table with oohs and ahhs coming from the guests. Chatter postponed while they savored their bites, and then lavished compliments on the proprietors for such gracious attention to detail.

Once coffee cups were filled, Irene asked a simmering question. "Halley, my curiosity won't wait another second. You must share with us how you've managed to orchestrate another holiday with us at Port Royal?"

Halley choked on her coffee. The coughing spell bought her time to gather her wits. Irene offered her the chance to do what Halley dreaded most—explain her return while omitting the part about having a benefactor. Over the past week, she'd failed at conjuring a story. Halley knew others in town would soon pepper her with the same questions. Showtime was upon her.

"Let's see." Halley paused as the words came calling, amused at what she was about to say. "I'm calling this a pre-mid-life crisis of sorts. You see, I've yearned to write a novel since college and discovered my love for writing working at the local newspaper. A few weeks ago, I sort of had an epiphany that now presented the opportune time, and why not go for it? And if I'm charting a new path, I want to begin in my favorite place, Port Royal."

"Why, Halley, how exciting for you. For us, too. And you're single and without dependents, which gives you the freedom to write that book. We get to enjoy having you become a full-time resident." Irene clapped her hands.

"Making this big change takes courage," chimed Joe.

"What about your sister and your job?" Irene's practical side awakened.

"Oh, Beth's positive input cinched the move. Imagine my shock when Beth declared I must grab hold of my dream, and my boss agreed, even assuring me he'd find a place for me at the company if I decided to return. All the obstacles melted away, and so here I am ready to embark on—"

"On a shrimping trip with Captain Mick. Let's all toast to this lass's success." Mick raised his coffee mug. "To our Halley penning a story." Mick paused. "What's the tale about, gal? Mayhap, a fine, dashing sea captain name of Mick Duffy?"

Laughter filled the room as glasses clanked, and faces turned back to Halley.

"Mick, you're a natural storyteller. Tell you what. I promise to name a character after you if you'll excuse me from a day of shrimping. How about it? Do we have a deal?" Halley grinned, enjoying the banter and realized there's no place she'd rather spend her first night back in Port Royal. "Mick?"

"I'm a-thinkin' on this barter. Do ya believe yourself a good writer?" Mick stroked his beard, with a countenance as bright as stars in the late summer sky.

"I'll tell you what I'm not. A good mate to have on your boat."

More laughter erupted around the table. Mrs. Nelson waved her napkin as a fan.

"Then a dashing character I shall be," Mick replied, raising his mug again high in the air.

"You're a character all right," Joe said with a chuckle.

Halley relaxed as the subject changed to the Chesters' and Nelsons' plans for the next day. She'd avoided housing questions, at least for the moment. She understood finding a cottage would reign supreme, as staying at the Buttercup Inn provided only a temporary solution. Tomorrow morning, a call to Oliver, the local real estate agent, should get her moving. She smiled at her pitiful pun but celebrated she could cease dodging Mick. No doubt he'd bait some other naïve person to go shrimping. A second pun marked her limit. She would bid the group goodnight, find Éclair, and take stock of her senses one more time before closing out a perfect day.

Chapter 4

Halley entered the kitchen, looking for a quick breakfast she could hold in one hand, and a cup of tea in the other. She'd succeeded in scoring a meeting with Oliver at nine o'clock to begin the search for a cottage oozing charm and with a view of the bay. A picturesque bay ought to deliver plenty of creativity for a romance novel. She did her best work using water as a creative muse. Some of her strongest newspaper feature stories had been written from a campus park bench by a small pond.

"Good morning, Halley. Craving a tasty something to start your day?" Irene slid a tray of toasted multi-grain bagels and a crock of cream cheese toward Halley.

"A bagel is perfect. And a—"

"A cuppa." Irene grinned, handing Halley a mug with hot water and a basket of assorted tea bags. "You're always easy on breakfast."

"And I guess as predictable as my old Aunt Tilly's arthritic rain knee as she called it." Halley parked on the kitchen island's wooden stool and smeared the cream cheese on her bagel. She dropped a tea bag into her mug.

"What's your day asking of you?" Irene leaned across the island and snagged a teabag.

"So far, I have a meeting with Oliver in less than an hour to cottage shop. I'm jazzed about finding a small place, getting settled, and of course, busting to write." Halley's face turned wistful thinking about story ideas.

"Wow, I'm impressed you're committed to buying a home right off. Joe and I love the idea of seeing you more than one month a year. You've certainly surprised us in the best possible way." Irene's face brightened. "This news needs spilling."

"What needs spilling?" echoed Joe entering the kitchen with a tray of dishes.

Halley laughed. "Oh, only that I'm starting the hunt for a cottage this morning with our local broker, Oliver. Speaking of that—" Halley stole a glance at the kitchen rooster clock. "I must dash. Thanks for breakfast, and scold Éclair if you need to." She took the bagel and disappeared out the side door.

***

What Halley desired in this moment was parking karma. She'd made herself late to town by driving around searching home-for-sale signs. "Fantastic!" she declared, spying an empty place smack in front of Oliver's office. "Ugh, parallel parking. Not my thing. Still, I'm going to nail this."

Halley put the German SUV in reverse, began the maneuver, and failed. She ignored the glowering man waiting behind the wheel of a ginormous white pickup truck and tried again. "I'm no quitter," she muttered. "The guy can show some patience." She straightened the wheel and looked out and saw the sidewalk four feet away.

A tap on the driver's window got her attention. Halley touched the button and the window rolled down. The man outside didn't look particularly friendly. He *did,* however, look rakishly handsome with grey eyes contrasting black hair, which needed a barber's scissors. He bent down and presented a square jaw that only Michelangelo could chisel stronger. The fit of the jeans and tee-shirt testified to muscles that certainly weren't hiding away.

"Listen, you obviously failed parallel parking in driver's ed, so you've got two choices here. Either hop out and let me park this vehicle or find yourself a nice pull-in place around the corner. You're making me late, and I'm never late."

Halley gathered a huff. "You listen, Mister Rude, or whatever your name is, this parking place belongs to me, and I'm perfectly capable." She broke off and glared at the man. "What *are* you doing?"

He opened Halley's door and held out his hand. "I'm proving that I'm not Mister Rude, but Mister Helpful. I'm Ben Shaw, who's going to park this vehicle for you. Would you mind stepping over to the sidewalk? I know it's a mile away, but I'm going to fix that for you too."

Halley ignored his hand and hopped out. "Well, Ben Shaw, I don't need your assistance. What I need is one more chance—"

"To practice your parking skills? Do it later. I'll have your buggy parked in a second. Watch and learn." Ben closed the SUV's door and engaged the gear shift.

Halley scurried to the sidewalk, refusing to let her temper ignite. She seethed, watching Ben park the vehicle with ease. She snubbed his engaging crooked grin as he exited.

"Here's your key, and if you want to show gratitude, ignore future parallel parking places in town so others who are adept can have them." Ben turned toward his truck.

Halley felt her face flush. "You beat all. Listen up. I happen to think parallel parking slots waste too much real estate. Pull-ins seem a better use of space," she hollered to his retreating back. With a toss of her head, she marched toward Oliver's office door. "Pushy and rude man."

"Who's pushy and rude?" asked a familiar voice.

"Ginger. Hey there." Halley hugged the owner of Port Royal's favorite coffee shop. "I planned to drop in Deja Brew and see you after I met with Oliver."

"I certainly hope so." Ginger clipped her auburn hair in a twist. Freckles splashed across her face and added a dose of cute. "Before I get the low-down over a latte, answer me two questions: What are you doing back at Port? And who acted pushy and rude? Tell me that name and I swear their next coffee will be so weak they can read a newspaper through it. Colored water in a cup." Ginger wrinkled her nose, causing the freckles to meet.

Halley broke a laugh. "You make an awesome friend. Okay, here's the quick scoop. Prepare yourself. I'm planning to make Port Royal my home. More on that later. As for pushy and rude, two words: Ben Shaw. Know him? Wait, you know everybody."

"You're going to live here? What fabulous news. I love the idea of you as my full-time friend. I'm excited to hear lots of details, so hurry and claim a large latte on the house to celebrate. As for Ben, of course, I know him and his brother Andy. They're two of the nicest guys living in Port. Oh look, here comes Ben down the sidewalk."

"What?" Halley turned and saw his legs taking long strides in their direction. "Geez, not him again. Listen, I'll stop by later and share my flight of fancy. Right now, Oliver's waiting to help me find a place to live. Wish me luck."

Ginger reached in her handbag and held out her hand. "You want luck? My Irish means to help. Doesn't get better than this." She placed a sealed shamrock in Halley's hand.

Ben came alongside and glanced at Halley's palm and winked at Ginger. "She could have used that a few minutes ago. The woman can't park a bicycle." He walked up the steps and entered the real estate office.

Ginger hid her smile from Halley.

"Did you hear that nonsense? Nicest guy in Port my foot. I fear my lousy kismet has returned. He's gone into Oliver's. I need that clover." Halley planted both hands on her hips and released a breath.

"Girl, get yourself to Deja Brew soon. I promise the tastiest hazelnut latte with almond milk will be waiting. As for hunky Ben, that may take a different kind of brewing," Ginger said cryptically and squeezed her friend's arm. "Go find that home."

"That's what I was trying to do before he commandeered everything. Oh, never mind, I'm going. See you later for my java." Halley managed a smile.

Chapter 5

"Okay, Oliver, I'll get in touch with Miss Wellington today about the renovation job. I appreciate the referral," Ben said. "Getting a big project sure would help with recognition as a respected construction company." Ben shook the agent's hand as Halley watched, trying not to look as if she were eavesdropping.

Oliver glanced toward her, seated in the reception, and smiled as he waved her over.

"You're welcome, Ben. And if Libby approves of your ideas, I feel sure the gig is yours. I wasn't shy with my compliments about the quality work you and Andy do. All of the clients I've sent your way have come back singing the praises of Shaw Construction. Go nail this. Pardon the joke."

As Halley drew closer, Ben pivoted toward the door, and she found herself staring into his grey eyes.

"You again," he murmured. "Who are you anyway?" Ben stepped back, the start of a grin forming on his face.

She chose to ignore his charm-laden smile, which completed his all-too-masculine package. "I'm Halley Bowen, thanks for asking. Please excuse me." She straightened the drooping handbag shoulder strap and turned to Oliver. "Are you ready to meet?"

Oliver's face looked puzzled over the terse exchange between Ben and Halley. "Of course. Come on back to my office. See you later, Ben."

Halley followed Oliver down the hall, hearing voices as they passed each office. "You all seem busy. Is it a seller or buyers' market right now?" asked Halley.

"Unfortunately for you, we're in a tight sellers' market with low inventory. Have a seat." A bulletin board displayed active and sold listings on a nearby wall. The broker plucked a blue file from a stack and shoved the rest to the side. "Let's see. I ran a search for current listings this morning that might fit your criteria." Oliver re-positioned his thickset frame in the chair.

"Super. Can we look at the properties? I'm anxious to find my cottage and get out of Irene and Joe's way." Halley scanned the board.

"Hold on. I'm afraid you may need to temper the enthusiasm. I found three maybes."

Oliver handed over the listing sheets and turned his attention to a ham biscuit.

Halley took a glance and frowned. "None of these speak to me. Is this all?"

"I'm afraid so. The one residence on Sea Oats Drive is worthy of a look, though I warn you the view of the bay requires effort." Oliver chuckled and took another bite.

"Effort?" Halley's disappointment mirrored her tone. She'd hoped to visit a few cottages.

"Let me drive you over. You can see it for yourself. If this property doesn't work, I'll get creative in my search."

"Okay, I'm willing to at least look at the listing. First, finish your biscuit," Halley encouraged with a grin.

***

"I guess you'd better get creative, Oliver," Halley sighed, stepping out of the agent's vehicle. She glanced around the town's sidewalk, relieved Ben Shaw wasn't lurking nearby. "That house isn't for me. And who wants to stare out a laundry room window to see the bay? Plus, I need two or three bedrooms that aren't painted flamingo." Halley tried to find her sense of humor.

Oliver laughed. "I guess beauty is in the eye and all that. Okay, I've got one long shot that I need a little time to explore. May I call you if my idea proves viable? Give me till tomorrow."

"Sure. Thanks for the effort, Oliver. I'll keep hoping the cottage I've envisioned presents. Guess I'll mosey over to Deja Brew and chat with Ginger. She's always great at finding the silver linings. And right now I could use one."

"Don't worry. We're going to get you situated somewhere with a desk and computer to write that novel. By the way, I hear Mick's

bragging around town that you're naming a character after him."
Oliver's jolly nature was always evident.

"Gossip sure travels Port's sidewalks with the speed of light."
Halley couldn't help laughing. "Yes, Mick's character will have a
minor part. So minor, you might miss him."

"I get it. Go and enjoy that coffee and chat with Ginger. Oh, and
I hear she's baked lemon bars this morning. Don't miss them. I'll
ring you later." Oliver hurried toward his office.

***

Outside, Halley noted her parked SUV was centered perfectly
between the two white stripes. "Maddening man," she muttered
under her breath and decided to avoid another parallel parking
exercise by walking the four blocks to her latte. She'd use the time to
ponder where to find part-time employment. Before entering Deja
Brew, Halley beamed as an idea percolated.

The coffee house served as the locals' gathering place, but new
visitors soon found a welcome, too. Halley paused to savor the
aroma of coffee beans and the eclectic décor of the turn-of-the-
century building. Wingback chairs upholstered in earthy tones
invited customers to relax. Ginger allowed local artists to display
paintings on the brick walls, which showcased their interpretations
of coastal living. Tables with non-matching seats enjoyed a
reputation of closing deals, igniting romance, and encouraging
mothers to plan playdates for their kids. And Port's rowdy book club
members livened the place each Wednesday afternoon to dissect
their latest selection. Halley avoided visiting during their meeting
time after the women cajoled her into breaking a tie on their next
novel to read. She'd made the mistake of saying neither and
suggesting something else, not to their liking.

Seeing Ginger behind the bar letting the espresso machine hiss at
her, Halley sauntered over. "I'm ready for my hazelnut latte and to
spill the beans on what lunacy has claimed me, if you've got the
time. Aren't I witty? Beans. Coffee. Get it?"

Ginger grinned and turned to the guy working next to her.
"Walker, take the wheel and make Halley's usual, only large. We'll
be over in the corner far from the maddening crowd. Is that the right
cliché, Ms. Writer?"

"I do believe you're correct, Ms. Barista Extraordinaire. Thomas Hardy would be so pleased with the mention of his book. Maybe you could suggest it to the PR Book Club," Halley teased.

"The only thing I dare mention to those hens is my pound cake for the day."

The two friends claimed their chairs, and within moments a tall, lanky Walker placed two lattes on the small table and hurried back to a waiting couple.

Ginger tossed her apron over the back of the chair to discourage patrons from approaching. "I'm all ears. I've been anticipating this telling all morning."

Halley leaned in and lowered her voice. "As I shared earlier, I want to make Port Royal my permanent home. I'm calling this a pre-mid-life-crisis."

Ginger opened her mouth.

"Don't say anything yet. I know that we're the same age. Here's the scoop. I used to write for a local newspaper and never stopped wondering if I had a book living inside of me. I believe I do. When I returned home, the longing to live in Port Royal and write stayed with me. So, a couple of weeks ago, I'm preparing for this contentious meeting with clients, and I had sort of an epiphany." Halley grabbed a breath. "Here's the way I see my life at this moment in time. In the now is how I live my dream life. Not tomorrow. Not next year. Now. Waiting made no sense. Do I sound nuts?"

"Nope, more like inspired and passionate. I'm going to share a secret with you." Ginger paused. "Becoming inspired is how I ended up opening Deja Brew. After an unpleasant divorce, I found the idea of becoming a coffee house entrepreneur appealing. Let's say I had something to prove to myself. Enough said there. Anyway, I left the cold northeast winters, my unhappy memories, and discovered Port Royal. Like you, I checked into the Buttercup. And day one, I felt an odd connection to the seaside town as if I'd been here before. Thus, the name Deja Brew to honor that link. I purchased this place, renovated, and made my dream come true. After four years, I'm still grateful to Port Royal and the amazing people that touch my life each day." Ginger's face reflected her happiness.

"Wow. What a wonderful story. You've given me more validation to stay on this path."

"I'm curious. Who else has validated this move?" Ginger sipped her drink.

"The two people who possessed the power to keep me chained to Charlotte: my sister, Beth, and my boss. Surprise on me, they encouraged me to seize this chance and write the novel. Get a load of this. My boss even promised he'd find me a position if I ever wanted to return. He made the financial risk and worry evaporate, so here I am all revved to find a cottage and write a grand romance."

Ginger grew quiet for a few seconds before replying. "I sense your happiest days on the horizon. Welcome to the magic of life in Port Royal, Halley Bowen." Seeing both their coffee cups empty, Ginger rose. "Time for refills, and you need a lemon bar."

"Thanks for your words, coffee, and of course, celebrated lemon bars. Could you make my order to go? Buttercup's pool awaits, and I'd better check in with my muses so that they know I'm available. And, Ginger, maybe tomorrow I can toss an idea your way?"

Chapter 6

"Good afternoon, Sam. I've been anticipating your call." Libby smiled hearing Sam Langdale's voice. She'd known him for some time, ever since law school, and he was a steadfast friend. "Please do tell me how our young lady is settling?"

"Libby, from our sources, I hear Halley wasted no time engaging the local broker, Oliver, in searching for a cottage. For now, she's staying at the Buttercup Inn. Based on my brief time with Ms. Bowen, I think she's results-driven by nature."

"Well, that's most encouraging. Let's see what the enterprising young woman produces." On the other side of the phone, Libby heard Sam tapping a pen on his desk as he continued.

"I agree. As usual, I'll ring you in a couple of weeks or sooner if there's news. Halley understands she's to email me a full accounting on the first of each month. I'll forward that to you."

"Thank you, Sam. She needs time to set her new life in motion. As usual, we won't interfere."

Sam chuckled. "You're an extraordinary woman, Libby. Only you could listen to someone's wish on a bench at the marina and decide to make their dreams come true."

Libby tutted. "You know I love doing it. There's something about hearing someone talk to a seagull and lay out all their future dreams when I have the means to give them what they want." She laughed softly. "That delightful young woman had no idea I could hear her. And I feel quite sure the bench is enchanted."

"It was certainly fortunate for Halley to be vacationing in Port Royal when you heard her. And as I said, you are one of a kind. Come to Charlotte one day soon. I still owe you dinner at The Club."

"And so you do. One day you'll learn never to bet against me on baseball games." Libby smiled as she disconnected.

She sauntered into her flower garden, the place offering daily doses of joy. With garden shears in hand, Libby snipped a bouquet of violet hydrangeas to provide company at the dinner table. Despite her sixty-three years, Libby's agile body allowed her hours of pleasure gardening each week. She'd entrusted her passion to nature's beauty, which was loyal and reliable.

Libby had inherited her family's majestic old brick two-story manor ideally situated on the bay's point. The home's architecture represented Port Royal's most elegant of that day. Magnolia trees lined the winding driveway and led to the front entry door opened by Libby's devoted houseman, Rupert. His wife, Jasmine, served as housekeeper, and Mrs. Cookson ran the kitchen like a Marine drill sergeant, her face at mealtime daring intrusion by any human or varmint around her cooker. The gardener, Miquel, executed Libby's grand vision for the grounds and elicited his two brothers' help when needed. The staff of four represented Libby's family, and she theirs. Providing them a permanent home and a lifetime salary relieved future worry and fostered a long-term devotion, which cut both ways.

The mistress of Magnolia Manor surveyed the grounds feeling pleased until her gaze landed on the pool house structure and a large gazebo. Both flirted with shabby to Libby's discerning nature, a fact she was about to remedy. Glancing at the vintage pocket watch pinned to her blouse, she walked toward the veranda and the man holding a tall glass of Mrs. Cookson's lemonade.

"Miss Wellington, thank you for the opportunity to meet today. I'm Ben Shaw." His smile exuded charm.

Libby extended her hand, fashioning gentility in the gesture. She paused a tick to appreciate the handsomeness and evident charisma of the younger man. "Thank you for making the time. Shall we walk a bit? I want to show you the two structures that most need a refresh. Depending on your vision and quality of work, the next phase I'm envisioning might take you inside the manor."

"That sounds great." Ben matched her pace and smile. "I must tell you, Miss Wellington, your estate captivated me from the moment I moved to Port Royal and heard about Magnolia Manor. Its timeless beauty and architecture can't be duplicated. I respect the hands which created this splendor."

Libby paused. Keeping the upper hand in business dealings was a skill in which she'd taken pleasure. "Mr. Shaw, I've done my homework on you personally and professionally. You've got the job."

"But you haven't shown me the pool house and gazebo, or heard my ideas," Ben said in confusion.

"Ah, but I'm about to. And I fully expect to be impressed by your designs. Want to prove me wrong?" Libby teased.

They both shared a laugh.

"Lead on, Miss Wellington. I aim to impress."

***

They returned to the veranda for Ben to sketch ideas, each one seemingly building enthusiasm in the manor's mistress. With his plans spread before them, he finished outlining his ideas and waited nervously for Libby's reaction.

"Ben, you've delivered in spades what needs doing," Libby exclaimed in delight. "You've no shortage of talent and confidence. I respect those qualities. In fact, I require them. And your bid to do the work is reasonable."

"I appreciate the compliments." Ben tucked the drafting pencil in his pocket.

"Yes, and I'm feeling inclined to tack on a nice bonus if you meet two requirements: Finish on budget and on time."

Ben nodded. "Can do on both, Miss Wellington." He gathered his drawings.

Libby signed the work contract and slid it across to Ben. "Last question. When can you start my project? I don't want to schedule any gatherings while work is underway. You understand?"

"I do understand. The crew is wrapping up a remodel job on Pelican Way this week. How about seven a.m. next Monday?"

"Make it eight, and I'll have Mrs. Cookson bake some of her delectable strawberry scones for the workmen." She nodded when Rupert appeared.

"Those scones cinched our deal." Ben grinned, accepting Libby's hand once again, and the houseman's encouragement to follow him out.

***

Sitting in the truck, Ben dialed his brother, unable to contain his excitement. "Andy, we got the contract and a bonus if we finish on time and within budget. We'll be working for the grand dame Miss Wellington of Newport Society. What a fantastic opportunity. And, you know what else, brother? I like her a lot."

"Way to crush it for us, Ben. Thanks, man. Shaw Construction will make payroll next month. We'll still need a chunk of cash to carry us until we start the nautical museum renovation in the winter. Hopefully, another job will materialize soon."

"I know. Something will open up. Let's celebrate that Libby's project gets us major recognition and endorsing." Ben started the truck's diesel engine.

"That it does. Where you headed next?" Andy asked.

"I guess back to the office and the day-old BLT waiting in my refrigerator upstairs. I might go to work on the boat for an hour or so." Ben turned onto Bay Drive admiring the charming homes along the street. "You there, buddy?"

"Hang on. Okay, sorry, I'm back. Sally and I want you to come for dinner tonight. We can celebrate the Wellington job. Hamburgers on the grill and Sally said she's making your favorite key lime pie. Real food, bro."

"I don't want to intrude… Key lime pie, huh?" Ben grinned.

"And, Tulip, your niece, your *only* niece, has been asking when Uncle Ben's going to play tea party again."

"I'm a pushover for Tulip and her dimples. Tell your girls I'll be there by six. Thanks, Andy."

Ben flashed to the dimples on another face he'd met that morning and wondered what Halley Bowen's story was. He hadn't seen her around town, but during tourist season, it was easy for people to slip in unnoticed until the population dropped to three thousand and the busybodies claimed control once more. He forced his mind to dismiss pint-sized Halley and her feisty persona. His life didn't lend itself to female entanglements. His kind of commitment rested with growing Shaw Construction and garnering the funds to finish building his bungalow, ironically situated a few blocks from Magnolia Manor.

He'd never met anyone quite like Libby Wellington. Stories abounded about her life and times at Port Royal. Ben didn't put stock in much of the telling, preferring to draw firsthand conclusions. Growing up in foster homes, he and Andy learned at an early age that people lied to suit their purpose. Ben withheld trust except for his brother and one other. He was glad Andy found love with Sally, and Tulip's sweet self was proof, but that kind of love wasn't in his future.

He pulled into the restored house that served as Shaw Construction's office and his temporary home in the upstairs apartment. He and Andy had discussed finding a vacation renter for the one-bedroom furnished bungalow located out back. He'd taken the word "quaint" and applied it to the exterior and interior design, hoping to garner more appeal. They needed the extra income it could provide.

Ben hurried upstairs to grab a shower before heading to Andy and Sally's. He'd make sure to stop at the To Your Health store and buy Tulip some mom-approved animal crackers for their tea party.

***

Back home from a relaxed evening at Andy's, including the tea party that his niece had tried to extend way past her bedtime, Ben checked his watch.

Still early enough to work up a lumber order for Miss Wellington's job. His cell phone chimed. "Hi, Oliver, what's up?"

"Sorry to bother you after hours, Ben, but I have an interesting proposition I'd like to discuss tomorrow first thing. I can swing by your office on my way in."

"What's this about?" Ben's skepticism rushed to his head.

"Income and a chunk of change. Both of which you're needing, buddy. See you tomorrow." Oliver clicked off.

Ben put down the phone with a frown. Oliver was a bit of a town institution, acclaimed for his real estate expertise and genuine kindness. If the town needed volunteers for any endeavor, Oliver's name appeared on the list. If there was anything he could do to help the man, Ben was in.

Chapter 7

The next morning found Halley and Éclair in search of a quiet place to relax. The feline had grown weary of Chaucer, shadowing Halley's every move as both females craved solitude.

"Morning, Halley," Irene said, arms laden with fresh towels. "You and Éclair seem on a search. Can I help?"

"Good morning. Yep, we're on the hunt for an undisturbed place. Today I plan to work on the novel, or at least that's my intention."

"How exciting. Follow me. I know the perfect place." Irene moved down the wide hallway to a closed door. "Here you go. Joe's gone fishing with the guys. His den is yours." Irene stepped aside for Halley to enter.

"This is perfect. Thank you, Irene." Halley placed her laptop on the desk and squeezed the soft leather chair.

"You betcha. And, Éclair, don't worry. I won't tell Chaucer where you're hiding." She laughed and closed the door.

Éclair settled on a plaid sofa cushion, activated her purr, and watched Halley make a call.

"Hi, Beth. I'm checking in. What's up?"

"I'm so glad you called. Great timing. I'm packing. I'm off to the London office for several days. The company's making another acquisition, and I need to implement a plan to meld their employees into our organization."

"Wow, that's quite the feather in your bonnet. Congrats. Wait, what about Percy?" Halley had sudden second thoughts about gifting her sister Éclair's cuddly cousin.

"I've got that all worked out. Promise you won't yell, and I'll tell you."

"I probably won't yell." Halley's frown set.

"My friend from work recently said goodbye to her elderly cat and is feeling bereft. She begged to have Percy stay with her until I return. They know each other from movie night. It will be fine. Promise." Beth waited.

Halley massaged her temple with one hand. "I suppose. Look, I'd take him, but right now, my situation isn't conducive to having a second kitty."

"Percy's personality is super friendly and adaptable. My plan's fine. Plus, I may get home sooner. And should I stay longer, Percy will cross the pond and be with me. He's my guy, and I'm committed to him. Stop worrying. Before we hang up, do you have any news? Found a place?"

Halley relaxed. "Sadly, no news except meeting this super annoying guy who insisted on parking my car."

Beth giggled. "Parallel parking, right? When I visit, I'm making it my mission to teach you the parking trick. Hey, how old is the annoying one? Is he like, a hotsie?"

"Geez, maybe early thirtyish? And parking lessons aren't needed. Go. Have a safe flight. Text when you land." She ignored her sister's silly 'hotsie' question and rang off. It didn't stop Ben's too handsome face flashing in her mind's eye.

Halley walked to the window. Beth seemed fully engaged with her job and excited about this trip. And didn't she want Beth to become less dependent on her? The answer was yes. Fresh out of delay tactics, she went to the desk chair. A blank page awaited her attention. Halley loved Carl Sandburg's quote from his poem, An American Classic, "This is where I dirty paper." She wanted to dash out at least twenty pages starting this moment.

Halley arranged her notepad and pens to the left of her open laptop. A cup of tea sat on a lighthouse coaster to her right. The screensaver presented an inspiring collage of Jane Austen's book covers. The temperature of the den felt right. She pulled her golden hair away from her face into a ponytail. Her tank and elastic-waist shorts felt super comfy. Éclair had settled on a cushion for a nap. All was well, except it wasn't. Something was missing—words to type. Halley had none. Not even a title.

A writer's dread was a blank screen staring them down, and she had hers. Fear shot through her body. The adrenaline pump kicked on. What if she didn't have a great romance to tell? Maybe her dream life was nothing more than wishful thinking? Still, she owed her benefactor a story. After all, this woman must have faith in her.

Eyes closed, she waited for direction—her next step. She heard the words *"Take a walk."*

For some inexplicable reason, Halley felt compelled to stroll toward the marina. She loved the sounds, the smells, and the activity there. Boredom didn't exist around the water, and that fact fed her love of Port Royal. She adjusted her baseball cap to hide the sun as the marina came into sight. The sailboats chattering to each other welcomed her, their riggings clanking against the masts. She plopped down on a bright yellow wood bench adorned with painted daises. Halley felt a curious magnetism to the bench, discovering the special spot on her last visit to Port Royal. Watching the sailors tack in and out of the bay while fishers showed off their catch of the day helped distract her mind's chatter.

Halley checked her cell phone and sighed, seeing no missed calls or texts from Oliver. Nothing had jelled for her. A cottage seemed unattainable any time soon. Her story was at best hiding in the abyss and at worse non-existent. And the clock ticked on.

"Isn't this the loveliest of days? Of course, one must be present and accounted for to take notice." A surprised Halley turned to see who'd sat next to her. An older woman, perhaps in her late sixties, attractive and regal with beautiful porcelain skin, offered a knowing smile.

Halley smiled back. "Be present. Funny you should say exactly what I've been struggling with all the livelong day. Hello, my name's Halley Bowen."

"It's my pleasure to meet you, Halley. I'm Libby. You look like a newcomer to our seaside town." Libby removed her sunglasses and nodded to a man passing by.

"I've vacationed at Port Royal for the last few years, but only recently decided to make it my new home. However, right now, I'm wondering if I've made a huge mistake and—"

"Please forgive my curiosity. I am told I have an oversupply. Who told you moving here was a mistake?" Libby's amusement lit up her face.

"Who told me?" repeated a confused Halley. No one was telling her she'd made a mistake. Quite the contrary. Her friends seemed super jazzed she'd returned. "I guess I told myself."

"Ahh, the mind sure can ruin a perfectly sound plan if we allow it. Wouldn't you agree?"

Halley chuckled at the truth of Libby's words. "Yep, I agree. In one sentence, you've described how my mind led me right into the trap of doubting my decision. Would you by any chance know the secret to getting confidence back? Maybe you have a magic wand?"

Wow. What made me ask a total stranger for help? Maybe because the refined woman sitting next to her seemed wise and certainly friendly.

Libby smiled and waved a pretend wand in the air. "See here? You're in luck. I brought my wand with me. Let's get you back on this exciting journey once more and this time with abundant faith. Abracadabra, Halley will now receive happy news and know her next step. Faith restored." Libby reached for her straw bag.

Halley's cell phone chimed. "Wow. That wand of yours works fast."

Libby smiled. "Answer that call. I must be on my way. Nice chatting with you."

"Hi, Oliver." Halley watched the curious woman take her leave.

"Halley, I've got ten seconds here. Wish me luck. I'm off to meet with the owner of your dream cottage. Keep the faith. Bye for now." Oliver disconnected.

Halley's mouth opened and closed as her mind struggled to understand what had happened. Two people telling her to "have faith" and "keep the faith" within a few minutes of each other? Libby's virtual wand possessed magic. Halley chuckled at that thought. Port Royal's vibe offered something special, something unique, something that drew her home.

Chapter 8

Oliver arrived late to Ben's office, wearing a Cheshire grin as he chose the most generous-sized chair. He shrugged rounded shoulders and laid a white sack on Ben's desk, loosened his tie, and failed at crossing one leg.

Ben shook his head. "Okay, Oliver, you're here, all nicely tucked in. I'm listening. Make it quick. I've got a cement truck scheduled to pour footings this morning." Ben emptied his coffee cup and returned to the brewer. He filled a second mug for Oliver. "Here's your fuel. What are you selling?"

"I don't know if you ever had a godfather, but you're looking at yours. Here's my take on what's causing you to lose sleep and what I'm offering to get your Zzzs back. Number one, the way you explained things earlier this week is that Shaw Construction needs a healthy infusion of funds to manage bigger jobs like Miss Wellington and the Nautical Museum renovations coming up. Number two, you need the right tenant for that charming bungalow out back, which will give you more dinero." Oliver cocked an eyebrow.

"Pretty much." Ben gulped his coffee.

"Get ready to find ways to thank me for I, Oliver H. Moretti, am here to solve both needs. Yes, sir." The broker opened his sack and took a whiff and closed it again.

Ben studied his friend. "Tell me more, Godfather," he replied, attempting a heavy Italian accent.

Oliver chuckled. "Accent needs some work, *paisan*. Anyway, here's the lowdown. I have a client who needs a cottage exactly like the one you're building on the bay lot. There's nothing in inventory that meets her needs. Zippo. Yours does. Sell it to her. And, while you finish the cottage, she rents the cute little bungalow. Bam. One golden goose delivering two golden eggs. If I'm mixing metaphors, so be it. Focus on that money streaming into your account. Besides, she's a nice person, and we like nice people moving to Port. Problem solved. Bam." Oliver smacked the arm of the chair.

"Need I remind you, Oliver H. Moretti, that you're pimping my own house? The one I've waited years to build on that primo lot. Are you asking me to give that up? You need to lay off those rum drinks with the umbrellas that you and Mick partake of at The Wharf."

"Leave my rum swizzles out of this. Let me finish. You've heard the saying you can take the girl out of the city, but you can't take the city out of the girl?"

"Oliver, it's 'you can't take the country out of the girl.' Country. Not city."

"Well, I customize my pitch for the situation, and in your case, it's a city girl. I'm talented that way. My formula still works. Listen, this buyer's got access to cash. No loan hoops to jump through. She's ready, willing, and able to close if she likes your house plan, and I know she will. The back story is she's taking leave of her big la-di-dah job for a year to write a book. My crystal ball predicts at the end of the year, a bored city girl's back in the bright lights climbing that corporate ladder. Port Royal is but a long vacation."

"And then what?" Ben began pacing.

"Stay with me. For now, I'm keeping your names to myself. Let's do this negotiating verbal and see if you two can agree on a price. Then, I'll get the attorney to draw up a purchase contract giving you first right of refusal when city girl's ready to sell. By this time next year, I'm betting you get your house back at the appraised value. Your company is flush with cash and has paid you back. All legal like. Bam again." Oliver pounded one fist into his hand.

Ben rubbed his chin. "I don't know, Oliver. It pains me to think I've got to finish my house for some corporate uptight pencil skirt and hope she returns to her old life. And, does she get to pick colors and all? That worries me. What if she likes something hideous like flamingo?"

"I can assure you flamingo will not be on your walls." Oliver laughed, recalling Halley's reaction to the Sea Oats house. "Details, only details. All of this can get worked out. Did I mention cash, with a hefty down payment? You can start the draws right away. Remember, it's a construction contract. Money flows your way as phases are completed. Another bam." Oliver smacked his hands again.

"Would you please cut out the bams? They're annoying. And yes, Oliver, I know how draws work. Still, I need to call Andy even though it's my house you've sold down the bay."

"I think it's sold down the river." Oliver grinned.

"I customize my sayings for each person, too. I'm talented that way. It's a bay for you," Ben replied.

"Touché, my friend. Touché. Make the call. I'm going to sit here and eat my ham biscuit." Oliver laid the contents on Ben's desk and tucked a napkin under his second chin.

"Man, how can you eat the same thing for breakfast?" Ben grabbed his cell phone.

"It's a no brainer." Oliver took a giant bite.

"On that, we can agree. Hi, Andy. Listen, I need to run something crazy by you before I make a decision." Ben stepped onto the porch to talk in private.

Oliver watched from the window and devoured his breakfast, waiting for Ben's return. "Well?"

"Andy said it's up to me. He'd never ask me to give up my house to keep the company afloat. Though he believes if I loan Shaw Construction the money I get from the cottage, I will get it back with interest by early next year." Ben sat down and tossed his cell phone aside.

Oliver closed the food bag and dusted crumbs from his ample lap. "Well, that sounds encouraging. Listen, I know this is hard, but I'm trying to help all concerned. It's not always about the commission with me."

"Hey man, I know that," Ben said gently. "I've watched how you take care of clients. I've seen you forgo getting paid so a young couple could buy their first home."

"Don't be telling those stories around town, or I'll never see another commission check." Oliver laughed and pulled out his legal pad and pen.

"All right, because of how this proposal came to me, I'm going to do it. I didn't chase the money, but the money chased me. Godfather, you've got a deal, but only if she accepts my price. Hand over that pad and pen. I'm going to jot down my terms, and you'd better bam me with a signed contract before I come to my senses."

Chapter 9

A mystified Halley took a slow walk back to Buttercup Inn determined to stay out of the past or future in pondering this whole "keep the faith" reminder delivered by Libby and Oliver.

Faith and trust had landed her back at Port Royal. So when did she shift into doubt?

Halley cut through a children's playground and stopped to retrieve a little girl's runaway red ball and handed it back to her. "Here you go, cutie. I sure like those pigtails. I've got one pigtail myself." Halley tossed her hair, smiling at the mother and daughter.

The child clasped her ball, frowning at Halley. "You need two to make pigs. It's okay 'cause you've got a pony. That's what you call hers, right, Mommy?"

"Yep, Tulip, a pony or a single pigtail is right. Thank the nice woman for returning your ball."

"Thank you, nice woman, for returning my ball." Tulip ran giggling over to the park slide.

"She's adorable, and so is her name. I bet there's a great story that goes with it."

"There is. Hi, my name is Sally Shaw."

"I'm Halley. Shaw? Related to a Ben Shaw?"

Sally smiled. "Ben's my brother-in-law. Do you know each other? Excuse me," she said, turning toward her daughter. "Tulip, do not climb the big slide." She grinned and shook her head. "Sorry."

"Oh, I met him yesterday when he decided to show off his parallel parking skills." Frustrating Ben Shaw memories came intruding on her day. "Never mind. Please tell me about Tulip's name."

Sally glanced over to where the little girl squatted picking clovers. "When I met Andy, now my husband, he was walking down Main Street carrying a bouquet of tulips with this puzzled look on his face. We were both waiting to cross at the red light, and I blurted out, 'Who's the lucky girl to get such beautiful spring flowers?'"

"What did he say?"

"He gave me the cutest grin and said that he'd felt compelled to buy them at the Cheerleaders Club fundraiser happening over on Chestnut Street. Then he melted me with his next words." Sally wiped a tear.

"Tell me before I bust," Halley replied. She felt an immediate fondness for Sally and guessed they were close in age. She detected a slight Midwest accent in Sally's speech.

"Andy said, 'I guess they're meant for you.' He handed me the red and yellow tulips and kept standing on the corner staring at me with that sexy grin."

"That may be the most romantic first encounter I've ever heard. Those tulips had magic." *Again with the magic*, Halley sighed, recalling Ginger welcoming her to Port's magic.

"Yes, they did come with magic and still do. Andy gives me tulips at the most unexpected times. Wonderful times like when he guessed I was pregnant before I even knew. And, of course, our baby girl could have no more perfect name, than—"

"Tulip," Halley finished. "Wow, you two must have an amazing connection and love."

"We do, Halley, and we don't take our love for granted. Andy had a lousy growing-up life and lacked faith in ever finding real love until we met." Sally gave a wink. "Anyway, that's the story of our Tulip's unusual name. Funny, I don't usually share so much."

"I'll take that as a compliment. I've recently moved to Port, so maybe we'll run into each other again."

"Welcome." Sally grinned. "And I already consider you a new friend. If you like coffee, I expect to see you at Deja." Sally turned the direction of her daughter and hollered, "Come on, Tulip. We need to get home and make your peanut butter and pickle sandwich."

Halley laughed and tilted her ball cap. "Did you say pickles?"

"I did. Tulip is in her creative phase with food. We go along with it. Andy tells me to have faith she'll soon move onto another creative area."

"Have faith. Those two words keep finding me today," Halley said, partly to herself. She smiled her goodbye to Sally. "Be seeing you. Bye, Miss Tulip." Halley reached down to tweak one of the little girl's curly brown pigtails.

She giggled again. "Wanna come to my tea party? We're having peanut butter and pickle tiny sandwiches. Mommy cuts them in shapes. My Uncle Ben comes to my tea parties. We could ask him, and then you'd have a friend. Can we, Mommy?"

Sally shook her head. "Out of the mouths—sure, Halley's welcome to come."

Halley bent down. "Thank you, Tulip, so much for inviting me, but I've got something to do right now. Would you pretty please ask me again?"

Tulip's lower lip pouted for a brief second, but her face brightened. "Come Sunday afternoon. It's my daddy's birthday, and we're having barbeque and cobbers. Tell her, Mommy." Tulip danced around the two women before joining their hands and declaring them friends.

"We'd love to have you. Do say yes. It's only a small gathering and casual. We live at 212 Harbor Mist Court. Come around four."

Halley guessed 'cobbers' must be corn on the cob in Tulip speak. She nodded and turned back to Tulip. "I'll be there. I adore cobbers. They're the best with lots of butter. Thank you for asking me."

Tulip hopped on one leg, showing off. "Yay. Yay. Yay," she said in a singsong.

"Boundless energy." Sally grabbed the ball and Tulip's hand and started walking. "See you Sunday."

Halley paused, replaying this last encounter. She felt a lightness, buoyed even. She'd made a new friend—their connection to annoying Ben Shaw she planned to overlook, but not Sally's lesson on faith. Things come in threes. A potent reminder of the role faith could play had happened three times in the last hour because her inner voice sent her on a walk. She dared not question the source.

***

Pet comb in hand, Halley moved through Buttercup's public rooms in search of Éclair. She saw the Nelsons and Chesters lounging by the pool. Judging by the colorful floats moving in the water, they were enjoying a laid-back afternoon. Mr. Chester must have said something lively to his wife. Halley watched the woman wallop him with a straw hat, but the entertainment continued when Mr. Chester lifted his wife off the lounger and dropped her in the deep end. Halley howled watching the shenanigans, a testament to love. She sighed.

"What's up, kid?" Joe came alongside.

"Thought you were fishing today." Halley turned from the glass doors.

"I thought I was fishing, too, but the fish didn't agree. I came home without tonight's dinner, and Irene's smacked a grocery list on me. You didn't answer. What's up?" Joe grinned.

"For starters, a nice combing session if I can find where Éclair is hiding and after that, well I'll be shown. Don't you think?"

"I certainly do. Things are sure to come up roses for you. You've only been here a short time. Hold on to that faith, gal."

Great, more faith talk. Did she need to wear a sign saying, *I got faith already*? "Not you, too."

"Pardon?" Joe's expression showed confusion.

Halley hugged him. "Private joke. Get to the market. I'm already feeling peckish." She continued the search for the cat and ended up in the kitchen, where Irene was emptying the double dishwashers. "Have you seen Éclair?"

Irene tilted her head to the right and grinned.

Halley tiptoed toward the walk-in pantry and saw sleeping Éclair on top of the flour sacks. "Found you. You're late for your beauty appointment with me." Halley winked at Irene and scooped up a sleepy Éclair, taking her upstairs for the grooming session.

The comb had passed through the cat's coat once when Halley's cell phone rang. Éclair took advantage of the distraction and high-tailed it out of the room. "You're bad," Halley hollered, clicking on the call.

Oliver's excited voice found her ears. "I read this cool quote online today by someone named 'Anonymous.' You know him?"

"Aren't you funny. What's the quote?"

"Yes, I'm most entertaining. Here goes: 'Faith is like Wi-Fi. It's invisible but has the power to connect you to what you need.' Good one, huh? Thought I'd start by sharing that. Hello? You there?"

"Yep, I'm here and brimming with faith. So much faith. My cup runneth over with faith."

"Hmm, that all sounds—I'm not sure what that sounds like but mosey down to my office. We're going on a short outing."

"You sound pretty amped, so I'm on my way. Whatever it is, don't sell it until I get there." Halley hung up. She'd need to change clothes. She tugged on white jeans and grabbed the first blouse her hand touched. Bright yellow daisies and tulips greeted her, and she thought of the bench and adorable Tulip. "Could this day get any weirder?" She finished buttoning and ran to the bathroom mirror. Applying coral lipstick was the only attention her face received, but her hair needed a fast restyle. Releasing the ponytail and waking up the brush, she frowned at the crazy bends in her hair. "Beach waves—maybe. Can't be helped." Halley reached for her handbag and jogged down the stairs in anticipation.

Chapter 10

Halley hurried into Oliver's office. "I'm here ready for this mysterious outing. What is that you're eating?"

"This is a pizza slice gone wrong. Some dumb high school kid working at Dano's Pizza topped my takeout with chopped pastrami. I've had enough." Oliver tossed the remainder in the plastic container.

"And to think if I'd been two minutes later, I'd missed seeing my first pastrami pizza. Unforgettable, I fear."

Oliver groaned. "Come on. Time to wow you with my creative real estate genius."

As the two walked around the corner to Oliver's vehicle, she saw Ben exit the Rolling Pin Bakery with a tall model-type hanging on his arm. *Who wears heels in Port Royal?* That California blond hair styled in real beach waves had probably cost the woman a few hundred smackers. "Figures," she muttered aloud.

"What figures?" Hop in. Oliver pulled on the handle.

"Who's the girl over there with all the flash?" asked Halley, emphasizing *flash*.

"Oh her. That's the mayor's daughter, Cara." He cranked up the AC. "We're headed toward Bay Street. It's five minutes, tops, to what I want you to see."

Halley dismissed Ben and Cara and tried to tame her eagerness when Oliver named her favorite street in Port Royal.

"Here we are. Let's go take a peek." Oliver pulled a paper from his pocket.

Halley stepped out of the vehicle and squinted. "Wow. I admit the bay view has no peers. It looks like the cottage is close to completion, so that's a plus. What's the story with the property?" She followed Oliver balancing on wood boards that served as a temporary walkway.

"The story comes after I show you around, and you fall madly in love with me and what I've found." Oliver waved his arms for Halley to proceed.

Halley burst into laughter. "I've never been in any kind of love, madly or otherwise, but I'm open to the experience. Can we see what the inside looks like first?"

Oliver grabbed the key from above the door frame. "After you. Note my chivalry. It's my Italian upbringing."

"Duly noted, Mr. Moretti." Halley grinned. She couldn't help but like the guy. He was easy and fun with banter. She stepped into a cozy, welcoming area with the walls covered in beadboard and envisioned pewter coat hooks, a pot of ferns tucked in the corner, and a nifty hanging light fixture. She ventured toward the great room with a wall of glass doors showcasing the bay and stopped breathing. The dining room adjoined.

"Pretty groovy, huh?" Oliver cracked.

"Super groovy." Halley walked out to the expansive porch savoring the view and watched a passing pontoon boat. She'd never grow tired of the changing show outside but contained her excitement until she heard the catch. *Wait.* Course correction needed, she reminded herself. For the last several hours, she had faith that things would sync. She came to Port Royal to live a different kind of life, and her benefactor wanted that for her too.

Halley found Oliver waiting in the kitchen. Her voice dropped to a whisper. "I'm home. Show me more."

"Well, I call this the kitchen," Oliver replied comically. "Use your imagination because you're looking at the sheetrock. The double sink will sit in front of this window. You won't mind dirty dishes when you can gaze out and see—is that Ole Mick's boat going into the marina?"

"It sure is. And it looks like Mick's snookered some poor sap to help him and Gus on today's run. Please continue the virtual tour of the kitchen."

"Yes, ma'am. Against the wall will be the cooker and a nice-sized refrigerator. The island's designed with a vegetable prep sink and an overhang so you can fit—" Oliver peered at the space. "Easily four stools. I believe the cabinets and countertops will be neutral colors. Around the corner is a small pantry and then the laundry room. It's not big."

"Oh, it's more than adequate. What's this cubby?"

"The contractor likes built-ins, though I'd better ask him what his intentions are for the cubby. This door leads out to the garage." Oliver released the door for Halley to see. "On to the two bedrooms. It's a split plan and feels like two master bedroom suites. Follow me."

They entered the first suite off the dining room. Double French doors opened to the porch. The bedroom size felt cozy, but the sloped ceiling let the room breathe. The bath area design made excellent use of space and built-ins for towels. The builder had a knack for creating niches.

"This space makes me feel nesty. I'll have to donate my entire corporate wardrobe to have enough room for my clothes to fit in this closet." Halley pivoted to face Oliver.

"You won't need those threads in Port. We like our vibe relaxed, as you know. Hey, I'll even help you find them a home. Drop the clothes off whenever you want. Come on. I want to show you the second bedroom. It's down this short hall."

Halley took in the space. "It's a tad smaller than the other suite and doesn't have the bay view. This will make an ideal guest room, but Oliver, I need an office or a study for writing." Back in the hall, Halley approached a staircase. "Where do these stairs lead?"

Oliver pulled her back from starting up. "Hang on. I'm not sure the treads are nailed down yet. They lead to unfinished space above the garage. The contractor plans to leave it as attic storage, but you could maybe get him to finish it for you."

Halley shrugged, undeterred. "It seems a waste to me not to use the space. Can we go outside? I'd like for you to show me the lot lines."

Oliver locked the door and hid the key. "To find a half-acre on the bay is pretty incredible. The property sat undeveloped for generations. The owners didn't need money. Folks were surprised when the contractor found a way to get them to part with it. I never could get the full scoop from him. Guess I'm too nosey. Anyway, that leads me into why you're walking around this jewel."

Halley strolled down to the water's edge and noticed the beginnings of a dock that had newly constructed u-shaped seating. "Want to sit down here and chat? Looks safe enough."

"Good idea." Oliver extended his hand to help Halley navigate the steps. "Okay, I'm going to dive in with you. Let's start with: Do you want to try and buy this cottage?"

"Absolutely. Even if there was something else on the market, this is the one. It's spanking new and I'd like to hope I can choose the remaining things like paint and finishing touches. My only hesitations are finding out the price and if I can live in Buttercup until the cottage is completed. Or, maybe I could find a short-term rental, but those are probably impossible to snag in vacation season." Halley laced her hands, pondering any other frets.

"Those are legit concerns to explore, but remember you're working with a real estate genius." Oliver checked his phone. "Sorry. Life as a broker. On-call seven days a week. Back to you. First, the price is at the top of your limit, but within your budget. The cottage isn't on the market because the seller is building it for himself. Circumstances of late have him in need of cash. Otherwise, you and I would not be sitting here."

"Wait. The contractor's willing to sell me his home that's near perfect for me? What's the catch? There's always a catch." Halley twisted to face her agent.

Oliver chuckled. "Not anything I'd call a catch. Let me show off the rest of my creative brokering. So happens the seller finished a great little bungalow behind his business, and he's willing to let you rent it while he finishes the cottage. How about that?"

"No way. And, I can move in—"

"As soon as we strike a deal and sign on the dotted. Here's a stipulation that I can't imagine you'd mind. Let's say after the year you've given yourself to write, you decide Port Royal isn't your cuppa. You give the seller first right of refusal to buy back the cottage. We'd get an appraisal to keep things on the up and up." Oliver pulled out a pack of gum and offered Halley a stick.

"No, thanks. I need to be able to talk," Halley laughed. "This seems too good. Nothing ever comes to me easily like this, Oliver."

"Told you to keep the faith. If you want this cottage, and the bungalow all freshly cutesied up, agree to the typical new construction contract terms, and allow the seller first right of refusal to buy the cottage. Then you've got a home on a spectacular bay lot. My advice is for you to sign the documents now before he changes his mind."

Halley frowned. "Do you think he might?" She couldn't lose this meant-for-her enchanted place.

"Not if you autograph the papers I happen to have with me. Are you ready to go over the documents? He's already signed, proving to me he's unwilling to negotiate any terms set out in the contract. Once you sign, and I tell him, you're bound." Oliver paused. "Listen, if you need to see the bungalow first, I can try and arrange that."

"No, let's not bother him. After all, I'm not going to live there that long. You said it's cute and remodeled. I'm sure it will work. Before you go fetch those papers, I need to do something." Halley leaned over and hugged Oliver. "Thank you so much for the grand effort. You are a humdinger of an agent. I promise to cook you dinner as a thank you once I move into the bungalow."

"And, I promise to clean my plate. Back in a jiffy."

***

Oliver shoved the documents into his portfolio and turned, smiling to Halley. "Let me be the first to congratulate you. Now, how about I drive you over to meet the seller, and I can give him the contract? You can chat a bit about some of the next steps, ask any questions, and lay those baby blues on the bungalow, too. Sound good?"

"Can't happen soon enough. I forgot to ask, is this guy easy to work with?"

"A real pussycat," Oliver chuckled, moving toward his vehicle.

Chapter 11

Halley stepped out of Oliver's sedan, admiring the two-story home oozing vintage charm but didn't notice a business sign anywhere. What did that matter? She had more important details to focus on—like having signed a contract, a mental list of questions ready for this meeting, and, of course, a heartfelt thank you. She couldn't help feeling sympathetic to the seller giving up his home. Maybe there'd be another bay lot for him at a better time.

Oliver and Halley entered the front office. She noticed the tidiness of the desk and bookshelves lining one wall. Blueprints were tacked on a bulletin board, and others rolled up stood tall in a corner basket. It was a functioning office without unnecessary frills.

"Halloo? I've come bearing gifts and a happy buyer." Oliver peered into the next room and shrugged. "He's around. I told him we might stop by."

A door closed, and the sound of footsteps brought Halley face to face with Ben Shaw. Neither spoke.

Oliver lifted his arm in greeting. "Ah, there you are, Ben. Great news, you've got a bound contract. I think you know Halley. At least, you two were in my office at the same time talking as I recall. Anyway, you're officially in a purchase deal together and also landlord and tenant. That's a lot of connections." Oliver stopped talking, sensing a chill in the air. "Is there a problem?"

Halley pounced. "You bet there's a problem. I can't be in a relationship with—he's rude, and he commandeered my SUV."

"Hold on a second. I was not rude. I was in a hurry and late for a meeting with Oliver here. You were married to that empty parking place, but no way could you ever in a gazillion—"

"Hey, Uncle Ben." Tulip came running and grabbed Ben's hand. "Hi, Miss Halley. Are you still coming to Daddy's party?"

Halley smiled and gave the little girl a wave.

A surprised Ben hoisted Tulip into his arms and planted a kiss on her cheek. "How do you know Halley? Does everybody know her but me?"

"She's Mommy and my new park friend. We like her a lot. She's going to eat cobbers with me Sunday. Aren't you?" Tulip pointed her finger toward Halley.

"I sure am."

Oliver chuckled and walked toward the front door. "Well, this little reunion has turned ever so friendly now, and I only wish I could hang around for more, but I've got to dash back to the office. Ben, please show Halley the bungalow, and you two discuss particulars of your arrangement." The agent closed the door only to open it back. "Ben, would you mind giving Halley a ride back to Buttercup? Thanks, buddy. Congrats, you two."

"Tulip, come on we're leaving," a male voice called from the back of the house.

Ben put Tulip down, and she planted a kiss on his cheek. "Bye, Uncle Ben. Bye, Halley."

She disappeared through the adjoining door.

"Shall we continue?" Ben gave a lopsided grin. "Let me go first."

Halley parked both hands on her hips and assumed her best defiant stance. "Go ahead."

Ben moved toward two chairs, which invited the middle ground. "Come sit over here. Let's turn to a fresh page."

She moved slowly, bringing her loyal companion of skepticism with her and sat in the matching wooden chair. Hands folded, she grabbed a breath. "Okay, fresh page. I'm Halley Bowen, who is grateful to purchase such a charming cottage for me to call home and the opportunity to rent your place out back, which P.S., I'd like to see before I leave. Additionally, I look forward to going over the particulars of the contract and what selections I'm able to make. There. Those are my words for our fresh page. Your turn." She flashed a grin and her dimple. Blast Ben Shaw for exuding a hard-to-resist magnetism. She'd even forgiven his rudeness—mostly.

He acknowledged Halley's friendly grin and raised her a generous smile, his best. "I'm still Ben Shaw, builder of your home-to-be, it seems, and your landlord, too. And I want you to know I am sorry for acting so—"

"Brash?" Halley's eyebrow lifted. She couldn't help baiting Ben to see if he'd own the behavior.

"*Brash?* I was brash?" His voice rose an octave. He studied Halley's expression before replying. "I was brash," he said, agreeing. "To continue, selling my dream home isn't easy, but it is necessary. Thank you for appreciating my design. Come on. I'll show you the bungalow." Ben rose and extended his hand toward the back of the office.

Halley walked through the wide door opening into an office she suspected belonged to Andy. She followed Ben through a small kitchen filled with abundant sunlight. She now understood what a 'cheerful kitchen' meant as she took in the pale lemon walls with white cabinets and marble countertops. An antique round whitewashed dining table was tucked in a corner. "This room is delightful. I can envision my Nana canning bread and butter pickles here."

Ben paused. "And I'd be begging the first jar. They're hard to come by around here."

They walked the stone path to the rental. Oak trees with moss dangling from the branches created an inviting archway. A stocked bird feeder had two robins sharing an early dinner, while a nearby squirrel plotted how to climb the pole and get his share. A vivid red hammock was tied between two trees and swayed gently in the breeze.

Halley hesitated. She took in the peace, the absolute tranquility of where she'd live for the next bit of time. "Say, Ben, will you let me use the hammock over there? It looks lonely."

Ben laughed. "Oh, it is lonely. Andy and I are too busy right now to keep it company. It's yours to enjoy. Here we go. Meet your temporary home." He entered the small living room "As you can see, we went with a shabby-chic beach style, and I think it works. Don't you?"

Halley didn't expect the interior to enchant her within seconds. She adored the place and wondered how she'd ever want to leave. "Ben, I'm completely beguiled by what you've done here."

"Wow. I wondered how others might feel vacationing at the bungalow. If I'd nailed the look. Tell me what you like. I'm interested."

Halley moved to the room's focal point. "Well, for starters, this old brick fireplace with the curved hearth and mantel the color of driftwood drew my attention as soon I entered. The shelves flanking it anchor the wall. It looks like you've mingled some cool sea life objects amongst the books. Your color scheme of aqua and sand with white metal accents complement Port Royal's location. The bay and all." Halley paused, taking in the entire room.

"Please continue. You've got a decorator's vision."

Halley smiled. "I do think a home needs to reflect inside what's outside and feel inviting when you enter. How about you?"

"I do, and that's always my goal as a constructor."

"I'm going to ramble around the rest of the place, and I'll finish my little critique afterward. Feel free to anticipate your final grade, Ben Shaw." Halley disappeared down the hallway, seeing Ben relax on the sofa and glance at his phone. The rest of the home was as wonderful as she'd expected.

"You get a giant gold star, Ben," Halley said when she returned. She wasn't a fan of aqua walls, but the rest suited her. "This place is too stinking cute. I don't know where you found such perfect pieces of furniture and finishing touches, but does it have a name?" Her eyebrow lifted.

"The bungalow?"

"Yes. It needs a name to up the cute quotient for vacationers." Halley noted the builder's bewildered face. "No worries. Let me come up with a few choices and see if you like one. If you do, I'll get you a routed sign made to put in front. That's my thank-you gift." Name ideas started popping into her head.

"Sure, that'd be great, but you don't need to buy—"

"Yes, I do. Let's move on. I want to rent this unnamed bungalow. When can I move in?"

"Umm, how about in two or three days? I need to finish a few things remaining on the punch list. And, I'd like to plant a few flowers around the front."

"That works for me. Did Oliver tell you I have a Persian named Éclair who's perfectly behaved?" Halley wanted to make sure they'd both be welcome.

Ben nodded. "He did. You and Éclair consider this home, for now anyway."

Halley watched him close the bungalow's front windows. Maybe she'd been too hasty bestowing the name Mister Rude on him. Harmony flourished around Ben and his work. The home and office both reflected his talent to create a relaxed environment, though she sensed Ben was a complex man. Geez, she'd missed his last words. "Sorry?"

"I was wondering if you'd like to grab a pizza and go over some of the details of the cottage's construction specs. That is if you don't have plans because I'd totally—"

Halley jumped in, seeing Ben falter. "Pizza sounds super, and I'm excited to get more details. Be warned, I'm inquisitive—a lot inquisitive."

Ben groaned. "A woman with a running list of questions. What has Oliver visited upon me?"

"Oh, you'll soon get used to me. Here's a tip my dad would share if he were still around: Give in and let me have whatever I want." Halley winked and headed toward the vehicle. Seeing the waiting truck's impressive ground clearance, she fretted how best to climb into the cab.

"Come hither, fair maiden. I can hoist you into my chariot." Ben opened the vehicle's door and took a deep bow.

Halley tossed her head and huffed. "I can manage, kind sir. Can I step on this chrome thing? Whoa."

Ben lifted her onto the seat, grinning. "I'm starving. And I've learned that you operate from the adage if you don't succeed, you keep trying again and again." Ben strode around to the driver's side.

"If you didn't hold two keys to my future, I'd be tempted to give you one of my witty retorts and set you straight on my parallel parking. For the moment, I'm going to smile pleasantly and say the pizza is on you, mister." She had her to-do list organized in her head and meant to follow it to the letter. Ben would soon hear about her milestones to hit and completing the cottage on schedule would be their primary focus. Writing awaited, and the sooner she got settled at the bungalow, the sooner she could officially start living her dream life. Ben was a means to that goal. Only a means, she felt the need to remind herself. Besides, the mayor's daughter owned his arm.

Chapter 12

Dano's Pizza was Port Royal's single destination for Italian. The restaurant time-traveled its patrons back to the fifties, and not on purpose. While the food was authentic Sicilian and delicious, the place needed a major refresh into the twenty-first century. Halley shook her head at the dark-paneled walls with photos of Al Capone and his entourage and other renowned wise guys from that era.

"A dose of Americano, huh? Check out the jukebox in the corner. It still works. Hang on." Ben darted out of the booth with quarters jingling in his hand.

Within seconds, Halley heard the first notes of an old rock-and-roll band playing "Rock Your Socks." More surprising were the couples who appeared on the round vinyl dance floor doing the bop. Halley immediately recalled memories of cotillion dances that her mom made her and Beth attend.

Ben returned. "We've got ambiance. Now let's order. Want to share a pizza? You can decorate your half the way you like, and I'll do my side. Is that okay?"

"Yep, and I know pastrami won't be sitting on my half." Halley chuckled. "Poor Oliver's pizza order got messed up earlier today. Pastrami and not peppers were the topping, and trust me, our real estate guru acted majorly chapped."

Ben smirked. "Chapped describes Oliver perfectly when his food disappoints."

The waitress appeared, interrupting further conversation. "What you want tonight, handsome guy? First time here this week. We've missed you." The woman, in her fifties, certainly knew how to flirt, Halley thought with a grin.

"Yeah, Mel, work has kept me running, but my appetite for one of Dano's deep-dish pizzas got me here. Halley, you go first. What did you decide for your half?"

"Make mine sausage and black olive, and thanks." Halley handed the waitress her menu.

"Well, how about that, Ben? This gal ordered your standard fare." Mel smacked Ben in the shoulder with her order pad.

"That's pretty crazy. Make mine match hers." Ben looked at Halley. "Well, I guess we've found something in common tonight."

"Guess so. And, if I can't devour my half, you can finish it. Right?" Halley smiled and got to business. "Can we chat about the cottage? Where do you want to start?"

Ben unfolded a spec sheet from his pocket and flattened on the table. "Before we get to the cottage, do you mind waiting to sign the short-term lease on the bungalow? I don't have it drawn up."

"Not at all. I assume you'll put me as month to month. You can leave it inside the bungalow for me to sign."

"Oh, here's the key. I'll call you when it's ready to move into, but plan on a couple of days." Ben grabbed a pen off Mel's tray as she passed. "Thanks," he said, winking.

Halley put the key in her handbag. "Spec sheet, right?"

"Yes, ma'am. Here are the things you get to choose and the places to find them. As you can see, there isn't much left, interior paint color and some lighting. That's about it. You've got the list of what is going into completing the home. Pretty straightforward." Ben sat back, sipping his water.

"I'd like to ask about a couple of changes starting with finishing the attic. I need an office, a place to write. I suspect upstairs will have some fantastic views of the bay. Can you handle creating that space for me based on the roof trusses?" He was about to learn construction wasn't new turf for her. Having a designer mom who loved creating abodes with the latest innovation and style caused Halley to pick up on the lingo and a few of her own ideas. "Because if you didn't build to allow headroom—"

"There's headroom. I designed my house for later expansion if I ever needed more space. And while I'm impressed with your knowledge about trusses, I need to ask, are you prepared to pay more to have me do this work? This change wasn't negotiated before we contracted."

"You're right. It depends on the cost. Can you give me a bid?" Halley heard the music end and voices of diners replacing the beat.

"Sure. Give me a week or so, though. I'll have to work on it at night." Ben took a few minutes to jot notes then glanced at Halley. "What other questions are circling?"

"I want to make sure you've sized the HVAC adequately to cool in the summer. That's a biggy if we're going to finish the attic."

Ben nodded. "Duly noted."

Their pizza arrived, postponing any further business conversation. Halley and Ben turned their focus to eating.

"So, you're going to be writing a novel, huh? That sounds like a major commitment and endeavor." Ben grabbed another slice of pizza, taking a bite.

Halley laughed. "I'm trying not to think about that aspect, but hoping once I get settled at Driftwood, the words will find my computer." She waited for his response to the bungalow's name.

"Driftwood? You slipped that in to see if I was listening." Ben chuckled. "Driftwood. That's a maybe. Any more?"

"Blue Fin Bungalow symbolizes the color scheme and sounds right. Or, how about Shore to Please. Pretty bad, huh?" Halley grinned.

"Super bad. Give me a few more. We're going to decide this tonight."

"How about Sea Glass? I adore finding those beautiful pieces on the beach. It works with your obvious love for the color aqua, and I did notice a snifter with sea glass on a table. The last option is Wisteria."

"Halley Bowen, you do know that you're an easy read, right?"

"Only if I want someone to read me. Well? Name that bungalow." Halley hadn't enjoyed a guy's company as much as Ben's in many a moon. Yeah, his appeal came from wit and confidence that didn't seem to awaken an ego. A quality she found rare in any guys she'd spent much time around. She felt at ease in his company, a familiarity even. "Time's up." She reached across the table and waved her hand in his face.

"I vote Sea Glass. As if you doubted your pitch for that name. Thanks for supplying the names. That's one less thing on my list." Ben stole a glance at his diver's watch.

"Guess we need to go. I appreciate your dropping me off at Buttercup and for the pizza. The bop music, well, not so much."

Halley scooted out of the booth, already dreading the truck's passenger seat perched on the second story.

Once beside the truck's door, Halley looked over her shoulder as Ben approached. "So, I hopped down without mishap, but it's the mounting up—" Halley heard a motor, and a foot boost appeared from the running board. "You scoundrel." She quickly hoisted herself inside.

"I've been called a whole lot worse." Ben closed her door.

Outside Buttercup, Ben turned to finish the conversation. "You've got the suppliers' names and addresses. Go shopping in the next week. We've each got our to-do list. I expect I'll see you at Sea Glass in a couple of days. In the meantime, we'll wait for Oliver to send us all of our official documents."

"Yes, and I need to get the funds ready for transfer. Thank you, Ben, for entrusting me with your cottage. I promise to cherish it. Okay, well, goodnight." She didn't wait for his reply. Though he acted affable about the sale, she suspected the hole in his heart over the loss of his dream cottage wouldn't heal quickly.

***

Having enjoyed a pleasant visit catching Irene up on her incredible day of twists and turns, Halley cozied up in her room's loveseat to check email. The crackle of lightning warned of an imminent thunderstorm. Éclair scampered under the bed and probably wouldn't poke her head out until she heard crickets again. Halley wished she could follow her, but instead distracted herself by reading Oliver's email. His diligence had produced the documents needed to meet Langdale's requirement for releasing funds.

The email from Beth caught her eye. "Family before business," she said aloud.

Halley smiled, reading Beth's news full of cheerfulness—at least until she got to her struggles eating English cuisine, but even that had Halley rolling with laughter. Beth had discovered too late that Yorkshire pudding wasn't a delectable dessert. Still, Beth's personality was adaptable and one of her best traits. Her world was turning nicely.

She opened Sam Langdale's update and request form and began filling in the blanks. Having this unknown generous benefactor never left Halley's thoughts for long. She'd wondered herself near crazy about the woman's identity. Had she ever met her? Would she ever meet her?

Probably not, she sighed. If her benefactor wanted her identity known, she'd have handled things differently with the attorney.

I need to make peace with this wonderful gift, and not give her any reason to regret choosing me. She reviewed the documents from Oliver, sent her email to Sam, and closed the laptop.

The rain arrived, bringing wind. The lights in the room flickered. "Oh, please don't let Buttercup lose electricity," Halley muttered. A knock came at her door.

"Sorry to bother you, gal, but wanted to hand off these two candles and matches in case the power goes out." Joe passed the items. "Storm's got a punch, but it's a fast mover, kind of like Irene when she's chasing me into the doghouse." Joe hooted.

"Thanks, Joe, and it's good to see you out and about and not in that doghouse. By the way, where is it exactly?" Halley loved Joe's humor.

"It's that shed out back where the lawn equipment is stored. I have a chair and a battery-operated radio. Got my old bourbon bottle stashed somewhere. It's likely getting too old for keeping company." Joe closed the door laughing as he went to the next room.

Halley leaned over the side of the bed. "Éclair, won't you please come out? I've got your comb waiting."

There was nothing but silence. Halley retrieved a book from her briefcase. She studied the title: *Writing the Forever Romance.* After her failed first start, she needed a boost. The book promised to break writer's block and provide prompts to get a story moving. If need be, she'd burn the midnight candle supplied by Joe to learn the tips. Halley settled into bed, book by her side, and arranged Éclair's satin pillow for whenever the feline deemed the world safe.

After reading one measly page, Halley's mind took control. Port Royal fostered contentment, and her friends, both old and new, enhanced the feeling. She adored Tulip and her mom, Sally. Ginger, Irene, and Joe were loyal and supportive and truly good people. The encounter with Libby left her intrigued. And humorous Oliver, always chasing his hunger, had delivered on his promise to find her home. Surprise on her, it was Mr. Rude's real estate that answered her needs and wants. Remembering the parallel parking fiasco, she chuckled. Halley had experienced a day full of amazement. She closed the book to savor and appreciate the latest gifts and let her mind hit replay until sleep claimed her much later.

***

"I'd better savor this breakfast while I can. Day after tomorrow, I'll have to fend for myself with meals, and you know that's beyond scary." Halley sat perched on a stool in Buttercup's kitchen, watching Irene chop vegetables for a fish stew. She snagged another cinnamon roll off the tray and told her calorie-counting guilt to take a hike.

"Halley, you know that you can stop in and eat with us anytime your tummy rebels. What you need besides the book-writing genie is a boyfriend who can cook." Irene laid the knife down, signaling heartfelt words were coming. "My fondest wish is that you find your guy here and never leave us. You belong at Port, don't you know?" Irene came around the island and bestowed a hug on Halley.

"I *do* belong here. I'm content and will feel even more grounded once my cottage gets finished. Thank you, Irene, for always saying what I need to hear." Halley took a sip of her tea.

"Wait. Are you thanking me for encouraging you to find a nice guy to cozy up with?" Irene lifted a bag of carrots from the refrigerator.

Halley laughed. "No, no, you're getting thanked for the other things you said. Me to find romance, well, let's say you'd have better odds of Port Royal canceling the annual seafood festival." Yet, she knew too well the terms of her benefactor's gift revolved around finding love, never mind a guy that cooked. "You know something, Irene? I need both a writing and a romance genie. My genies must be multi-talented." Halley grabbed an onion, and a knife and began absently chopping and considering. A face flashed in her mind's eye.

Irene nodded and shoved another cinnamon roll toward Halley then took the onions back with a wink.

"Tell me, are you acquainted with someone named Libby? I met her by happenstance yesterday."

"Happenstance, huh? It sounds like novelist words are flowing. That's a word that gets read, not spoken." Irene paused, glancing out the window. "I bet you're referring to Miss Libby Wellington. I do know her. She's someone I'd describe as—complex. Yes, that fits our Libby. She's a woman of some wealth whose family always summered here when she was growing up. Once Libby became a young woman, she left Newport's high society life and chose to make Port Royal her permanent home. She lives simply, but with grace and elegance, if that makes sense."

Halley nodded. "It makes sense to me. Please tell me more."

"Libby never married, though a constant rumor persists that she had a beau in her younger years. That didn't work out. No one ever knew who he was or if he even lived in Port. One of those sad love stories." Irene shook her head. "Libby is friendly enough, passing you on the street, though most days you can find her in the gardens at her home, Magnolia Manor. I'd say Libby's joy comes from her flowers, which most agree are the most beautiful anywhere around. I understand from gossip the small staff that works for her are treated like family. She's done a good job creating the type of environment that suits her nature. How'd I do?" Irene went to the stove and slid the vegetables into the large simmering pot. "Tell me your thoughts about Libby." Irene joined Halley, taking the opposite stool.

Halley's impressions of the woman matched Irene's. "I felt intrigued the moment she sat on the park's daisy bench next to me. It was unexpected. She looks at you with wise eyes. And the last time wise eyes looked at me was when the bishop confirmed me at our Episcopal Church. Oh, and the time my Nana took a read on me and knew I'd nicked her plate of fudge. Of course, the fact that I had chocolate smeared all over my mouth and hands helped her Sherlock me as the pincher. I digress."

Irene laughed.

"Anyway, back to Libby, I hope our paths cross again soon because she's someone I'd love to spend time with. I like her energy. How'd I do as a newcomer?" Halley parroted.

Irene took a moment before responding. "I'd say you're sure to see Libby again. Port is a small town, and that's one reason people here try not to make enemies." Irene took a plate to the dishwasher. "So, what's on your schedule today? Plenty I suspect. I still can't believe how your stars aligned with the rental and cottage. I'm so happy for you, Halley."

"Thanks, Irene. I hope I can work and get along with Ben Shaw. We started rocky with his taking over my vehicle and all, though he seems to have mellowed. Anyway, to answer your question, I need to make a fast trip to Star Isle and order a sign and then to Deja Brew to share my abode news with Ginger. I plan to postpone writing until I get settled at Sea Glass and can focus."

"Sea Glass?" Irene looked puzzled.

"Sorry, that's the new name for the bungalow I'm renting from Ben. I came up with Sea Glass, and he seemed to like it well enough. I'm buying a sign as a thank you. I can tell you the guy's obsessed with the color aqua, so naming the place Sea Glass fits."

Irene smiled. "Hmm, I have a hunch you may be developing your own thing for a certain contractor—"

"What? No way. Besides, I've got a novel to write and a cottage to get completed. And with that, I'm leaving you to that soup pot. See you at dinner time."

Chapter 13

Halley smiled as she drove to the coffee shop, pleased with the routed sign she'd chosen for Sea Glass. Hopefully, that gesture bought her good juju with Ben. They needed to get along, at least until he completed her cottage. Halley dismissed Irene's words for the umpteenth time about her having a thing for Ben. Simply absurd. She spied Cara ducking inside Deja. Great. *I bet Ben's in there waiting for her. Whatever. I need a parking place. A pull in one, yes, right here.* Halley whipped her SUV into the slot.

Ginger's roving eye connected with Halley before the shop's door closed. "Hey there. I was wondering when you'd make an appearance. Come sit on the stool and talk to me while I finish these two espressos." Ginger shoved a cup under the machine's dispenser in time to catch the first dark drips.

Halley plopped down and stole a glance to see where Cara had sat. She felt instant relief seeing the mayor's daughter chattering away with another young woman. Stop thinking about Ben, she admonished herself silently and turned her attention toward Ginger.

Walker appeared with an empty tray. "Want me to take those over to Cara?" He cleared his throat and his voice dropped a bit. "Before I do that, umm, Ginger, I got this thing to do, and I need to cut out early this afternoon. I know that I'm scheduled to work and all, but—"

"Is she that cute?" Ginger placed one cup on the tray. "This afternoon's going to be crazy busy. Your timing is lousy to hit me with this, Walker."

"Look, I'm sorry, but actually, it's more than this afternoon I need off. You see, my sister decided to have her baby a month early and my mom's insisting we help out for a week."

Ginger's face softened. "Walker, that's wonderful news. I trust your sister and the new baby are fine? Of course, you must go. I'll figure something out. Here's the second cup. Deliver this, and you can scoot."

Another of Halley's agreement stipulations hung on her next words. Miraculously she'd been given the opening to pitch her idea. "Sounds like you're in a bit of a lurch and need some waitressing help?"

"You're right. Walker's got his new niece to see, and then classes begin soon, so he'll need fewer hours. I guess I need to find someone else part-time. What ya having?" Ginger grabbed a cup.

Halley grinned. "I think I'll have a frothy cappuccino and that part-time job of yours."

"Are you serious? I'd love having you with me at Deja, but why?"

"That's easy. I need the money to supplement expenses while I write. And, let's be honest, I'm not the type to tuck myself away from the world and type a day away. I'm a social being, and your coffee shop meets that need in spades. Come on. Say yes," Halley pleaded.

Ginger hurried around the bar's corner and gave Halley a big hug. "Of course, I say yes, and I'll even throw in free coffees. When can you start?"

"Well, that brings me to my news I came to share." In between Ginger waiting on customers, Halley told her friend the details about the cottage and where she'd live until construction got completed. She omitted the part about sharing a pizza with Ben. That would raise Ginger's antenna. "All this to say, I can start Monday. Want me here at nine?"

"Perfect. I'll get with Walker and write the schedule for the rest of the month. It's September, but business stays brisk until after the holidays, and then winter chases even the hardiest tourists back home. Halley, are you sure this job is what you want?"

"Absolutely. We're helping each other." Halley paused. "Confession time. Yesterday I had the idea to work for you and hoped you might need me. I love Deja Brew. It's the first place I came when I discovered Port Royal."

Ginger grinned. "Isn't it amazing how destiny works?"

"I'm becoming a believer." Halley prepared to leave. She needed to follow up with Langdale about funds. "Listen, I've got to run. Oliver needs a down payment from me, and he's one man I won't keep waiting. See you later, and thanks again. I'm excited about this job."

Ginger managed a wave and turned to the line of customers.

Halley snaked around the line and once on the sidewalk produced a deep, throaty, "Yes!" Her little skip surprised even her

"My, that was quite a performance. The skip added a certain something. Might I inquire the reason for such happiness?"

Recognizing the voice, Halley spun around and stared up at Ben. *Why must he be so tall?* She couldn't decide if his smirk was condescending. She'd had her fill with those smirks in the corporate world and knew how to deflate the source, but this was Port Royal. She would play nice. Halley planted a smile on her face and let the next words match her mood. "Hi, Ben. You caught my nanosecond celebration of Ginger agreeing to let me work part-time at Deja."

"That's cool and congrats for nailing a job so quickly." He hesitated. "I'm confused. Aren't you planning to write?" Ben nodded to a passerby.

"Sure, but the job gives me the chance to get out and meet people. I can't sit in front of a computer screen all day long without going buggy. My muses and I need time off. It's a writer's thing." Halley realized her long, beaded necklace was hanging off her shoulder from her jig. Embarrassed, she straightened it.

Deja's door opened. "There you are, Ben." Cara claimed his arm and sent an icy stare to Halley. A polar ice cap seemed warm in comparison.

Halley ignored Cara. "Umm, Ben, I'll get the down payment money wired into your account for the cottage."

"Guess I'll see you tomorrow on moving day. I've got Sea Glass about ready for your arrival, but you'll have to make peace with our work trucks parked in the back."

"I can do that. Enjoy your coffee."

"Ben, whatever do you mean about moving day? What have I missed?" Cara's voice could drip faux maple syrup.

Halley hurried away, starving a chance for a reply from Ben or his haughty Cara. And, the question following her down the sidewalk was, *Why does it bother me so much seeing Cara with Ben?* The guy wasn't even her type. *Huh. Do I know what my type is?* She wasn't sure she'd ever figured that out.

She continued walking toward her vehicle, craving a distraction from thinking about Ben Shaw and paused at the Book Worm's display window. Her too vivid imagination ignited, envisioning a book signing poster featuring her novel. She couldn't picture the title yet, but the call to get the story out was back to chasing her. That feeling was welcomed.

"Do you see a book that wants to go home with you, Halley?" Libby looked through the glass, spying an interesting title. '*Flowers for Every Season.*' I must purchase that one."

"Hello, Libby. What a surprise to see you again, but hey, Port is a small town." Halley smiled. The town's sidewalk was a magnet for conversing. "That book's cover looks exquisite with the colorful blooms."

"Yes. What about a book for you? Anything?" Libby asked again.

"To be honest, I need to be about writing one and not purchasing. I've committed to that project. Oh, it nearly slipped my mind." Halley's face lit. "Your magic wand's powers delivered me the most wonderful cottage on the bay. Better than I could even imagine. It's under construction, but so worth the wait. The view fills me with joy."

"Why Halley, that's lovely news. It sounds like your faith and trust rewarded you handsomely."

"Yes, that reward came immediately after you left. I'm still in awe."

Libby nodded. "Please excuse me. I must purchase the gardening book and get to my next appointment. It was nice to see you again, young lady, and learn things worked out so well."

"Of course, and I'm truly grateful for those wise words you shared." Halley stepped aside for Libby to enter. She waited outside, watching Libby make her purchase and reflecting on Irene's words about the woman being friendly enough in passing. Libby seemed to hold her emotions in check. Halley continued to her vehicle, reveling that she'd secured a part-time job, got an update from Ben, and the cherry on top was seeing Libby once more. Glancing at the town square's clock, she had enough time to check if Beth emailed before Irene rang the dinner chime.

Chapter 14

Libby sat behind the wheel of her vehicle, amused watching two twin girls try and manage melting ice cream cones. On the other end of the phone, Sam Langdale's cell phone rang. He answered with a smile in his voice

"Hello, Libby. I'd planned to ring you later with an update."

"Good afternoon, Sam. I hope I've found you at a good time? My call shouldn't take but a few moments."

"I've got some moments, and I'm a gentleman. You go first."

"Yes, you are that, Sam. I've had another chance encounter with our Halley Bowen. The girl's managed to find what sounds like an enchanting cottage on the bay. I'm quite impressed with her real estate acumen."

"Yes, she emailed me about the cottage and sent the purchase contract with terms. I reviewed the documents for her. I agree. She's succeeded in negotiating a prime piece of real estate that wasn't even on the market. There's a buy-back clause should Halley ever decide to sell. The current owner has the first right of refusal. Under the circumstances, that's reasonable, and I blessed that contingency. I'll email you the particulars."

"Yes, do that, and I'm pleased to hear her choice meets your strict approval. I understand it's still under construction. I'm curious, who's the builder listed on the contract? Also, do you happen to know if Halley will remain at Buttercup Inn?"

Sam cleared his throat. "She's saving you money by renting a little bungalow behind the contractor's office until her cottage's completion. She emailed me the whole story. It seems the cottage was to be Ben Shaw's home, but he must sell it. He and his brother, Andy, own Shaw Construction and need cash to fund an upcoming commercial job. I feel for the guy having to sell his place on the bay. Gotta be hard."

Libby stared into space, wondering how she might help Ben, besides her two small renovations and feeding him scones. He seemed such a fine, hard-working young man and worthy of success.

"Libby? You still there?"

"Yes, yes. I was sympathizing with Mr. Shaw making such a hard sacrifice. Noteworthy. I recently met and hired him to do a small project for me. Do you have anything further to share about Halley's activities?"

"Only that she needs me to move money into her account. I'm going to speak with her and explain how I plan to handle the draws and such. I don't want her involved with overseeing the construction. After all, I'll deed this property into your blind trust until such time Halley proves worthy, and then I can easily transfer the title and keep anonymity for you."

"You have my complete trust in this matter. Sam, if the finished price of this cottage exceeds her allotment, make an exception and provide the funds. No doubt it's a great investment, and she's quite elated over her find. She must have the cottage."

"Will do. Halley's a little thing but knows her mind and how to get things done. I say again, Libby, you've made another excellent choice."

"I couldn't agree more. Talk to you later, and thanks, Sam." Libby applied fresh lipstick using the rearview mirror. She ignored Mick Duffy's wave as he passed by and put her vehicle in gear, turning toward Magnolia Manor and a second meeting that now carried much more significance.

***

"Miss Wellington, I appreciate your making time to meet so we can discuss my new design ideas for the pool house. I know you were agreeable to the plan I sketched before, but I believe I've captured better what you want and even added a few extras that won't drive up costs." Ben spread out the drawings on an antique wormy chestnut coffee table in Libby's study.

Libby studied the builder's face. His caring persona failed to hide old hurt, and she knew the look well. She had it, too. "Ben, I'm most impressed with your devotion to this project and attention to even small details. Whenever did you find time to do this additional work? I didn't expect to hear from you until next week since I'd already approved the project."

"Yes, ma'am, but I kept thinking we were missing an opportunity to make the pool house function better. The feeling wouldn't leave me, so I worked on the drawings into the morning hours." He gave a lopsided grin. "I had an epiphany on how to increase the shower and dressing area without changing how the plumbing pipes run. See here?" Ben spent the next few minutes explaining and answering Libby's questions until Mrs. Cookson appeared with a tray.

"Oh, thank you, Mrs. Cookson. Please place the tray here on the coffee table."

Mrs. Cookson gave a solemn nod and did as asked. Hands folded, she stood back.

Libby turned to Ben. "As you can see, I asked Mrs. Cookson to bake some of her delicious strawberry scones. I thought you might enjoy sampling before she made a big batch for your workers on Monday." Libby poured the iced tea and handed the crystal goblet to Ben with a floral napkin.

"I'd like to do more than sample. I want to relieve that plate of at least two right now."

Libby placed the sweets on a Limoges plate and passed it to Ben. "Please, enjoy. I suspect Mrs. Cookson is waiting for her compliment."

The cook dropped her head in unexpected shyness. "Yes, ma'am, I'd like to hear how Mr. Shaw finds my baking?"

Ben swallowed. "Mr. Shaw finds your scones the best he's ever tasted. Be warned some of my single workers may try and marry you, Mrs. Cookson."

"Ahh, go on with yourself. I'm an old widow, but I confess that I am quite merry. Quite merry." They all burst into laughter at her words. Mrs. Cookson took a chair, fanning her flushed face with her apron, while Libby and Ben relied on their iced tea to calm them.

Ben spoke first. "I apologize. I don't think a scone has ever had such an effect on me. Maybe I should take that second one home and eat it alone." He couldn't contain the laugh bubbling inside. The two women joined in.

Mrs. Cookson wrapped the scone in a napkin and handed it to Ben, chuckling as she went back to the kitchen.

Libby dabbed at her wet cheeks. "I'm not sure exactly what sent the three of us into such a state, but I did quite enjoy it. We might need to consider having Mrs. Cookson bake some boring chocolate chip cookies for the men on Monday?"

Ben offered a mock solemn nod and cleared his throat. "I believe chocolate chip cookies are an excellent choice and much appreciated on all fronts. I probably should go. I've kept you too long, though I am glad you liked the changes."

Libby's expression grew serious again. "Before you depart, I have a personal question. Please, don't feel any obligation to answer. Port is a small community, and news moves quickly." Libby bestowed a gentle smile before continuing. "I understand that you're in contract to sell your home on the bay. If my project is causing a financial strain before you get the first draw, I'd like to remedy that concern and send you home with a check to cover two advance draws. Would that help?"

***

Ben wasn't used to new clients showing such faith and trust in him. He sat nonplussed, unable to speak. The unexpected kindness threatened to crack the wall he'd spent a lifetime erecting to the outside world. Here sat Miss Libby Wellington stealing his heart and affection, and by golly, it felt good. Emotions flooded him. He rubbed his jaw, searching for words. "Miss Wellington, I don't know quite what to say. You see, I'm not great at expressing myself. Well, except for humor, as you already know." Ben broke into a grin. "Yes, our growing company does need a cash infusion to carry us into next year, but I can't accept early draws. You see, I mean to earn your respect by exceeding expectations for this job you've given us, but thank you, Miss Wellington, for the offer and trust." An emotional Ben looked out the window. "Right now, I'm thankful I have a place to sell and someone who's going to appreciate it. At least, I hope she will, and if not, she can sell it back to me."

Libby leaned toward the young man. "You continue to impress me, and that's no easy task. Some might even say it's impossible." Libby rose and extended her hand. "My offer stands should you change your mind. I'm going to anticipate Monday when work begins, and Mrs. Cookson gets another opportunity to make merry. Rupert will see you out."

"Thank you again, Miss Wellington." Ben gathered his drawings and looked up to see Libby leave and Rupert standing in the corner, waiting expressionless. He'd analyze over a chocolate malt how Libby Wellington had captured his heart and respect in two meetings. As for Halley, soon to play a significant role in his day-to-day life, he'd need more than a malt to cope with her as a tenant.

Chapter 15

Saturday morning greeted Halley with abundant sunshine and a flurry of phone calls. Beth called to wish her an easy move and reminded Halley it should be a snap since Sea Glass came furnished. Beth also slipped in that London would keep her longer, and Percy was already there settling in with his British-sounding meow.

Sam Langdale begged ten minutes while Halley packed her suitcase, phone in hand. He seemed pleased she'd gotten a job in such a short time and found the cottage. She felt relieved when he avoided asking if any romance was budding. Port Royal wasn't exactly the mecca for eligible men meeting her requirements. *What requirements?* Great, she'd missed the attorney's last words.

Sam took time and explained the steps he'd employ to release funds and ensure the cottage was meeting specifications. The attorney had already hired an outside inspector to check on construction before the final draw. He surprised Halley by saying Ben was on board with the terms and had signed the agreement.

Halley had one major concern still hanging over her that the attorney needed to alleviate. "Mr. Langdale, I remain adamant that I don't want anyone to know about my benefactor or question how I have funds to purchase the cottage. I want to live a simple, uncomplicated life here. Can you assure me it will be kept private?"

"And, so you shall, Ms. Bowen. There's nothing unusual about having your attorney in Charlotte handle real estate and financial affairs. I find left alone, people assume their answers." Langdale chuckled. "Let the curious ones assume you've inherited or are an impressive saver from that corporate job. Regardless, it's no one's concern. I can assure you Mr. Shaw did not question your financial health, and if anyone should, it's him. Rest easy."

"Thank you for understanding and eliminating my worry." She hung up, knowing the gift of a year to live her dream life was indeed unfolding.

Halley's cell phone rang moments later. This time it was Sally calling to confirm Halley's attendance at Andy's birthday party the next day. The celebration had slipped Halley's mind from the whirlwind over the last few days. A gift—she needed to buy Andy something, despite never having met the guy. And of course, she could expect to see Ben there.

Irene and Joe greeted Halley with big smiles when she and Éclair entered the foyer. "Moving day. The next leg of your big adventure. What can I do to help?" Joe flexed his biceps. "I woke up my muscles this morning."

Halley chuckled. "Irene must have fed you spinach last night. Thanks, Joe. My suitcases are upstairs. I'm on my way out with Éclair's things and my tote."

"You do know we expect to see your face at Buttercup often? You've got a place at the table whenever you crave that home-cooked meal. And take me up on giving feedback on that story as you write. Remember, I taught English until Buttercup netted Joe and me." Irene scooped up Éclair. "Chaucer is going to miss your smushed-in face."

Halley smiled. "You two define wonderful and thank you for all the offers. Count on seeing me at your dining table."

Irene and Joe headed upstairs to Halley's rooms.

Mrs. Nelson appeared with her husband and the Chesters. "There you are, young lady. We're off and wanted to bid you goodbye. We've had such a wonderful visit."

The other three guests voiced their agreement and well wishes.

"Then you'll return. Be warned. Buttercup Inn is magnetic." Halley waved and headed out the door, arms laden with luggage.

***

Halley fell into the bungalow's chair, letting her legs dangle over the arms. Éclair jumped into her lap, purring. "So, you like our new digs, huh, kitty? Guess we're as settled as possible, given we won't be here that long." She glanced at her watch. It was late and she hadn't eaten much all day, distracted as she was with unpacking. No wonder her tummy was chatty. The refrigerator offered only cold, empty shelves. Halley jumped, hearing a tap on the front door.

Ben stood grinning, holding Chinese take-out in one hand and a potted plant in the other. "Welcome to Sea Glass. I thought you might like dinner and a—well, whatever this plant is. It looked kind of nice."

"Wow, thank you. Do you want to come—"

Ben zipped past her toward the kitchen, placing the plant on the dining room table.

"I guess you do want to come inside." Halley laughed and followed with a curious Éclair ambling behind.

Ben arranged the cartons on the counter and spied the cat. "Ah, you must be Miss Éclair. I brought something along for you, too, if Halley says it's okay? He held up a tiny container. "A morsel of fish."

"Éclair will love you forever. What else you got there, mister? I'm famished." Halley popped the lids. Oh, sweet and sour shrimp and chicken with snow peas, so good. Did you get spring rolls? Yes, you did." She took a bite. "Let me grab plates, serving spoons, and two glasses of water. Sorry. Grocery shopping is on my errand list."

"Water's fine." Ben took his glass.

Éclair tucked into her bowl, making happy smacking sounds.

Spotting the pot of flowers sitting on the table, Halley thought perhaps Ginger was right about Ben being a nice guy. Then an image of the pouting Cara flashed into her mind. She wondered what Ben's girlfriend would think about him sharing a meal with his new renter.

Ben pulled out Halley's chair. "Have a seat. That'll give you time to decide on the toast."

"A toast? With ice water? Sure, okay." She waited for her neighbor, landlord, builder, and maybe friend to settle. Halley raised her glass. "To the start of a beautiful working relationship."

Ben nodded and clinked his glass to Halley's. "So, would you like your own entrée, or do you want to split them?"

"I like both choices, so let's share." She grabbed the carton closest, scooped her portion, and passed it to Ben. "Do you cook?"

"Yep, but my menu is pretty basic. What about your cooking skills?" Ben snagged his spring roll, dragging it across the hot mustard.

Halley paused to consider how best to own the truth. "Well, let me say it this way. Irene exacted a promise from me when I left earlier. I must sit at Buttercup's dining table as needed."

Ben laughed. "Well, it's a good thing you've got a meal invitation for tomorrow at Sally and Andy's."

Halley laughed. "Yes, I'm grateful to Sally, but hey, I have other talents that make up for my culinary lacks." She poured Ben more water.

Ben took a sip. "Besides loving to decorate? I'm curious. What other talents belong to Halley Bowen?" His tone was teasing.

Halley considered her reply. "You might be interested to know that I'm talented, maybe even gifted, at removing the detonator from angry clients when, for example, we failed to deliver a product on time. Good, huh?"

"I suppose. What else you got to brag about?" Ben sparred back.

Halley thought about her new job. "Well, I'm excellent at waitressing and making the customer feel welcome. You should stop by Deja next week and experience my talented waitressing skills."

Ben grinned. "Wow, that's impressive times two. First, you like to waitress and second that you're going to work while writing this novel. I mean, do you need to work?"

"I do. I'm practical. Is that another talent?"

"I'm not sure I'd call that a talent." Ben shook his head and scooped up rice with his chopsticks.

"Okay then, being practical means I like to have extra jingle. Also, it helps my writing if I can observe others and draw off those experiences. What better place than Ginger's to check both boxes?" Halley peered into the near-empty carton and speared the last shrimp.

"That makes sense. Congrats again then on the new job." Ben lifted his glass to toast.

Their fingers grazed as they clanked glasses. Halley felt a tingle, then both of them pulled away as if they'd touched a hot outlet. Halley jumped up quickly to clear the table, confused by the feelings welling in her chest. Ben stood up and tossed the containers in the recycle can, not looking at her. She had no doubt they were both ignoring the spark that had flared between them.

Halley hung the dish towel over the faucet. "Thanks for helping and of course for the meal. Listen—"

"You're welcome. Look, I've got some plumbing bids to review. I'm going to leave you to settle in." Ben moved toward the door.

"Okay, sure, and I need to—to run an errand," stammered Halley. She held onto the door, feeling awkward, and watched Ben cross the yard and go inside the house. What happened to their cheery evening? She'd felt comfortable until that last stupid toast, and they touched. For pity's sake, she wasn't sixteen on a first date, but right now she felt like it. Hormones weren't overrated after all, but hers were sure latent.

Halley hurried to the bathroom and splashed her face with cold water. The much-acclaimed cold shower could wait until later. She did have an errand. Grabbing her keys, Halley went in search of a birthday gift for Andy, already fretting at the idea of seeing Ben Shaw the next afternoon.

***

Sunday morning ushered in a large serving of happiness. Halley felt pleased with the functionality of her writing niche. Once seated at her chair with her computer in her lap, the shift to writer happened, and three opening pages of her novel stared back. Writing the first few hundred words always proved the hardest while working at the newspaper. She'd learned that once words flowed, their constancy remained until the story's end, so she celebrated that cleared hurdle.

Later that day, wearing her favorite sleeveless maxi dress and strappy sandals, Halley glanced once more in the mirror at her makeup. An outdoor party asked for a light and natural application. She'd dusted bronzer along her cheeks, gave her lashes a coat of mascara, and finished with a rose lip gloss complementing the colors in her dress. Halley called this new signature style effortless and straightforward, and the reward for moving to Port Royal. She felt zero melancholy for leaving behind the rigors of a corporate job and the time and money wasted on appearance.

Placing Andy's present in her straw tote, she gave Éclair instructions to ignore the dining table's flowering plant and closed the front door.

The sound reached Halley before its source. Mick's vintage SUV chugged around the corner, his red hair catching the wind from the open window. Halley stood puzzled when he turned up the driveway, stopping next to her.

"Hey there, lass. I've direct orders to fetch you. Best get in and not risk Sally's wrath at our late arrival." Mick released the door handle and threw a newspaper behind the seat.

"Well, this is a surprise." Halley hopped in the passenger seat. "I guess this means you're a party guest, too."

"That I am, lass. That I am. I've known the two lads since they showed up at Port Royal looking for work." Mick turned toward town.

Halley laughed, not minding the open window blowing her ponytail. "Let me guess, you scoundrel. I bet you put them to work shrimping for you."

"Course I did. They were hungry, and I had their answer. You see, Ben had worked his way through college at State while trying to look after Andy. They were foster kids who'd seen their share of hard knocks but still managed to stay together. I couldn't help but take in those rascals." Mick grew thoughtful.

"You did more than get those boys on that boat, Mick Duffy. I bet you brought them home to live with you and helped Andy and Ben find direction. Didn't you?" Halley squeezed his forearm. "Such a softie."

"Well, they needed someone to care and help them figure some things out. Ben and Andy aren't one bit lazy, but man can they ever eat your larder empty. I should never have taught them how to cook." Mick chuckled. "At least I got Andy married off. Sally takes care of him, and she does a fine job of it. Now, Ben, he's been my challenge." Mick came to a red light. His arm flew out the window to wave at another local fisherman. "How'd the flounder behave today, Crusty?"

"Good, Mick. I dropped over a dozen cleaned ones at your Captain's Table." Crusty gave a salute before moving on.

A confused Halley cleared her throat to gain Mick's attention. "Uhm, Mick, I'm past curious. Answer me two things. Why did that fisherman call the Captain's Table Restaurant yours, and what makes Ben such a challenge?"

Mick slapped his knee and let a chortle rip. "Gal, you'd make a first-rate detective. Might want to consider it if that book you're to write can't find a home."

"I'll keep that in mind, but you're dodging. You better answer or I might feel inclined to tell Irene to stop feeding you. I've got clout with her, too."

Mick rubbed his chin, pretending to worry. "Okay, I own the restaurant. Fact is, I own a few of them around."

"How many of them around?" Halley mimicked. "Hold on. The Captain's Table is a chain of restaurants all along the Carolina coast. Mick Duffy, you old salty dog, I had no idea." Halley sat back in her seat, absorbing the revelation. Boy, she'd pegged Mick all wrong.

"So now you know. I have some fish houses scattered around. Truth be told, lass, I let my managers run things nowadays. They do a good job for me. Yep, I put together a top-notch group and that allows me to—"

"To shrimp, and lure unsuspecting young people aboard your boat. I'm starting to see the picture here. You have an ulterior motive for inviting them to work, maybe helping guys like Ben and Andy find their way," supplied Halley. Mick was proving quite the enigma.

Mick's mouth turned up at the corners. "More or less." He pulled the truck over. "Andy's house is at the end of this street, but I still owe you the telling of why Ben's my challenge."

"This I can't wait to hear because I don't get the guy. I mean he's super smart and all, but—"

"Ben's broken, Halley. Broken from years of hurt by adults when he was growing up—broken from years of neglect, hunger, and disappointment. None of which the boy had a lick of control over. Some fostering is only about people getting the government money, and that's Andy and Ben's story. They relied on each other to survive. Ben's drive to become something got the boys to our town, Port Royal. They were my first takers to work on the shrimp boat. They told me years later that time on my boat taught them what hard work could produce. And lass, I'm not talking about the obvious, but that mettle you need if you're a Ben or Andy coming from an empty place." Mick tapped his chest.

Hearing Mick's explanation, Halley had an epiphany. "Mick, when you invite young people to work a day with you on the boat, you see if they need your help in some way. I suspect the same way Ben and Andy needed you. Fess up."

"Why would I want to do that?" Mick joshed.

"For the same reason you kept offering me a day out to sea with you each time I visited Buttercup. You sensed I needed something more, that I wasn't thrilled with my life. Oh, Mick." Emotion filled Halley's heart. She leaned over the console and planted a kiss on his rosy cheek.

Mick stared out the windshield. "Aye, but you found a way back to us, without the benefit of my boat. You're a gal that knows how to chase a dream." Mick adjusted his cap. "And town talk, which normally I have no truck with, says you got yourself employed and a nice place to hang your bonnet."

"All true, especially the dream part. So, what are you wanting for Ben that's defying the powers of Mick Duffy? How can I help? I suddenly find myself a loyal supporter of your philanthropy."

"Pretty simple, lass. I'd like to see Ben find what Andy has. Real love. The kind he can trust. It's rare. I give you that, but it's what can heal what's broken—his heart. Do you get me?"

Halley dug two peppermints out of her tote and handed one to Mick. It bought her pondering time. She wanted to discover real love, too. "I get you. I don't know how you help someone want to let another person inside, especially a woman. Ben's had years to put up walls. Still, he has Cara. That should give you hope." Halley rolled the candy wrapper around her fingers, ignoring how saying Cara's name made her feel.

Mick puffed out a breath. "That ain't the gal for our Ben. She's as shallow as a tidal pool."

A laugh escaped Halley. "That's plenty shallow."

Mick put the vehicle in gear. "We're late. Promise you'll keep our little chat between us? All of it, lass?"

Halley pretended to seal her lips and toss the key out the window. "Sorry. I have no clue what you're talking about. Let's go sing happy birthday and eat cobbers." Halley pointed her hand forward.

"Cobbers?" Mick frowned, repeating the word.

"Tulip will explain. She's my new bestie." Halley knew what she'd learned this afternoon would linger long after the moon appeared outside her bedroom window.

Chapter 16

"Halley, you came. You came." Tulip ran and wrapped her arms around Halley's hips.

"Yes, I'm here and ready to eat three cobbers with you, or did you already gobble them all up?" Halley twirled one of Tulip's braids. "Say hi to Mick."

Tulip grew shy. "Hi, Uncle Mick. Did you bring me—"

Mick pulled taffy from his shirt pocket. "I sure did, lassie. You said banana flavor this time." He passed two sticks down to Tulip's waiting hands.

"Thank you," Clasping her taffy, a giggling Tulip pulled Halley outside. "Mommy, here's Halley. We can eat now." Tulip promptly sat in a chair with a booster seat and opened her taffy.

Sally's face brightened. "I'm so glad you both could make it. Tulip, do not, and I repeat, do not take even an itsy bite until you've eaten your dinner." Sally turned back to Halley. Mick had moseyed to the grill where the men congregated. "Come on, let me introduce you. It's a small group. Unfortunately for us, Irene and Joe have a full inn and didn't dare leave the guests."

Halley nodded. "Sally, first, I've got to say again thank you for inviting me, and that may well be the cutest pair of tomato-red sandals in Port Royal."

"Aren't they? I bought the shoes for July fourth and keep finding outfits to wear them with before fall makes me box them up." Sally pulled a face.

Halley gave an understanding nod. "I own shoes that refuse their box. Instead, they stay out and torment me."

"Don't you hate that?"

"I knew I liked you, Sally Shaw. Tell me, who am I meeting besides the birthday boy?"

"Follow me," Sally led her guest over to the woman stirring a giant bowl of potato salad. "Halley, this is my mom, Liz. She owns The Book Worm."

"Hi, Liz. It's lovely to meet you. I love your shop. Whenever I'm there, it feels like I've time-traveled, and Charles Dickens might appear from behind a stack of books at any moment." Halley smiled.

"Well, that's a compliment I shall savor. You must stop by again soon." Liz turned toward her daughter. "Is there anything else you want me to bring out?"

"Oh, let me help with something, too," Halley chimed.

"Thanks, you two, but all that's left is for Andy to finish grilling the burgers. Come on, Halley, more people to greet."

Halley locked on two other familiar heads in a huddle with Oliver. Smile in place, she followed Sally.

Ginger broke ranks and hurried to meet Halley halfway. "How terrific you came to celebrate with us. Sally told me how you'd met, and that Tulip invited you." Ginger offered a quick hug.

"Don't I have the best taste in girlfriends? You, Sally, and Tulip."

"Thank you," chorused the smiling Sally and Ginger. The other woman merely offered a bored stare.

Sally pulled Halley closer. "I don't know if you've met Cara yet?"

Cara stiffened and answered first. "We've not been properly introduced, though I do recall seeing you somewhere recently. It's slipped my mind." A plastic smile dressed her face.

Sally and Ginger got summoned to the grill, leaving Halley alone with Cara.

Cara touched her diamond hoop earrings. The long white gauzy skirt and matching sleeveless top showcased her model figure. She wore an expression of mild disdain. "*You* obviously haven't wasted any time trying to make friends. Emphasis on trying."

Halley's manners trumped her desire to say something snarky. "The people at Port Royal have always been so welcoming and kind whenever I visit. That's a big part of why I've chosen to move here."

Cara sipped her lemonade while studying Halley. "How nice for you."

"Yes, and I'm so grateful to Oliver for putting me in a contract with Ben, and of course, I'm thrilled by the bonus of renting the bungalow until I can move into my cottage. It's all been seamless."

"So it appears."

Halley noted Cara's attention moved to observing Ben and Andy pile burgers on a platter. "Guess it's time to find a seat."

Halley moved toward Tulip's table.

Cara came up from behind. "Find yourself another table. Ben insists he and I sit with the child." Cara rushed to Ben's side.

Mick passed by, grinning. "Tidal pool. I call 'em as I see 'em."

Those two words brought Halley's good mood back. She snagged Mick's arm, reeling him back. "Introduce me to Andy before we sit down."

"Aye." Mick covered Halley's hand with his and walked them to the grill. "Don't pull up anchor yet, Andy. It's time you meet my newest girlfriend, Halley Bowen."

"Hi, Halley. Glad you took the invite. My two girls told me about your meeting, and of course, my brother has filled me in on the real estate transactions. As for you being Mick's girlfriend, that's pure malarkey." Andy gave Mick a friendly shove.

Halley grinned. She liked Andy and his personality. "Happy birthday, and it's wonderful to be here with you all. As for Mick and me? He's for sure my friend, and I am a girl. So…" Halley grinned and shrugged her shoulders.

"Nice middle-ground answer." Andy chuckled.

Mick saddled up to Andy. "Told you, she's a charmer. Let's eat some burgers, birthday boy. Got an empty plate in each hand, one for me and one for Halley. I'm not sure about eating those cobbers I've heard about."

Halley took a chair at an empty table and waited for Mick to join her. She watched Cara act all sugary sweet as she served Ben from the buffet spread and asked herself why she cared how Cara behaved.

Mick sat down. "Here you go. I served you a sampling of it all and discovered what cobbers are, and I like them. Got two, in fact. How's your plate look?" Mick dabbed a hunk of butter on his corn on the cob.

"My plate is perfect. Thank you, Mick."

"Halley, aren't you gonna sit with me? You promised." Tulip came over, dragging her booster seat to the chair next to Halley.

Mick hopped up to help the little girl get situated and then returned to his food with gusto and renewed silence.

"Of course, I want to sit next to you. I'm so glad you found me. Is your mommy bringing your food?" Halley tucked a napkin around Tulip's shirt collar.

"Yes, Mommy fixes my plate, but can I have one of your chips?"

"Sure. Take two. One for each hand while you wait."

Ginger passed by and whispered to Halley, "You're one of us now, kiddo. Tulip deems it so." She and Oliver claimed the table for two.

Spying his niece, Ben did a U-turn, leaving Cara at the table abandoned by Tulip. "Hey jitterbug, I thought we had a date? May I join you?" He sat down, and Halley couldn't help an internal smirk at Cara's put-out demeanor.

"Okay, but does a date mean a tea party, too?" Tulip wrinkled her nose and crunched her potato chip.

"Absolutely, a date can mean a tea party. What are you serving this afternoon?" Ben took a bite of his burger.

Sally set Tulip's plate down and bestowed a kiss on her daughter's head before joining her husband, Cara, and Liz.

Tulip picked up her cob, taking a bite. "I think taffy sticks and lemolade."

Halley grinned. "Lemolade, huh? Maybe you mean lemonade?" She exchanged nods with Ben.

Tulip chewed, pondering the word. "Uncle Ben, we will drink lemonade in my teacups, but I broke one. Mommy said it's an oops. And, Halley, you come to my tea party, too."

Cara appeared and planted herself in the empty chair next to Ben. "I thought we had a plan to eat together?"

"Sorry, Cara. My niece's charm drew me right over. Please join us. We were discussing Tulip's tea party."

"I want Halley and Uncle Ben to have lemonade—lemonade and taffy with me," Tulip announced to the table.

Reading the tense scene, Mick put his fork down long enough to reply, "Lassie, methinks you'll have four of us at that tea table. And, mayhap more taffy sticks for all." Mick patted his inside pocket.

"Now, let's all eat our cobbers because our Andy's got presents to open and candles to blow out."

Ben winked at Halley and tucked into his meal.

Cara made a face and left their table.

Halley let the warm sense of belonging that even Cara's icy daggers couldn't extinguish envelop her.

***

Halley chuckled as Andy devoured two slabs of chocolate layer cake and stole the iced roses off his wife's slice, declaring birthday privileges. Gifts surrounded him. And like a kid, he tore into the first one using one hand while he finished his cake with the other.

He caught Sally's scowl. "Hey, I'm a multi-tasker. Let's see what big bro brought me." He tossed the wrapping paper to the side and held up a new putter. "Ben, this is a beauty, and I like that you think I'm going to have time to use the thing."

"Glad you approve. As for time, well, it's not as if the putter will break down or pine away. It'll wait to help you improve your game." Ben laughed.

"It's not like that boat of yours will go wanting either," Andy bantered.

Mick stood. "Now boys, you'll find time for your hobbies. You always have. Andy, open this one. It's from yours truly." Mick took a bow when the leather golf gloves got waved for all to admire.

Andy tore through his gifts, exclaiming his appreciation for each one. He raised the present from Halley up in the air. "Last one, and it's from our new friend, Halley."

Sally chirped in, "Halley, you didn't need to bring a present."

"Yes, she did. It's Daddy's birthday," Tulip piped in.

"You're so right, Miss Tulip. Now, let's see if your daddy likes it." Halley grabbed the little girl's hand and squeezed.

"Wow, super cool. A laser level, *and* it's the latest version."

Halley smiled, pleased she'd scored a hit. "I confess the guy at the hardware store convinced me it would be handy for a contractor. He felt confident you hadn't purchased that one."

Ginger and Oliver delivered a high-five to Halley.

Ben extended his arm. "Pass that over here. I may want one."

Cara mumbled something, excused herself, and went inside the house.

"Time for our tea party." Tulip jumped up and down, flapping her arms. "Come to my playhouse." She tugged on Ben's shirt. "Come on, Uncle Mick and Halley." They made a hand–holding-chain sans Cara, walking toward Tulip's clapboard playhouse.

Halley took a moment to appreciate the little house's charm. The exterior paint matched the main house complete with two front windows, but it was the darling front porch with two children's rockers that stole her heart. Of course, once inside, the adults had to forgo the chairs and scrunch around the table sitting on the braided rug while Tulip poured a thimbleful of liquid in each miniature cup. Mick made a big show of dividing the taffy stick's evenly between the four of them.

As soon as Ben lifted his cup, Halley lost her tea party manners. His little finger tilted to the heavens proving he'd received education on teacup etiquette. Laughter consumed her.

"What?" Ben asked with mock confusion.

Mick joined in laughing. "Next thing I may hear Ben, is you're having high tea over at Libby Wellington's. What do you think, lass?"

Halley tried to put a serious face on before answering. "I'm more worried Ben might want to borrow my grandmother's frilly parasol should the day look cloudy."

"Shut up, you two. I'm in character as any good uncle who's attending a lovely tea party should behave. Isn't that right, jitterbug?"

Tulip nodded, chewing her taffy with cheeks gorged like a chipmunk's.

Sally appeared. "Okay, you party animals, it's Tulip's bath time. The others have left for home and said to tell you goodnight."

"Not yet, Mommy. I want to see Uncle Ben's frilly parasol." Tulip's lower lip pouted.

"Sweetie, I'd like to see that, too, but we'll have to check out Ben's fashion accessory another time." Sally winked at Ben. "I'll want to hear more about this." She turned and led Tulip outside.

"No, you do not." Ben hollered to his sister-in-law. He looked at Halley as if daring her to speak.

"Guess we'd better get home. Mondays always ask a lot," Mick said. "Listen, Ben, how about giving Halley a ride since Cara high-tailed it? I mean, the lass lives out back of your place and all."

"I don't want Ben to feel—"

"No, it's fine. Cara's gone and likely going to snub me all week for not making her the center of tonight's universe." Ben led the way outside.

Mick massaged his back. "No more Tulip parties for this body. I got to stand here and flex some things. You two go straight home," he said with evident mirth.

"You're not tricking me again." Halley waited for Ben to activate the truck's power step so she could climb into the cab. "So much easier. This truck is twice as tall as me. I keep expecting an oxygen mask to drop down from the headliner."

Ben laughed. "Do you want another a gratis ride home or not, Ms. Bowen?"

"Why yes, kind sir, I so appreciate you extending me this itty-bitty favor in my hour of need." Halley's southern accent would garner any linguist's approval.

Ben turned the truck in the opposite direction of home. "Well, since you're acting so uncharacteristically accommodating this evening, might you accompany me to check on my boat? I promise it won't take long."

"Sure, I'd love to see your boat. Wanna tell me the story about how the two of you met?"

"Me and my boat? You have a way with words." Ben grinned

"Let's hope they serve me when writing my novel. About you and that boat?" Halley returned the smile.

Ben veered onto Bay Drive and glanced at the water noting the tide was out. "You could say Mick introduced us. Andy and Sally had married, and I was trying to find my direction. Mick kept me busy doing different jobs for him, and I suppose he ran out of things, waiting for me to chart a course." Ben's chuckle didn't hide a flitting pain on his face. Hayley guessed the memory wasn't all that sweet.

"I know that feeling all too well. Charting a course is daunting. We are simpatico on that one. Go on," Halley encouraged.

"Simpatico, huh? Good to know. Anyway, one morning Mick shows up at the house I'm renting, which so happens to be where I still live. That's a whole another story. He drags me off to the marina and introduces me to this cuddy tied at the dock."

"Cuddy?" Halley asked, confused.

"I'll explain in a bit. I can tell you the shoddy condition of the boat made stepping on the deck seem foolhardy." Ben laughed.

"On second thought, maybe I don't want to meet your boat."

"Yes, you do. Anyway, Mick tells me the boat is mine. A gift from him. He promised if I committed to restoring the cuddy, it would return the favor. Mick knew I was clueless about what I wanted to do but had plenty of pent-up ambition. I've always enjoyed working with my hands, creating, making something right." Ben paused.

"That's why you make such a fine builder. At least that's what I hear. You're going to have to prove it to me."

"That I can do." Ben's mouth turned up at the corners. "You know how the story ends. Guy gets boat, guy learns how to care for boat, guy restores boat, or at least guy is trying to."

"And guy learns commitment, gains direction, and—"

"And here we are, but yes, that's the super-condensed version."

Halley walked with Ben down to the dock listening to the marina's unique song. Sailboats' rigging tinkled with the breeze. Boats rubbed against the dock's bumpers, making deep thuds. But the sound she loved most was the water lapping against the boats' hulls. "I've got a question. It's personal."

"Shoot." Ben recoiled a rope that blocked the walkway.

"Why didn't you sell the boat instead of your cottage? I mean, Oliver said you had a mortgage on the cottage, but you own the lot. I know that bayfront lots should bring a nice chunk of change, but maybe the boat money would suffice? Maybe?"

Ben stopped and faced Halley straight on. "That's an easy answer. Selling the cuddy isn't an option. She's still teaching me lessons."

"Ahh, lessons. That I understand. Thank you for trusting me with the story."

Ben nodded and walked ahead a few yards. "And here she is. Come aboard." His voice changed to lighthearted again.

Halley took in the small boat and burst out laughing.

Ben looked surprised and confused. "I'm offended. My boat's offended. What's so funny?"

Halley covered her face, not looking at the vessel, trying to gain composure. "The color," she managed to get out before laughter took over.

Ben's eyebrows raised. "The color? The color is perfect. She likes this color. I like this color."

"Yes, you surely do like aqua. No commitment issues here."

Ben frowned, looking at his boat. "Hey, aqua and white look great on her. I even like the navy detail stripe running along the sides."

Halley's face broke into a smile. "Okay, I hear you. Tell me about your cuddy."

"All right." Ben shrugged. "I guess I won't take offense." His smile returned. "Here's your seat." He perched on the captain's chair and waited for Halley to settle. "A cuddy is a boat with a small cabin used for shelter. Mine is twenty-two-footer with a throaty outboard that can get her on a plane. I've outfitted the cabin by adding a head and berth. She makes a great fishing boat for these waters or simply cruising around. Though the boat has some age, she's getting pretty decked out. Pardon the pun."

Halley grinned. "This is a super nice boat and so pristine, Ben. You should feel proud of your accomplishment."

"Would you like to see a picture of the before?"

"I would." Halley watched him duck into the cabin.

"Here." Ben handed her a framed photograph.

"This can't be the same boat. No way." Halley took in the transformation and the man that had achieved what should have been impossible. Mick was a wise old coot. "You've done so much. I don't know how the boat in this picture stayed afloat."

"Imagine seeing her in real life that first day. I was convinced Mick had gone off the deep end." Ben smirked. "She continues as my steadfast and stern teacher. Sorry for the puns. They flow easily around the water."

"So I'm hearing. Maybe you should write?"

Ben shook his head and tucked the photograph away. He grabbed a rag to polish the windshield's chrome.

Halley peeked into the tidy cabin. The berth's tight coverlet would get a nod from any navy inspection. "Do you ever sleep on the boat?"

"It depends on how we're getting along when I'm here working."

Halley laughed. "I see. You've held back one important piece of information. The boat's name?"

"Ah, yes, her name is *Seas the Day*, and so far, that has been one of my most valuable lessons she's taught." Ben gazed at the bay. "Excuse me while I check to see if the guy installed the part on the motor."

Halley watched Ben walk to the stern and lift a cover off the engine. She tried to ignore how his bicep muscles flexed and how the knit polo shirt accentuated broad shoulders when he tugged on cables. Despite his addiction to aqua and parallel parking intimidation, there was plenty to like about Ben Shaw.

***

Ben threaded the truck up the driveway and swore. "No driveway lights. The circuit must have tripped them." He killed the engine and twisted to face Halley. "Thanks for coming aboard the cuddy and listening to my story. I don't usually run my mouth about—"

"You?" Halley offered. She held her tote but didn't release the door.

"Yeah, me. You're easy to talk to, and besides, you liked *Seas the Day*."

"Thank you for the compliment. And of course I like your boat. She's cute and sassy."

"Like you," Ben responded. He seemed surprised by his words as he turned and jumped out of the truck.

Halley came around to his side of the vehicle, witnessing the confusion play across his face. "Relax, Ben. I know Cara is your girlfriend. I'm going to say goodnight. Thanks for the ride." She didn't wait for an answer. She had enough to ponder, starting with Mick's revelations and Ben sharing parts of his story. What unsettled her the most was a silly flutter that had taken up residence in her solar plexus. Sitting next to Ben at Tulip's tea party and observing his affection for the little girl had melted her.

And his last words about her being cute and sassy had certainly thrown her.

Chapter 17

Monday morning found Halley at Deja Brew wearing her friendly smile, jeans, and a printed apricot-colored t-shirt. She'd copied Ginger's lead to dress down, which suited the vibe of the coffee shop. "I'm ready for training. We've got a half-hour before opening to get me useful."

"Let's get after it, girl," Ginger said. "Follow me."

Ginger used the allotted time for instructing and handed an apron to Halley. "See, I told you the job was easy. You're officially ready to launch into coffee service. Put that smile on, while I unlock the door for showtime."

"Before you open, I want to say again, thanks for hiring me. I can tell I'm going to love this job." Halley grinned.

"And the job's going to love you right back, and you get all the free coffee you can drink." Ginger tied her apron and moved toward the door.

Moments later, Halley scanned the line of waiting customers. Judging by Ginger's gyrations around the espresso machine, the morning wasn't cooperating. "I'm here ready to help. What can I do first?"

Ginger wiped her forehead. "If you know how to talk to a temperamental espresso machine, I'll give you a raise on the spot."

"A raise, you say? Step aside. Go take orders." Halley noted the error code displayed on the coffee maker. She grabbed the wire and followed it under the counter, crawling her way to the outlet. "Okay, you moody thing. It's Monday and time to get to work." She pulled the plug and counted to ten before reconnecting. She looked up to see a familiar face leaning over the counter, staring down at her. "You. Back in my world, and it's only nine o'clock?"

Ben stole a glance at his watch. "Looks like trouble down there to me, and I'm in dire need of my morning triple shot."

Halley stood, dusting her hands off. "You might want to get in line. That's how getting a coffee here works." She moved toward the machine, sensing him following along the counter.

Ginger beamed. "You did it, Halley. I'm giving you a fifty-cent raise. We're back in the coffee business." She placed a cup under the dispenser and nodded to the waiting couple. "Go find a seat. We'll get those vanilla lattes to you in a jiffy."

"Ah Ginger, I'm not worth that generous fifty cents. Wait and see how I perform today." Halley lived to spar. She grabbed the lattes, delivered them, and hurried back, relieved to see the other customers had left with their brews. Ben had found a corner seat and was chatting on a cell phone.

Ginger deposited the cup on Halley's tray with a wink. "Triple espresso, and you know where you're going with that. Make sure Ben gives you get a fat tip."

Halley scrunched her face at Ginger and tried to walk casually toward Ben. She ignored the return of the confounding teenage flutter. At this rate, she'd break out in zits and pop bubble gum within the week. "Here's your triple, guaranteed to amp you until next Wednesday." Halley's hand moved to place the cup on the table only to collide with Ben's hand trying to help. The cup shook and fragrant vanilla coffee splashed out.

"Whoa, that's hot. I'm awake now." Ben hopped up, escaping the coffee dripping from the table. He tugged at his shirt, lifting the material away from his skin.

Halley grabbed napkins and started blotting his shirt. "I'm so sorry, Ben. I've ruined your polo. I'll buy you a new one." She stopped her cleanup when Ben's laugh ricocheted around the shop. "What's so funny, mister? You're only my third tray delivery and look at you!" Halley stuffed a dry napkin into his belt. "Ginger's going to fire me—and after she gave me a fifty-cent raise, too. A raise and a firing in less than a half-hour. That's got to be some kind of record. Why are you laughing?"

"I'm amused because I recall you proudly naming talents you possessed the other day, with waitressing being one. I'm called to question—"

"Excuse me. What's going on here?" Halley heard a slight whine to the voice that could be only one woman. "Ben, why do you have a napkin hanging off your belt, and your shirt is a—" Cara fixated on

Halley. "You're using *that* old ploy?" She snagged the napkin and wadded it. "Please bring Ben another triple shot, and I want a frozen matcha."

"Cara, find some manners," Ben muttered. "Both of us caused this accident. Sit down. We'll get drinks soon. Sorry, Halley."

"Me too." Halley retreated to the counter and a somber Ginger.

"Had a little action in the corner, I see?" Ginger kept her expression neutral.

"Would you go ahead and fire me and put me out of my misery? I've never felt so embarrassed." Halley walked behind the counter and handed Ginger her wet apron.

"Fire you? Are you nuts? And miss out on other opportunities to see Cara diminished and Ben growing besotted? Forget it, sister." Ginger winked and handed Halley a clean apron. "I've got a triple and watered-down matcha ready to go."

"Would you please take the drinks over? You can keep the raise. I've had enough of the harpy in the short skirt that a breeze had better avoid." Halley flounced over to wipe the counter and accept a tip from the couple leaving. Out of the corner of her eye, she observed Ginger doing her bidding. She could keep the tip. Halley did a quick replay of the spilling debacle and Ben's shirt, now looking like a Rorschach inkblot test. Amusement bubbled up. Halley laid her head on the coffee bar allowing the hilarity to replace her humiliation.

"Are you okay?" Ben asked as he laid down sodden napkins onto the counter.

Halley raised her head to the level of the shirt stain. It looked even worse if that were possible. "Yeah, I'm over here enjoying the cornucopia of emotions of my first day on the job. I'm truly sorry about the shirt. I owe you a new one and the sign for Sea Glass. And, Cara, I don't know what I owe her, but I'm happy—"

"Stop. You forget you contributed fifty percent to the mishap. And, if you want to go shopping with me and buy half a shirt, well that might be fun. As for Cara, we have an understanding, or at least I thought we did until the last few days."

Halley poured herself water and dropped a lime slice in the glass. "Okay, I'll let you have your half of the blame."

Ginger joined them. "Sorry to interrupt, but Halley, I need you to put a batch of white choc macadamia cookies in the oven."

"On it." Halley pivoted. "And by the way, Ben, I *am* a talented waitress when I have customers that know how to let me serve properly." She walked a few steps away as Ben headed toward the shop's entrance.

"You two change humors faster than a three-year-old choosing an ice cream flavor," Ginger said. She turned, seeing no one there to hear her funny, and noted Ben's girlfriend had moved to a table with the town's young attorney. "If that fake smile got any wider, she'd need more teeth," Ginger muttered.

"I heard that. I forgot the cookie scoop." Halley held it up and disappeared to the small kitchen, pleased to witness Ginger's feelings about Cara mirrored her own. A kindred spirit helped ease the— the what? Halley didn't have that answer. And what did Ben mean he and Cara had an understanding? She had zero desire to get in the middle of any existing relationship. *I'll keep ignoring the flutters and focus on our business arrangement. At least I know there's hope for me to feel attracted to someone.* Maybe she was capable of having a romance this year and honor her benefactor's requests. Ben served as the much-needed proof. Nothing more. Her emotional self in control, Halley put the batch of cookies in the oven and returned to her customers.

***

Ginger hung up her apron and accepted Halley's. "Well, I must say this second apron of yours is as clean as when I gave it to you this morning."

"You're a real comedian." Halley parked herself on the stool while Ginger cleared the register. "Critique me, boss lady. Do you want me back?"

"Well, for starters, you managed to turn your day around nicely after the Ben encounter. Second, I saw big tips hit the jar. They're all yours. Third, I had some regulars make a point of telling me how much they liked you. One guy who owns a gift shop a few doors down even threatened to steal you away. And last, I love having you around. We don't get to hang out much because we're busy, but seeing you buzz around feels right." Ginger grabbed a breath. "Thank you, Halley, for taking the job, and yes, please bring your face back."

"Wow. I didn't expect to hear all of that. I'm grateful to be here, and yes, we're huffing it, but I enjoyed each minute. Well, maybe not those early minutes, which we will not speak of again, but all of them after that." Halley flicked off the lights and waited outside for Ginger to set the alarm.

Oliver wandered up to her. "Hey there, Halley. How did the first day at Deja go, excluding the splashing of Ben?"

"Seriously, you heard about that?" Halley asked, exasperated.

"Well, first, I saw it. That shirt was hard to miss." Oliver turned his smile to the redhead. "Hiya, Ginger. All buttoned up?"

"Sure am. Halley gave Deja a great day. Everyone adores her." Ginger tucked the keys into her handbag.

"Not everyone, but we don't need to raise that flag up the pole," Halley said. "You two going places?"

Oliver exchanged looks with Ginger. "Yeah, we thought we'd grab a bite at one of the restaurants on the wharf. Wanna come along?"

"Yeah, do come with us," Ginger replied.

"Thanks, but I have a kitty waiting on her dinner, and she gets crabby if I'm late." Halley suspected these two might have a little something brewing. She thought them ideally suited. "So, go enjoy a nice dinner. Ginger, count on me being here tomorrow. Night."

Halley paused on the sidewalk, knowing she needed to stop at the grocery store if she ever planned to eat at the bungalow. Finding something fast, tasty, healthy, and easy would challenge her empty cart. And her other challenge of keeping things strictly business with Ben would end if she found another guy. May it happen soon.

***

After a disappointing dinner of ham on rye and a bag of chips, Halley felt called to the backyard hammock, notebook in hand. She'd only written three pages of her novel, but some plot ideas kept swirling around. The brownie wrapped in a napkin was her reward for making it through her first day waitressing. As she settled in to explore if these fragmented story ideas jelled into anything usable, she heard male voices coming from Ben's screened porch.

"I stopped by to hear about day uno at Miss Wellington's. Did all of the crew show?" Andy asked.

"All the guys arrived on time except for Plug," Ben chuckled.

"Let me guess. More sparkplug troubles with the truck."

"Right. And I keep telling Plug if he junks the thing, we'll change the nickname. Man, he was plenty vocal earlier about how much he hates being called a car part. Wouldn't surprise me if he shows up tomorrow driving something new. The guy turned crimson when I introduced him to Miss Wellington as Plug. She didn't know quite what to say to him. The whole scene was comical."

"Too bad I didn't get to witness that exchange." Andy grinned.

"Yeah, all in all, the day turned out productive. The guys got the scaffolding set and did the prelim work. During the afternoon break, Miss Wellington's cook brought out some homemade cookies and sodas. The good chow pretty much sealed the guys on the project. I heard a lot of whistling at the end of the workday."

"When the crew starts whistling, we can count on quality work from them." Andy laughed again. "I'm close to finishing that kitchen remodel so that we can split days at Libby's. I know you've got a few projects to spec and bid on your desk. Those skills I don't have, but man, we could use more work in the pipeline."

"Right. So, why don't you take Miss Wellington's job for the next two days? I think tomorrow Mrs. Cookson is making a peach pie with homemade ice cream. I may have to drop by."

"Okay, I'll handle Tuesday and Wednesday. Listen, I'd better go. Sally's texted me twice in the last minute."

"See ya, brother."

Halley heard an engine start. She guessed Ben was sitting on the porch alone. And alone he'd stay. She wasn't breaking her new rule of business only. Nope. She'd swing the night away in this safe hammock writing essential things in her notebook and waiting as long as she could to devour the fudge brownie. She relaxed and let the sweet evening breeze steal her senses. A shadow fell over her and she opened her eyes.

"I see you're breaking in the new hammock." Ben smiled down at Halley.

"You scared me. Yeah, it's awesome. Listen, I don't mean to sound unfriendly, but don't you have work or something to do? I'm sort of busy making notes for my story."

"Notes, huh? You don't have a pen to go with that spiral notebook," he teased.

A bested Halley glanced down. "I must have lost it." She moved to exit the hammock only to discover getting in was easier than getting out.

Ben watched, amused. "Here give me both hands and turn a little more. No—"

Halley pulled Ben's arms instead of waiting for him to do the pulling. He lost his balance and landed on top of her, sending the hammock swinging at an impressive pace. Sprawled across Halley, he tried and failed to slow their swing by grabbing at the grass.

"Can't you do something?" she begged.

His face inches from hers, their legs and arms intertwined, they looked like a human spider. "Sure, I can thank you once again for getting me into another predicament, when all I was trying to do was help you get out of my hammock." Ben freed one leg. "Hold on. We've slowed enough, let me try and twist out of this Venus flytrap."

The visual of them being inside a Venus flytrap plant sent Halley into hysterics. "That's hilarious. Great image, Shaw. Wait." She felt Ben's arms from behind. "Let me do this without your help. I'm learning things go smoother when you stay at least five feet away from me."

Ben released her arms. "You're close to right. It's you that needs to stay five feet from me. Think espresso and my favorite shirt." He grinned as she planted both feet on the ground and pushed off.

"Fine, five feet. That's our force field. Now, what's so funny? I swear all you do is laugh at my expense. I'll have you know I was a senior corporate director and commanded the respect of—"

"Come closer." Ben curled his index finger, beckoning.

"I will not. Have you forgotten? I've implemented our force field."

Ben's cell phone rang. "I've been waiting on this call. Enjoy that chocolate mess on your butt—whatever it once was." He walked toward the house, talking on the phone.

Halley stood in the same spot, wondering what he meant about enjoying chocolate. Her brownie. Where was her brownie? She looked on the ground. When she tugged to straighten her shorts, she found the answer. It was smashed messily on her butt. *Why must humiliation keep visiting me?* Halley stomped into the bungalow to change and look for a pen. She'd sit in her porch rocker and work. At least it was on her turf.

Ben never reappeared outside. Inside her head—that was a whole other story.

Chapter 18

"Good Tuesday, dear Libby." Sam Langdale's fond words echoed down the line.

"Hello, Sam. I didn't expect to hear from you again this soon." Libby poured a second cup of peppermint tea. Having dressed informally for her day with the flowers, she'd already witnessed the surprise workmen's faces seeing her wearing loose-fitting denim overalls. She reveled in behaving unpredictably. "Are matters still satisfactory, Sam?"

"Yes, most satisfactory. I thought you might appreciate a quick call to say Halley worked her first day at Deja Brew yesterday. And, I heard customers took to her straight away. She does possess a certain charm," Sam said.

"That's lovely news. I'm so glad for Halley. I suppose it's too soon for her to experience any romantic sparks?" Libby went to the window and scrutinized the crew pulling old siding from the structure.

Sam cleared his throat. "We're going to need an extra dose of patience for Halley fulfilling the romance part of the agreement. She warned me that love had eluded her, but I'm giving the woman credit for moving rapidly in the other stipulations. By all indications, she lives frugally despite your generosity with funds. I continue to like this young lady more and more. Anyway, that's all for now. I'll wait for contact from her."

"I quite agree. Let her get on with life. I'm sure we'll speak again soon. Thanks, Sam." As Libby disconnected, there was a gentle rap on the study's door. Libby knew the knock. "Come in, Rupert."

"Ma'am, Mr. Andy Shaw is outside and would like a few moments with you."

"Please show him in." Libby went to her desk chair and settled behind it, wondering what impression Ben's brother would leave on her.

Andy walked across the expansive room, his keen gaze taking in the carved wood paneling and Persian rug. "Hello, Miss Wellington. I'm Andy Shaw. I wanted to stop in and let you know I'm managing the site today, so if you need anything or have questions, please let me know."

"Would you like to take a seat?"

Andy nodded and settled on a burgundy leather chair, looking uncomfortable in the elegant surroundings.

While moving papers around on her desk, Libby studied the young man. His frame was smaller than his older brother's, his features softer, the chin less angular. Eyes were what Libby read. They told truths that the mouth would not. Andy's doe-brown eyes were the type that made one relax and smile with him. The lines etching the corners testified to frequent smiles. She guessed he must have children to earn them. Libby gathered her words. "I'm pleased that you've come to say hello. I'm anticipating excellent craftsmanship with this first project and others I have in mind for you and Ben."

"We look forward to delivering a finished product that meets all of our high standards. Can I answer any questions? We've got a wood delivery due this morning, and I'd like to be out there to inspect it before the driver leaves." Andy glanced toward the door.

"I do have one pressing question needing an answer before you rush off. Do you have a fondness for peach pie and homemade vanilla ice cream? You see, Ben approved the dessert, but you're the one here today." Libby's serious expression gave way to a tiny smile.

"I admit that Ben told me last night about Mrs. Cookson's desserts and most especially the pie. Don't tell my brother, but even if he begged, I'd not trade back this workday. I'm watching the clock for our afternoon break time and that pie to appear. Thank you for that kindness. The men may never want to work anywhere else."

"I see you and Ben share one common character trait." Libby stood.

Andy rose. "What's that, Miss Wellington?"

"Charm, young man, an abundance of charm." Libby slipped out a secret door panel, knowing Rupert would show her guest out.

***

Libby enjoyed time with her flower gardens and planted a few varieties of azaleas with colors that mesmerized her. She'd acted on the nudge to take an afternoon stroll to the marina, and her charmed daisy bench.

When the bench appeared, she noticed it had an occupant. She nodded to herself, understanding the nudge now. Her face relaxed. Another gift awaited the giver. "Hello again, Halley." Libby sat and adjusted her bonnet to better snub the sun.

"My goodness, seeing you again has made my day perfect." Halley tucked her hair under the ball cap. "Are you out for another stroll?"

"Oh, yes, my gardens sent me away. They were tired of my touch." Libby chuckled at her words. "It's the construction noise and a little nudge that sent me here. You see, I'm having some renovations done at my home. The commotion seems a small price to pay for the finished result. Don't you think?"

"I do. Here's a coincidence you'll enjoy. I'm renting a bungalow from one of the contractors working for you. Isn't that something?" Halley said.

Libby's expression gave nothing away. "You're renting from Ben Shaw? Does that mean my abracadabra wand is still working?" She clapped her hands in excitement.

"That power wand delivers big time. You've no idea after you left the other day how even more things fell into place. Simply amazing." Halley watched a small sailboat tack out of the marina. She squinted but couldn't make out if *Seas the Day* was moored waiting for its owner. She twisted to face Libby, smiling at the unexpected overalls.

"What delightful news, young lady. I hope your doubts evaporated, and Port Royal's welcome feels genuine." Libby squeezed Halley's hand.

"Yes, each day, I feel more connected here. I've settled in nicely at Sea Glass. That's the name Ben and I decided for the bungalow. Once Ben completes the cottage, I'll move there permanently."

Halley grabbed a breath. "Libby, it's a bayfront cottage and not far from here. Talking about it makes my heart sing. It's what I envisioned for my ideal life."

"Goodness. A new place on the bay is impossible to find nowadays. That's a gift, young lady."

"Yes, an enormous gift which means that wand, and you, carry major sway." Halley grinned. "Promise to keep it handy should I ever have a need."

Amused, Libby patted her back pocket. "All tucked away. Tell me what other happy news you have to share?"

Halley took a sip from her water bottle. "I found this great part-time job at my friend's coffee shop, Deja Brew. Yesterday was my first day, and other than spilling hot coffee on Ben, our shared contractor, things went pretty well. Today I worked the morning shift with no mishaps thankfully. Well, except I petrified a batch of cookies in the oven." She glanced over at Libby, catching the smile before it disappeared.

"Ben seems like a forgiving person," Libby replied, returning to the mishap.

"Yeah, he came around. Then his girlfriend, Cara, showed up and made a big to-do about the coffee faux pas all over again. I'm going to buy Ben half a shirt since his hand contributed to the spill."

"Half a shirt? You have the most marvelous way of entertaining me with your adventures." Libby laughed.

"Maybe I should be the heroine in my romance novel, but alas, I'd need to find love." Halley placed her hand at her brow for effect.

"Maybe you should allow that exact story idea to unfold. I find the concept charming." Libby sat quiet and let the words penetrate.

Halley's face brightened as a familiar figure walked toward them. A smile broke through. "There's Mick. Do you know him?"

Libby's head swiveled to see his approach. Her body went rigid. "I'm afraid so. Halley, please forgive my quick departure, but I feel a headache coming." Libby rose. "We'll see each other again soon."

Halley frowned, watching Libby scurry off. What did Libby's confusing negative response mean about knowing Mick? Maybe in time, that answer would come. Halley dismissed the thought and watched her favorite sea captain approach.

"Afternoon, lass. I caught sight of you as I brought my boat into dock and didn't want to miss an opportunity—" Mick watched Libby turn the corner before finishing his sentence. "Miss an opportunity to say hello. Tell me, how's your world turning today?"

Halley chose to stay silent about Libby's departure. "I'm so glad you came over. My world is turning nicely. What about your world? Getting some good fishing in?"

"Aye, I've some snapper destined for Irene's dinner table tonight. She ordered me to catch them for you. I'm heading there after I escort you to the parking lot."

Halley stood and tucked her arm through Mick's as they walked toward the vehicle. "I do love snapper, especially with lots of melted butter and lemon. And yes, I did beg a meal this evening at Buttercup. Are you dining with us?"

"If she and Joe have an empty chair, count on seeing me." Mick opened the SUV door. "In you go. Mayhap I'll see you later."

"No mayhap. Don't worry, Mick Duffy. I'll find you a seat at that table." Halley waved him off.

***

Halley pulled the list of errands from her handbag and wondered how many she could check off before dinner. Thinking about the snapper made her mouth water. She could eat seafood daily and never grow tired of the ocean's many offerings. Learning to cook something of consequence had to make the list of future to-dos. So far, she wanted to learn to sail, master parallel parking, take yoga classes, and plant an herb garden. Libby flashed into her mind as a potential guide to starting an herb garden. With a sigh, Halley put cooking at the top of her mental list.

She made her first stop Oliver's office. As promised, Halley lugged two bags of her corporate drone clothes toward the office's entrance.

Oliver opened the door. "Let me take those bags from you. I assume that I'm toting all manner of suits and such that once dressed Halley Bowen for endless meetings."

"Pretty much." Halley grinned. "I'm happy to pass that baton to someone else, you know. This batch of threads represents my entire corporate attire."

Oliver moved the bags to the corner of his office. "Have a seat. If you have a few minutes, I'd like to catch up." He grabbed a file as he sat down.

Halley moved books and an umbrella from her chair seat. Oliver was a magnet for clutter. She pitied any woman with tidy tendencies who said "I do" to the guy. "What ya got for me?"

"The funds for the cottage transaction have moved around the horn and settled in Ben's account. The first draw happens in a couple of days, assuming completion of that work. I understand Ben gave you the spec sheet for selections and the places to go?"

Halley nodded.

"I think it's time you start shopping. Ben mentioned this morning he'd need the paint selection later this week. Something about an upcoming paint promotion discount and he wants to get the order placed."

"Thanks for reminding me. What else?" Halley checked her watch.

Oliver pulled a yellow sticky note from the corner of his desk and frowned. "I can't read my writing. What do you think this says?"

Halley held the note out and squinted. She turned it sideways. "Oliver, my cat could scratch neater words than these. I think it says "Logan," and maybe a date." Halley turned the paper over. "With Halley. Logan something date Halley. What does this mean?"

Oliver reached across the desk and snatched the paper. "Forget it. I'm an idiot, and this may be the last time you see me alive. Ginger's going to kill me."

Halley couldn't resist a chuckle. "Why would Ginger kill you? Are you two up to something that involves me? Who's Logan?"

Oliver's handkerchief came out for a swipe at his forehead. "I can't tell you. You got to forget this little slip-up. Ginger's worse than any of the wise guys up north."

"Okay fine. I'll visit Ginger and see—"

"Don't you move. Here it is neat. Ginger wanted me to call Logan. He's Port Royal's new attorney. I've sent most of my clients his way, and he's done an excellent job getting the deals closed." Oliver paused.

"Oliver, have you taken leave of your senses? Stop pitching. I don't need an attorney representing me on the cottage. I have Sam Langdale," Halley said, a little confused.

"Um, I didn't mean Logan as your attorney, but your date." Oliver coughed. "I can't believe I'm going to have two women trying to kill me."

"My date? Wait. Are you trying and failing at saying you and Ginger are setting me up with this guy?" Halley's expression changed to disbelief. Her life in Charlotte seemed mundane compared to the last few days at Port Royal.

Oliver's face brightened. "Yep, you got it. Only you aren't supposed to know that set-up part when Ginger asks you to join us for dinner at Mussels tomorrow evening. Halley, you must promise me you'll keep quiet and agree to go. Please tell the woman yes. Besides, it'll be a fun evening, and you get a free meal."

"I swear if you weren't so comical, I'd bop you on the head with this umbrella. Answer me a few questions, starting with: Does this Logan know about this set-up?"

Oliver smiled. "He does, and he…"

"He what, you big blabbermouth? Don't stop now." Halley raised the umbrella in the air.

"Well, Logan might have checked you out at Deja yesterday. He must have liked—anyway, he's already made our dinner reservation hoping you'll agree."

Halley's mind flashed to the attorney she saw Cara join once Ben left the coffee shop. She didn't want to invite more wrath from Cara. "Oliver, I don't think—"

"Don't think. Do it. I wasn't planning on using my trump card so soon, but you leave me no choice. Need I remind you who found that perfect cottage for you and a place to lay that pretty head until it's finished?" Oliver thumped his chest, nodding.

Halley laughed at his antics, acknowledging he had a valid point. If not for him, she and Éclair and all of their belongings would reside at Buttercup. "Okay, this get-out-of-jail card only works once for you. I'll play my part when Ginger calls, but you'd better not play matchmaker again. Walk me out and do us all a favor. Leave your big yap locked in a drawer."

Back in her SUV, Halley tossed her errand list into her purse. "Change of plans. I need a cookbook if I'm going to live where fresh seafood is plentiful. It's my duty to support the local fishing industry." Great, Oliver had her so rattled over this Logan character she was talking out loud. If anyone saw her, maybe they'd assume she was on her cell phone. Feeling better about appearances, she exited her vehicle, deciding to walk the few blocks to the Book Worm.

The doorbell jingled, announcing her. "Hi, Liz. Are you still open?"

"For another thirty minutes. It's so nice to see you again. Did you have a good time at Andy's party?"

"Yes, I had a great time and felt so welcome," Halley said.

"That's exactly how you should feel. Want to browse, or do you need help?" Liz left the counter, joining Halley.

"Oh, I need your help, and feel free to laugh. Do you have the most basic of basic seafood cookbooks? Did I say basic enough times?" asked Halley.

"You did." Liz grinned. The round glasses perched on her nose, along with her simple navy shirtwaist dress, made her the perfect backdrop for the Book Worm. "And I'm guessing pots and pans aren't something you've spent much time around."

"As little time as was necessary, but I mean to change that. In Charlotte, I had a loft uptown surrounded by restaurants that delivered. But I'm in Port now and somehow, I can't see Ben Shaw sharing his dinner with me at the bungalow, so I'm forced to—"

"Cook. That four-letter word," Liz finished, smiling. "Follow me to the display." The shop owner thumbed through a few books before presenting one to Halley. "This cookbook is meant for you."

"*Seafood Meals in Fifteen Minutes*. This author knows me. I'll take it." Halley laid the money on the counter.

"Here you go. Please drop by and tell me how your dinners turn out. If you get stuck, ring Sally. She's an excellent cook."

"Thanks for the book and idea. I won't tell Sally you sicced me on her." Halley glanced at her watch. Reading the mouthwatering recipes awakened her hunger for Irene's dinner. She'd make an early appearance at Buttercup and offer to help. No time like the present to begin her culinary education, and tomorrow night promised a refresher on dating etiquette, all thanks to her matchmaker friends.

Chapter 19

The evening at Buttercup reminded Halley why she loved Port Royal. Life felt easy with a unique type of rhythm, which fostered an enterprising spirit. A spirit Halley delighted in awakening as a writer. Dodging Chaucer in the butler's pantry, she found Irene in the kitchen, her mixing bowl taking a beating. "I came early to help. It's time I learn how to feed myself." Halley washed her hands at the sink. "What can I do?"

"Well, let's start you with something simple. Chop these vegetables and make something happen while I finish this brownie mix." Irene slid the cutting board across the large island and returned to her bowl.

"I'm cool with chopping, but that 'make something happen' part—"

Irene laughed. "You've got this. After you finish, visit my herb containers at the window. Inspiration will find you."

Minutes later, Joe came into the kitchen. "Umm, Halley, what ya doing there?"

"I'm sniffing herbs to find one for those waiting vegetables I chopped. Irene's trying to inspire me as a cook and I'm not feeling it." Halley scrunched her face.

Joe moved into action. "Watch and learn my way." Joe tossed the veggies on a sheet pan with salt and olive oil. He sprinkled fresh rosemary and whispered, "Roast them." Joe left an amused Irene to introduce the new cook to the wonders of convection cooking.

Halley stood like a sentinel at the oven door, watching vegetables morph into crispy morsels. The morning memory of the rock-hard cookies she'd ruined at Deja taught her the importance of oven vigilance.

Irene took the opportunity to inquire about Halley's last couple of days. "It sounds to me like your new job is a nice fit. You and Ginger's friendship will benefit from spending time together. I hate that we missed Andy's party. I understand you and Ben shared your first tea party with that adorable Tulip."

"You heard about me at the party? Honestly, I can't believe how fast things get reported around here. Do you happen to know what time I woke up?" Halley shook her head. "And, yes, Tulip did invite me to the tea party. She's quite the hostess. Mick and Ben are putty in those little cherubic hands."

Irene looked inside the oven. "You're so right. I've witnessed our Tulip's talent. And to answer your other question, you got up at seven a.m. and the veggies need to come out."

"Ha. You had me for a moment. Of course, you know what time I like to get up. After all, I've been a guest here for years. Dumb." Halley bopped her forehead.

Irene smiled and handed her assistant the oven mitt. "Let's get you fed. And I've noted your avoidance of any Ben news-sharing, and that's only piqued my interest more."

Halley set the sheet pan next to the cooktop. "You're wasting your piquing on Ben. He's involved with Cara, and besides, I bet you haven't heard yet that I have a date with Logan, the new attorney in town." Halley disappeared through the kitchen door, smiling. That tidbit should satisfy Irene's curiosity gene for a few days.

The Buttercup dinner table welcomed only four that evening. Tuesdays were what Irene referred to as transition Tuesday. The free day, sans guests, which allowed her and Joe time to catch up on tasks and grab some personal time. Having Halley and Mick to dinner was purely social and provided no shortage of banter. For Halley, these three caring people were her anchors as she charted this new life at Port Royal.

***

Halley prepared to leave. She hugged Joe and then Irene. "Thank you for feeding me another delicious meal and for the cooking class."

"Glad I was around to contribute a little guidance," Joe said with a wink.

"Yeah, husband, you're always a big help toting platters. Halley, it was my pleasure on all counts." Irene leaned in to whisper, "Enjoy that date. Romance is in the air. I sense it, though I'm not sure which guy is meant for you."

"I'd call that wishful thinking, Irene," Halley replied.

Mick appeared in the doorway, cap in hand, a smile plastered on his weathered face. His beard looked scruffy, testifying to the extra hours logged on the boat. "My turn for some appreciation."

Halley hugged Mick. "I know shrimping is your first love but catching the snapper for dinner earned you even more of my affection. How's that?"

The sea captain winked at Joe. "That's dandy, lass. I'll try my luck at oysters next. I know your fondness for them."

"Mick, if you'd don an apron and cook for me, I swear I'd marry you next week," Halley teased. She left her three friends laughing over the notion of Mick Duffy sporting an apron.

The evening breeze carried a gentleness like a lover's caress to her cheek. That thought courted Halley as she strolled toward her bungalow. It was a thought lacking any romantic foundation, yet she claimed the image, unsure of its purpose.

"I'm glad you're back. A storm's brewing," a husky voice said.

Halley caught Ben's shadow. The inky night sky hung overhead without the benefit of the moon's light. He abandoned the Adirondack chair, guarded by the branches of an old oak tree, and moved to Halley's side.

"Why else are you glad I'm back?" Her voice matched his, somewhat low and throaty. Halley tilted her head back as Ben's grey gaze locked on her, and the bothersome flutter returned.

A pause surrounded them. The kind of pause that brought only questions—questions lacking answers. The breeze returned, blowing a wisp of Halley's hair across her face. The same breeze that moments ago portended a caress. Ben reached out and tucked the piece behind Halley's ear. His hand felt like a feather against her cheek, and she released a pent-up sigh. The startling sound of a horn and headlights traveling up the drive forced them to part.

Andy hopped out of the truck holding a plate covered in foil. "Sorry, kids, for the late delivery. It was my turn to read Tulip her bedtime story and wait an exhausting twenty minutes while she arranged her 'fluffies' in her bed. I swear, brother, if you buy her any more stuffed animals, I'm putting you on the bedtime schedule."

Andy lifted the plate and grinned. "Who's in charge of serving Libby's outrageous peach pie?"

"Libby sent pie? To me too? Why?" Halley asked.

Ben grabbed the plate. "I know why she sent me a slice. She likes me, and I am a growing fan of Mrs. Cookson's baking." Ben looked at Halley. "But I have no clue why Libby Wellington sent you a slice of peach pie. Obviously you know her?"

Andy walked back to his truck. "I'll leave you two to solve the mystery. I've got two slabs of pie waiting for me at home." He hopped into the truck and waved goodnight.

Halley waved a hand. "Bring our pie to the bungalow. I've got plenty of unused dishes."

Ben closed the front door and joined Halley in the kitchen. He lifted the foil and took a sniff of the pie. "Man, that Mrs. Cookson and her rolling pin can bake some mean desserts."

Halley transferred a piece to each plate. "Here's a fork and a napkin. Wow, this is going to taste amazing. Let's not waste time getting placemats out for the table. Grab a stool. We can eat at the counter." As soon as they sat, Halley popped up.

"Where are you going? You can't leave this pie unattended next to me." Ben took an enormous bite of his.

"Don't you dare touch mine. I forgot to offer you something to drink." Halley reached for two glasses.

"What are my options?" Ben forked another bite then sat the fork on his plate.

"Well, I can offer you water... or iced water? I've got a new grocery list waiting for tomorrow to come. What's it going to be, Mr. Shaw? Hurry, my peach pie is waiting."

Ben pretended to weigh his options. "I think I'll have ice water."

Halley came around and sat down. She gobbled a bite before replying. "When you're sure, let me know."

Ben left the stool and filled the glass with water, omitting the ice, and sat back down. "You're too literal, Ms. Bowen." He grinned, watching her savor each bite. "So, tell me, how do you know the illustrious Libby Wellington?"

"I've had the pleasure of encountering Libby on the daisy bench. Do you know the one I'm referring to?"

"What in blazes is a daisy bench?" Ben rinsed his plate and motioned for Halley to pass hers.

"The daisy bench is a welcoming sweet addition to the marina park, and besides, it kind of calls to me."

Ben rubbed his neck muscles and nodded. "Oh, I think I know the bench. Hard to miss. Bright yellow and close to the dock?"

Halley grinned. "Yep, that bench. Be warned if you plant yourself on the seat you'd better be open to its magic. That's my word to describe the daisy bench. Things happen when you sit there."

The corners of Ben's mouth turned up. "Magic, huh? I didn't know a park bench carried any special invite or vibe. I'm glad you told me so I can avoid anything painted with…?"

"Happy, sunny, bright yellow daisies with the cutest faces. My favorite color and flower." Halley interjected, laughing. She moved to the cushy aqua living room chair, turning on the table lamp. "Was that thunder?"

Ben sank into the sofa cushions. "Probably. I told you a storm with high wind is coming through tonight. When you drove up, I'd recently returned home from checking to make sure my boat was tied down. Hurry and finish telling me more about you and Libby so I can beat the rain home."

Halley was comfortable in the chair until a crash of lightning sent her to the sofa and Éclair under the dining table. "Sorry. I'm not a fan of lightning. It unnerves me. That strike seemed close." She started to scoot over to the opposite corner on the sofa.

"It's okay. Stay where you are. Tulip hates storms, too." Ben reached for Halley's hand. "You know I recently met Libby Wellington. I mean, sure I've seen her around town. I've even had indirect involvement with one or two of her town projects, but our paths never crossed until Oliver recommended our company." Ben squeezed Halley's hand. "Better?"

"Yes, as long as the lightning and thunder stay quiet." Halley pulled her hand back, resting it on the cushion. "Okay, back to me on the bench where Libby first appeared. Our meeting happened a few days ago when I felt discouraged that Oliver hadn't found me a place to buy. Anyway, I like watching the action at the marina, so I always go there to hang out when I vacation at Port."

Lightning and thunder returned for an even louder encore. The flash lit the living room like a stadium. Ben extended his hand. "Scoot back here and finish your story before the sun comes up."

"Humor helps. Even yours." Halley tried to grin past the fear. She moved to the center seat cushion and accepted Ben's hand. A working man's hand, a strong and capable hand that could cause her heart to flutter in the middle of a lightning show.

Ben threaded his long fingers through hers. "Pray, continue. I hear a few drops of rain on this metal roof."

"There's not much more. When I was feeling uncertain about things, Libby shared some wise words about having faith in one's path. You know. 'Trust the process' as I used to tell my staff." Halley left out the wand and abracadabra part. No point in having Ben think she was a complete nut. "Anyway, her words that day were what I needed to hear. Right after that encounter on the daisy bench, Oliver showed me your cottage, and things shifted. Only then did I feel like I'd found home. I saw Libby again today, sitting on that charmed bench. I swear it felt like she expected to find me there."

Ben twisted to face Halley but held tight to her hand. "That sounds sort of weird."

Halley's expression turned to puzzlement. "Maybe a little unusual, but then that's the daisy bench. Anyway, we only chatted a few moments before a headache made her leave. She asked if things had smoothed out, and that's when I told her the condensed version of contracting on the cottage and renting the bungalow from you. That's how she knew of our connection." Halley stopped. Holding Ben's hand rattled her, though she knew it meant nothing to him. He probably saw her as a scared older version of Tulip. "Hang on. I didn't mean connection. I meant a working relationship."

Ben chuckled, allowing her hand to leave his. "I knew what you meant. And, so now I understand why two slices of peach pie came to us for sharing. I must thank thoughtful Libby next time I'm at Magnolia."

Halley stood. "Libby does seem thoughtful, but there's an aloofness about her, too. Hey, I think the rain is getting closer. You'd better go while you can, or risk getting soaked. My umbrella is out in the SUV, so I've got zip to offer you." Why did she suddenly feel awkward?

Ben stood. "Yeah, I should go. I need to answer a few emails."

Éclair appeared and escorted Ben to the front door. Halley stood back, unsure of what to say next. "I'll get the paint colors selected in the next couple of days." Could she have come up with anything lamer?

Ben nodded, opening the door. "Well, good night."

Halley held Éclair close as the downpour erupted. In mere hours, she'd blown her vow of keeping things with Ben strictly business. Sharing pie wasn't business behavior. She'd do better next time. Yet one question tumbled around in her head: What made Libby Wellington decide to send peach pie slices to her and Ben?

Chapter 20

Halley had her Wednesday mapped out all neat and tidy. Not a single minute was unaccounted for, which eliminated surprises like peach pie or unsettling visits by the guy next door. She'd work the morning shift at Deja Brew, nab one of Ginger's multi-grain bagels for lunch, devote the afternoon to writing, and end the day with her traitorous matchmaking friends and some guy named Logan. His name sounded like it belonged to a dude riding the range in Montana. Halley smiled. Maybe a cowboy hero would make for a rugged-style romance novel. Nah, she'd need to do too much research on the west and cowboys. Better to choose a setting she'd experienced, like a metro city or a quaint seaside town. Yes, a seaside town felt right.

Éclair sauntered by and released a loud meow over an empty bowl.

"You're next on my list, Miss Thang." Halley filled the bowl to the brim and waited for the thank-you purr. "You're welcome. Is there anything else, your majesty?"

The cat swished her tail and buried her face into the dish.

Cell phone in hand, Halley sent Beth a quick email. They were doing a decent job of keeping each other updated on things. Beth promised to visit once the project in London wrapped. That date remained elusive, but Halley's bungalow and sofa bed awaited Beth when the stars deemed it.

She glanced in the mirror and felt satisfied her jeans and yellow blouse looked work appropriate. The gold hoop earrings were a birthday gift from her mom and always brought something good when she wore them. Snagging the navy cross-body bag from the hook, she left to honor one of the generous benefactor's requirements, a part-time job.

While driving, Halley's mind peppered her with questions about the woman who had swooped in and changed her life. Where did her benefactor live? The most likely answer seemed Charlotte. Was the benefactor pleased by Sam's updates? Halley tried to be succinct in detailing her doings and careful with expenses. She'd found a job, the perfect cottage, and begun her novel, albeit only a few pages. One stipulation hung out, taunting her. The one she'd voiced concerns to Langdale about achieving. The one that had eluded her since the braces came off. Romance. A steady boyfriend. She'd keep reminding herself there were scads of time yet. And absolutely no reason to fret, except for the niggling reminder she'd never, not once, ever loved any guy.

She'd tried once to lower her high standards and ended up dating a work peer, James, who proved to be the same self-absorbed jerk in or out of the office. Halley kept pardoning his late arrivals at restaurants or while he excused himself in the middle of their conversations to take calls. James's ambition always seemed to eclipse hers. Despite his impressive financial worth, she tallied his emotional worth at zero and ended things months ago.

Maybe it was time to toss the old list of what qualified as her ideal man and create a new template. Thankfully, Port Royal didn't attract corporate types. What types of men found Port appealing? Ben and Andy came to mind. "Two nice guys," like Ginger told her that first day when Ben had hijacked her vehicle to park. Now that time had passed, Halley could appreciate the humor of that first encounter. She thought about funny, big-hearted Oliver, which also described Mick and Joe. Still, not her type. This Logan might fit an unnamed category that she'd find attractive. Yep, a refreshed list of the *Ideal Man's Traits* should get her on course. She had a plan. A confident Halley flicked on the music, not even minding it was a love song.

***

Inside Deja, Halley hurried to put her things away, don the apron with an embroidered steaming coffee mug plastered in the center, and discovered Ginger blending frozen coffees. "I'm here. What's first, cleaning tables or delivering brews?"

"Hey, am I ever glad you're here early. It's been a circus." Ginger set two coffees on the counter. "Here you go, folks. You'll find straws and napkins to the right." She rinsed the blender and wiped her hands. "Okay, it'd be great if you grabbed the cinnamon rolls out of the oven and put them under this glass dome. By then, I'll have a tray of drinks ready."

"On it," said Halley heading for the kitchen. She hated all ovens, and they hated her back. This one had already bested her the first day. Cookers were pure stress. She peered inside the oven's window and muttered, "That doesn't look anything like cinnamon rolls. Ginger needs to see this."

Halley went in search of her friend. "Uhm Ginger, stay calm, but what's in the oven looks nothing like a cinnamon breakfast roll. Maybe you should take a peek."

She waited at the kitchen door, unsure whether to laugh or wring her hands. She did neither for fear of making things worse.

"Okay, let's see what oven karma you brought in this morning," chuckled Ginger. "Hang on people. I'm coming right back."

Halley let the karma crack slide and followed Ginger back to the perpetrator.

"Oh, no, I baked pizza rolls. I grabbed the wrong bag. I hadn't put my contacts in yet and was busy taking a phone order." Ginger shook her head.

Laughter overtook Halley.

Ginger joined in. "Don't you dare tell this story." Ginger pulled the pizza rolls from the oven. "Hurry and get the cinnamon ones baking. The Quilting Bees will arrive any minute, and cinnamon rolls and hot chocolate kick off their meeting."

Halley scurried to the freezer. "Get back to brewing. I'll take care of the Bees' needs. Trust me. I can manage this. I had an oven cooking lesson last night from Irene. I'm primed to impress and burn off that oven karma." Halley tossed a grin to Ginger's back.

In between delivering coffee and checking on the buns, Halley wondered why Ginger hadn't said anything about dinner at Mussels. Halley placed the pastries on the server with her spatula and approached Ginger. "Voila. Perfectly golden cinnamon rolls awaiting the Bees. And, while you have a sec, isn't there something important you need to ask me?"

"Wow, gold star on the oven duty results. Do I need to ask you something? How about a hint?" Ginger sipped a green tea, raising one eyebrow in question.

"One word should revive your memory: Mussels." Halley's hands found her hips.

"Ohhh, that."

"Yes, that. Time to pitch me how nice it would be if I joined you and Oliver for a lovely dinner overlooking the bay with tiki torches, and—"

"Save yourself while you still can," laughed Ginger. "Okay, Oliver confessed he blabbed yesterday about the set up with Logan and saved himself harm by saying you agreed to go." Ginger shook her head. "Men. Anyway, I planned for us to discuss our fun night once I recovered from the morning. Halley, our intentions are the best. We honestly think you and Logan might jell, and besides, we want you to get to know our friends."

Halley hugged the matchmaker. "And, that's why I said yes. I'm looking forward to our evening and the seafood and—"

"The tiki torches. You're a mess. Ooh, battle stations. Here come the Quilting Bees in procession. Help them settle over in the corner and pull the folding screen out. They get loud when deciding on their next design." Ginger lined up the mugs for the hot chocolate.

"Running a coffee shop sure asks a lot." Halley stepped into the gaggle of ladies approaching. "Hello, I'm Halley. We've been looking forward to your visit this morning. Please follow me."

The leader tapped Halley's arm. Her colorful muumuu covered a lot of real estate, and the clanking bangles announced her. "Make sure the chocolate is steamy and bring our rolls right out."

Halley nodded and smiled.

"I want mine frothy. I like froth," requested a Bee who was shorter than Halley.

"Gloria, froth doesn't agree with your digestion." The leader turned back to Halley. "Do *not* bring her froth."

Halley glanced back, catching Ginger's wink. "Ladies, I'm going to grab those warm cinnamon rolls as soon as you all get settled, and I promise the most delectable hot chocolate is coming right behind." As she returned to the counter, writing inspiration found Halley. She'd weave the Bees into her novel, only she'd name them something else to protect the guilty. The benefactor was right to declare a part-time job a necessary stipulation to experience Port Royal life. Taking along her gratitude, Halley hurried to do the club's bidding.

***

"Are you ready to quit yet? What a crazy morning, and the Bees topped it off." Ginger looked at the clock. "Grab your bagel before you leave."

"Quit? No way. I'm getting scads of character ideas. This place is the mother lode for inspiring a writer. I should pay you to work here." Halley bagged the bagel and slung her purse over her shoulder.

Ginger swiped her brow for effect. "That's a relief. You're doing an awesome job, and surprise! Even the oven made nice to you."

"Not funny," said Halley.

"Okay, about tonight. Oliver and I can swing by the bungalow around seven. There's no need for you to drive yourself."

"Seven. I'll be ready, and thanks for the ride. See you later."

Halley rushed to her vehicle. The gold earrings were about to deliver on their promise of something good. She sensed her muses were at last ready to work. Writing outdoors held colossal appeal, but where? Not the Venus flytrap. That hammock would wait a long time before her behind touched it. Ben's wooden picnic table in the shade might suffice, assuming her lower back agreed. Halley sighed, thinking about her cottage's porch making an ideal place to write. Tomorrow she'd devote time to visiting it and choosing paint. In the meantime, the picnic table won, and may Ben not cast a shadow on her writing afternoon.

***

Dressing for informal dining at Mussels didn't ask much of Halley's time, but her feminine nature did. She'd laid out her makeup and primped until satisfied she'd created a natural look. She chose her muted rainbow tank and matching shirt and paired it with cream-colored jeans.

Éclair reclined on the bed, watching.

"Do I look like a unicorn in this rainbow blouse?"

Éclair blinked slowly.

"Great, I look like a unicorn." Halley stripped off the set and stared inside a closet that lacked Port Royal-style clothes. She'd go with the designer black lacey top. The style screamed classy and fit after hours in Charlotte, but not dinner on a deck with sun setting probably in her face. She had precisely five minutes to pull herself together. *Not the black top. Hmm...third time's the charm.* Halley yanked a matching cream top to her jeans off the hanger, tossed a lavender printed scarf around her neck, added amethyst stud earrings, and headed outside to her rocker. *It's not like I'm dining with the prince.* She took the few minutes left to savor her official first writing day. Fifteen pages had come forth, a beginning worthy of celebrating.

Oliver's vehicle whipped into the driveway. A toot of the horn and waves from the two occupants brought Halley to her feet, grinning. She climbed inside. "Hi there. Thanks for swinging by."

"No problemo," Oliver said. "Ginger and I had a bet you'd cancel the date."

Ginger slapped his arm. "You are, without a doubt, the biggest blabbermouth in Port Royal. I don't know why I ever agreed to date you, Oliver Moretti."

Halley chuckled. "Don't go getting into a tiff. I want to know who won."

"I did, of course. Men don't have a clue about how we work." Ginger glanced back at Halley and winked.

Oliver jumped in. "Let's change this subject and talk about our evening. Appetizers. She-crab soup, Logan and—"

Halley interrupted. "Somebody, please tell me about Logan?" She took note of Magnolia Manor as they passed by.

Ginger twisted around to face Halley. "Logan has depth and intelligence. He's lived in Port a little over a year. Oliver, do you know why he chose our town to open a practice?"

"I think he—actually, no, I don't recall how Logan ended up here. We should ask him." Oliver waved to a couple riding a tandem bike. He tilted his head toward them and explained, "New clients who wanted out of Florida. I closed on a great little fixer-upper in town with them last month. Buyers come here with a goal and idea."

"You're right about that. I surely did. I love living above the coffee shop. I have the best commute."

"And no yard to keep up." Halley realized she'd need to find a lawn service at some point.

Ginger pointed. "We're here. Geez, the parking lot is already full. Oliver, if I promise to give you a big kiss later, would you let Halley and me out at the door?" She puckered her lips.

"Sold." A smiling Oliver looped the vehicle around. "Here you go, ladies. Chauffeur service compliments of Oliver H. Moretti. I'll see you inside."

Ginger spotted Logan first, studying a tank of lobsters. "There's your date, Ms. Bowen. Trust me, he's a better catch that what's in that aquarium."

Halley grinned. "I'll let you know if that's true later, Ms. Matchmaker. Come on. You might as well introduce us."

Logan caught sight of the two women approaching and waved. "Good evening." His attention settled on Halley. "I'm—"

"Let me do this properly." Ginger laughed. "Halley, I'd like for you to meet Logan. Logan, this is my friend Halley, who I've told you about."

Halley and Logan stood smiling at each other but didn't move or speak.

"Uhm, this is the part where you shake hands and say something vanilla to each other," Ginger encouraged.

"Vanilla?" Halley and Logan said in unison.

Logan nodded and reached for Halley's hand.

"Vanilla? What are we ordering that's vanilla?" Oliver asked coming up to the group.

Ginger sighed and hugged her beau. "Don't try and explain it to him. Let's get seated. I'm hungry enough to chew on an oyster shell."

"Oh, I like the sound of that," Oliver said. "Oysters will make you frisky." He snatched Ginger's hand, leading them toward the hostess.

"Halley, something tells me we're in for a night of bad jokes." Logan offered his arm.

"Counsellor, I think you've made an excellent assessment of our situation." Halley chuckled and found her hand willing to clasp Logan's elbow as they followed behind Ginger and Oliver. She liked his friendly tone. That was one point, and she awarded him another point on appearance. No, make that two points for looks upon closer examination. Funny, Logan had the look of the Montana cowboy she'd imagined earlier.

The four weaved through tables of noisy diners as the hostess led them outside. A silver metal roof covered the array of planked wooden tables that had suffered diner's hammers cracking oysters and clamshells. A trio of musicians near the bar returned from their break and began to play a jazz piece. Logan held the chair for Halley while the hostess left menus and words to enjoy the meal.

Oliver hid behind the menu but managed a few words. "Excuse me while I eat this menu."

Ginger piped up, clearly trying to break the ice. "I enjoy dining at Mussels. The atmosphere is so Port Royal. Not fancy, or super casual either. Right in the middle. And the scallops are the best. I always order them, but to be sure I'm not missing out on a new scrumptious dessert, excuse me while I peruse the menu."

"Sure. That's fine. Logan and I will muddle through somehow without your wit and charm for the next few minutes." Halley grinned at Logan.

"Yes, I'll do my best to string a few words together and sound somewhat interesting to my dinner partner." Logan sipped his water and signaled the waiter.

"Yes, sir?" The waiter produced a pad.

"Halley, what beverage sounds good this evening?" Logan turned his attention to the woman sitting to his right.

"I'd love a sparkling cranberry juice with a splash of lime. Thank you." Halley caught Logan's surprise at her choice.

"You know, that sounds like a refreshing drink. Same for me." Logan nodded at the waiter.

"Excellent, sir." He turned to Ginger and Oliver.

"I want that cranberry whatever, too. You game, Oliver?" Ginger asked, peeping over her menu.

Oliver laughed. "I'm game. Four cranberry sparklers, waiter."

Halley tucked her cloth napkin onto her lap. Her face glimmered with merriment. "Well, aren't I quite the influencer tonight? Surely, I need to take advantage of this lofty position."

Logan chuckled. "I admit to finding you a most persuasive woman. And, I'd feel most honored if you'd order dinner for all of us this evening."

"Geez, man, you sound like one of those guys in that Jane Austen movie Ginger made me watch last week." Oliver rubbed his chin. "I'm particular about my food, so I don't—"

Ginger chimed in. "You, particular about food? Ha. You eat everything, and I do mean everything, except anchovies. I'm for Halley ordering. Please get me out of my rut with the scallops."

The evening was starting out lighthearted and fun, the perfect first date atmosphere for Halley. She released a breath and joined in. "Oliver, stay in the 'I'm game' mode with us. Allow me this influence in choosing your bill of fare." Halley's eyebrow rose in question, but her grin stayed in place.

The waiter returned with their drinks. "Ready to order, folks?"

Halley looked at Oliver. "Well?"

"Oh, all right, but no squid. I don't care what the chef does to it." Oliver sat back, a look of concern on his face.

Logan spoke first to the waiter. "Halley is ordering for us this evening. I bow to the lady."

"Thank you, kind sir." Halley collected the four menus and presented them to the waiter with a nod. "We'll have four hearts of palm salad with the pistachio lime sherbet on top, and four fried seafood platters with your famous twice-baked potatoes. Oh, and extra tartar and cocktail sauce."

"Excellent choice. I can tell you're a fun group." The waiter left.

Halley caught sight of an unwelcome someone approaching.

Uh-oh. Here comes trouble.

Chapter 21

The perfume arrived before its wearer. A pale blue silk blouse whose neckline plunged to the equator met tight linen slacks cut to show off shapely legs. A sliver of gold chain belted the outfit. Hair pulled tight in a chignon allowed the observer to focus on the flawless illusion expertly applied makeup could create.

"Hello, Logan. What a surprise to run into you at Mussels." The smile didn't reach Cara's eyes, but in Halley's opinion, it seldom did.

"Hi, Cara," Logan answered, standing up. Logan gestured to the table. "Won't you say hello to—"

Cara rushed on. "I must say, Oliver and Ginger, you two make the cutest couple ever."

"Gee, thanks," Ginger replied, giving a disinterested Oliver a kick under the table.

Oliver perked up. "Yep, we're plenty cute, all right. You remember Halley, don't you, Cara?"

"Yes, good evening." Cara's voice dripped icicles. She tossed her head dismissively.

"Anyway, Logan, Daddy's taking a few important people out on his boat tomorrow night, and I've managed to procure you an invitation. You simply must join us." Cara's manicured nails twisted her diamond pendant.

Logan's expression changed. "That's nice of you, but—"

"No buts. See you at eight. Oh, to be clear, this is a single invite." Cara sent a dagger toward Halley. "Ta-ta all." She turned with her nose high enough to drown her if it rained.

Oliver spoke first. "I've got two words: She's something. Now, I say let's get back to anticipating those palms and sherbet."

Laughter erupted, and heads nodded as the waiter arrived with the salads. "Can my wife and I be included in your next outing?" he said as he passed out the food. "I'm laughing, and I don't even know why. Enjoy."

Halley turned to Logan. "I've got a question."

Logan grinned. "Shoot."

"Where are you from, or maybe I should ask, where you were born?"

"That's your first get-to-know Logan question?" The attorney placed his fork next to the plate and stared amused at his date.

Halley nodded, taking her first bite.

"I like her question. Where you're from answers a lot of questions in my real estate world," Oliver defended.

"Thank you, Oliver, for that valuable input. Okay, I'm from Helena, capital of Montana." Logan speared a piece of lettuce.

Halley's mouth dropped open. "Montana? I knew it." Her hand smacked the table's edge.

Ginger looked confused. "Wait. How did you know?"

Halley burst out laughing. "The name. Logan. I envisioned a dude on the range in Montana herding—something."

Logan shook his head in amusement. He's a good sport, thought Halley. "Well, little did I know my name could conjure up such visual interest. Halley, you should write one of those cowboy romances that my sister reads incessantly. I think you'll get a charge out of this. When my mother was pregnant with me, she discovered my name in one of those romance books. Embarrassing now that I think about it." Logan's face colored as red as the table's vase of hibiscus.

"Actually, Halley *is* writing a romance. Aren't you, girlfriend?" Ginger popped a pistachio into her mouth.

Halley glanced at Logan. "I am."

"Wow, I'm impressed, dining with a writer. And, if needed, I bestow permission to use my name for inspiration—with a couple of caveats."

Halley's mouth turned up at the corners. "This ought to be good. Go ahead and caveat me."

"Happy to oblige, ma'am." Logan turned cowboy. "You make me ruggedly handsome and strong. Maybe a cattle baron. Oh, and I want to win the lady's heart. That's a non-negotiable, as we lawyers like to say."

Oliver puffed his chest. "Hey, I happen to think Oliver is a name that denotes dashing sex appeal. You should consider that name for one of the heroes."

"Hold on. The name Ginger adds spice to any heroine," Ginger piped in, fanning herself for effect.

"You three are incorrigible. Gosh, I didn't expect such helpful input on my story. I promise to take your suggestions under careful deliberation and discuss it with my characters." Halley glimpsed the waiter's tray carrying their entrees, stopping any further novel discussion.

***

Four napkins lay folded neatly on the table as final sips of coffee got savored. The dinner crowd had thinned out, but a few tables' occupants enjoyed the live jazz trio's last few songs. Halley let the melody take her. She appreciated how jazz evoked the emotional freedom to meet the music in the present moment. It invited memories for the listener, but most of all, Halley liked the genre for its unpredictability, the way the songs often lingered in search of their ending.

Logan touched Halley's arm. "Are you tired or grooving with the bass player?"

"Grooving. Good word. Those guys sure get inside their music." She licked her lips, realizing the lip gloss was long gone. Halley scooted her chair back. "Please excuse me while I do a bit of freshening."

Halley entered the ladies' room and pulled the gloss from her handbag. Looking in the mirror, she saw her image but also caught another one staring back at her. "Hello again, Cara. You want to say something?" Halley turned to face the mayor's daughter.

Cara moved in closer, sizing up her adversary. "I most certainly do have something to say. Let me start with you being tiresome and annoying. I don't like you. And more, you'd be wise to stay away from Ben and Logan." Cara plastered on her fake smile.

"Wow. You get right to the point and so will I. You do realize me staying away from Ben and Logan is impossible? Surely you know I'm in a working relationship with both since Logan represents

Ben in our real estate deal?" Halley turned to the mirror and applied her gloss.

Cara moved closer, glaring into the mirror. "I'm going to clarify a few things for you, Halley. First, tonight doesn't look like business dealings to me. Next, the town knows that Ben and Logan are vying for my hand. Until I decide which one I want, they're off limits to you. Are we clear?"

Halley tucked her gloss in her bag and pivoted. "You've made your point, though your position seems pretty weak from my observations. Is there anything else?"

"Take some friendly advice. You do not want me as an enemy. I have a lot of influence in Port Royal, more than you can imagine." Cara spun on her heel and walked out the door.

Halley splashed cold water on her wrists, a trick her mom taught her to cool emotions. Right now, she'd like to climb in the sink to get her chill back. Cara's threat lacked teeth since Halley planned to live a quiet life in Port and not run for elected office. She had established mature friends with Joe and Irene. And Ginger and Oliver were great, too. Halley didn't yet know how she felt about Ben and Logan. Geez, she'd moved to town only days ago and already had a cottage to finish and a novel to write. Both enterprises demanded a lot of time. The fact that both guys offered a type of budding friendship felt nice. Halley's mind asked, *where's the harm?* One truth Halley felt secure telling herself was that sassy-pants Cara's intimidation style wouldn't work on citified Halley Bowen. She'd keep playing nice and hope Cara would cease viewing her as a threat. With that thought, Halley waltzed out.

Ginger frowned as Halley sat down. "Did you get a makeover in there or something?"

Halley joined in the laughs. "Yeah, I got something. So, what did I miss?"

Logan wisely ignored the "something" and replied, "You missed our waiter asking that we request his table again. And me offering to drive you home if that's agreeable? Ready?"

Oliver's sense of humor came calling. "All rise. The honorable Logan—"

"Cut it out, Moretti. I'm not a judge. Clearly you can't keep a guy's career ambitions quiet." Logan shook his head.

"You're not a judge yet, but we've got high hopes that can happen down the road. You've got our support," Ginger interjected.

"Becoming a judge is a lofty goal, Logan, one I'm sure you can achieve. And, yes, I accept your offer of a ride." Halley felt her arm tugged.

A wise Ginger whispered in Halley's ear. "Whatever Cara said, ignore her. She behaves like a gnat. Annoying, but harmless."

"I won't ask how you pick up on things, but your advice is appreciated." Halley turned, smiling at Logan. "Shall we, your honor?"

Logan shook his head. "Oliver, you're a dead man walking."

Once outside, Halley and Logan said their goodbyes to the other couple and headed toward his sports car. Halley was able to get good insights on a person from what they drove. Logan's sleek, black performance vehicle spoke to his passion for driving and building a reputation.

"The air seems cooler tonight. Fall may be knocking on Port's door." Logan closed the driver's door.

"I felt it, too. I adore the seasons, so I don't mind the change." Halley buckled the seat belt appreciating the sound of the engine's power.

Logan touched the screen, and soft rock filled the cabin. "There. Now, I'm taking you to the place behind Shaw Construction, right?"

"Yep, that's my temp home until I close on the cottage, and I'm hoping that happens in a month or less." Halley peeked at her phone and saw a missed call from Mick.

"You lucked into that cottage. Ben's loss is your gain as they say. Don't tell Oliver, but he amazes me with the deals he puts together. The guy starts from a genuine place of wanting to help others, like tonight. He and Ginger decided you and I needed to meet, and I knew better than to dismiss the opportunity." Logan grinned.

"Same for me, though Oliver did make a mess of the invitation." Halley chuckled.

"You know what? I never asked where you're from. I don't detect a native Charlotte accent." Logan turned onto Bay Drive.

"Good ear. I'm originally from Miami, which always gets mixed reactions." Halley glanced out the window, thinking about growing up in a city that exuded "local color." She and Beth always felt blessed to have exposure to fascinating culture, food, and the greatest pull, the beaches. "Growing up in Miami polished and honed me, which left me well equipped to enter the adult world when I graduated from college."

"And, yet, you jettisoned city life for us in Port Royal. Why?"

Halley sensed Logan's words were wrapped in genuine interest, but also something else which surprised her. He recognized the magnitude of her shift. *How do I want to answer? I don't know him.* Go shallow and light, her mind instructed.

"Hey, did I lose you to Miami memories or something?" A perceptive Logan changed the music to classical.

"Wow, I like your tunes, Judge. Rachmaninoff *Piano Concerto No. 2* impresses me. Sorry, I got sidetracked. Since we're close to the bungalow, I'll give you the condensed version. Corporate burnout served as my catalyst to honor a yearning to tap into what brought me joy. Living in Port Royal and returning to writing met both desires. Gandhi summed it up for me best: 'The future depends on what you do today.'"

Logan stayed silent for a few moments. "I'm honored to know you, Halley. And I predict a happy life for you here. You brought all the makings for success." Logan turned into the driveway. "I'm ignoring your calling me Judge, but I am going to inflict serious payback on Oliver tomorrow for his blabbing."

"Poor unsuspecting Oliver. I do thank you for the affirmations, which I collect and need." Halley released her door.

The two walked side by side toward the bungalow's front door. Logan spoke first, "I like anyone who enjoys Rachmaninoff, so might you consider going out with me again?"

Halley hesitated a few seconds.

Logan's confidence ebbed. "Nothing intense. We could grab a movie or even coffee. What if I promise no Oliver or Ginger?"

"You had me at the movie, if you let me choose." Halley laughed.

"You're on. I'll call you soon." Logan placed a light kiss on Halley's cheek. "Goodnight."

"Night, Judge." Halley watched him jog to his vehicle and drive off. She plopped down in the rocker to replay the evening and missed seeing a silhouette move toward her.

***

After surprising her, Ben now sat in the opposite rocker from Halley and stared into the darkness. "You're dating Logan?" There was bluntness attached to his words.

Halley rocked, letting her mind fight the war on what response to give Ben. What had her unsettled wasn't that he appeared on her porch, but that she cared what he thought. She rocked another minute, waiting for the answer. Most men recoiled from this type of silence, but Ben seemed willing to wait no matter how long she took to answer. She awarded him another point. Halley stopped the rocker's movement and felt warmth creep from her stomach to her face. Great. Blushing was an unwelcome addition. "I might be dating him. Why?"

"Honestly, I don't know why. Nor do I know why I'm rocking in this chair next to you when a pile of invoices is screaming for the checkbook." Ben released a pent-up breath.

"Maybe you know something unflattering about Logan and want to warn me off?" Halley replied, mystified but somewhat amused.

"No, Logan's a respectable guy. I like him. My dealings with him are geared strictly toward business. It sounds like you're considering dating him. Listen, I'm sorry. Your personal life—"

"I met Logan tonight for dinner with Oliver and Ginger. Those two morphed into matchmakers and set us up. I fear they're on the prowl for any eligible guy with hair and teeth." The thought made Halley laugh. She glimpsed a disappearing smile from Ben.

He clasped his hands behind his neck. "I'm hurt. They haven't approached me." Ben hid behind the façade, but she could see he was truly put out.

"You're not eligible, Ben Shaw." Halley tried to sound upbeat, despite horrid Cara's claim on both men. The flutter was back in her chest. Maybe it was heart-related? Ben's voice brought her back.

Ben waved his left hand in Halley's face. "See that? No ring, lady. That makes me—" He grabbed the cell phone as it lit up and held it to his ear. "Andy, your timing is lousy." Halley rose and he watched her.

"Night, Ben," she mouthed and closed the bungalow's door.

She spent the next hour closing out her day. Halley answered a few emails, including her ex-boss needing guidance on a problematic account. The call back to Mick left her more perplexed than Ben's baffling declaration of dating worthiness. The sea captain needed a favor that involved Libby Wellington, which Halley found herself agreeing to deliver. Her affection for Mick had grown, and she felt privileged to have gained his trust.

The clock said midnight, which meant Halley could catch her sister home. She needed help before Logan called. Rather than bother Ginger with this "Ideal Man" exercise, she'd enlist Beth who knew her history. Beth could offer unbiased opinions on men. Halley opened her laptop and found the old list of Ideal Man Traits and hit delete. New day. New town. New list. New guys. She dialed the number.

"Beth Bowen here," a sleepy voice said.

"Hey. I know it's early, but you can get a speedy start on your day. I need your input." Halley grabbed a breath readying for Beth's waking wrath.

"You do know it's only five in the always foggy London morning?" Beth growled. "This better flirt with life or death, sister."

"It sort of is. I mean, romance is after all part of my benefactor's requirement, and that affects my life. Look, I'll get right to it. I find myself needing a refresher on how to determine if someone is worthy. I might go on a second date with this guy named Logan. I'll fill you in on that back story in an email. Please help me create a new Ideal Man Evaluation. You know my horrible history with dating. Mom used to threaten to send me to Picker School to learn how to choose the right guys. Remember?" Halley stretched out on the bed and covered her head with the sheet hearing Beth's gales of laughter.

Once composed, Beth responded, "Oh my gosh, you may have a second date already? That's incredible and surprising. I forgot about Picker School. I wonder if it even existed? I know charm school did 'cause she sent us there. Mom's sense of humor always challenged us. I recall that Dad hated each guy that showed up at our door to take you out, especially the surfer named Sandy, who said 'gnarly' like every other word."

"Shut up. This reminiscing isn't helpful at all. Can we please create this check sheet? Your history with guys is respectable, and I bet you've already got some poor Brit on a string. It's time you help me out." Halley missed her sister. No one knew her like Beth.

"Make that two Brits. There wasn't a school, right? Because if there is you should—"

"Would you stop? Of course, there's no Picker School. Come on, it's late, and I want to get on the right track to finding romance. You know I'm no dilly-dallier. Here's what I'm thinking. We make a list of important character traits, career aspirations, financial health, throw in some particulars on looks, you know, the window dressing. Then we assign a value for each. The final score determines if he's date-worthy. What do you think, Beth?"

"I think you needn't have woken me. You got this all worked out. I'm going back for my two hours of sleep."

"Don't hang up. I need you to fill in all the blanks. I've come up with the template. Start naming qualities I should look for in a man. I'm ready to type. Beth?" She propped the laptop on a pillow.

"I'm here. Okay, I expect a fantastic Christmas gift this year. Stop it, Percy." Beth pulled the phone charger from the cat's paws.

"All noted. Start talking about my future hunk of burning love."

Thirty minutes later, Halley stared at the computer screen, pleased she had an evaluation checklist that awaited any man that acted beau-like. No more time wasted on guys that weren't a fit. She had a foolproof system. Halley decided to wait until morning for scoring Logan. She grinned, thinking that if he passed muster, Cara might need to start worrying.

Chapter 22

Halley liked Thursdays. She wasn't sure why. They never seemed exacting or demanding like other weekdays. Having the day off, she expected to breeze through her errands. She looked forward to visiting the paint store. Colors excited her decorating genes.

Oliver emailed that Ben had assigned a full-time crew to finish the cottage, which boded well for an earlier move date. Later in the afternoon, she'd spend time at the cottage measuring and figuring out what she needed in furnishings. As for Mick's request, she'd fit that into her day somewhere.

Pouring a second cup of coffee, Halley took her newly named Ideal Man Evaluation to the porch. Time to try it out on Logan. She caught sight of Ben leaving and waved. Why she noticed how his muscles flexed as he climbed into the truck, she couldn't say. Dismissing the thought and an annoying flutter, she returned to tallying up the Judge. Halley admitted Logan had appeal, and the funny nickname suited. Did she have appeal on her list? Nope. She did have physical attraction. Ben getting into his truck came to mind. *Ben's not in the running. He's not interested in anything serious.* As for what understanding he and Cara had, she couldn't care less.

She studied Logan's high score, wondering why she didn't feel hopeful. Here was a guy that qualified as a possible grand romance, but something was missing. The flutter? Why hadn't she talked to Beth about the blasted flutters? Maybe they symbolized some intense physical attraction that had evaded her in the past? She'd never reacted in such a fashion around the few other men she'd dated. Halley needed to understand if the physical feelings were normal, but who did she trust with this sharing? Not Ginger. She was too close to the situation to bring objectivity. That left wise Irene. Yes, she'd stop by Buttercup later for Irene's interpretation and guidance. Feeling better, Halley glanced at a blank evaluation sheet.

Torment chased her mind, followed by fear of knowing. *Stop acting silly. Score Ben and be done wondering.*

Halley went over the evaluation three times, getting the same results. Ben missed the ideal man score by one point. One point declared him not a candidate. So, why did she feel disheartened? Yeah, her heart was feeling dissed, all right. She needed Irene to make sense of the mishmash of emotions. Halley dashed inside and shoved the two evaluations into her handbag. Stopping at Buttercup moved to the top of her tasks.

***

The B&B always felt welcoming from the moment she crossed the threshold. Halley entered the kitchen in search of Irene's calming influence. Chaucer tagged behind. "Sorry, fellow, Éclair's at home." Halley found Joe wiping the kitchen counters. "Morning, Joe. It's so quiet. No guests in the dining room."

Joe straightened up and tossed the cloth to the side. "Hi, Halley. They're already out and about. What can I do for you?"

Halley nodded. "Well, I was hoping to chat with Irene for a few moments. Is she around?"

"I hate to disappoint you, but Irene's gone to Star Isle on errands. I expect her home after lunch. Swing back later. I know she'd love to see you."

"Thanks, Joe. I'll see if I have time." Halley hugged Joe. "Keep working. I'll see myself out."

Plans thwarted by Irene's absence, Halley drove to her second stop. Decorating always buoyed her spirits. She put the paint store's address in her GPS and counted that as a form of guidance.

Halley entered the paint shop and approached a dapper gentleman restocking drop cloths. She zeroed in on his name badge.

"Hi, Harvey. I'm Halley Bowen, and Shaw Construction sent me to pick out paint colors. Can you direct me to the brand and display samples they use?"

"Happy to help. Let me pull up Ben and Andy's account and confirm what they've specified. What's the project?"

"It's the cottage on Bay Drive." She followed Harvey to the checkout.

"Let's see here." Harvey's fingers swiped the screen in search. "Here we go. Come with me, young lady. We'll get this task completed in a flash."

"Great." She dodged some painters getting supplies. The cottage's color scheme danced in her mind. She felt pangs of excitement.

Harvey stopped at an impressive-sized paint chip display. He pulled out ten samples and passed them to Halley. "Here you go. Choose any of these. Come find me when you've decided, and I'll note them for Ben."

Halley fanned out the samples, as a myriad of emotions claimed her. They were all variations of aqua. Ben's favorite color. "Aqua. I'm not painting anything in my cottage aqua. There must be some mistake," she mumbled, feeling some better. She'd check with Harvey.

"That was fast. What did you choose?" Harvey moved toward the register.

"I'm confused. These samples are all aqua. I don't want aqua. I want sunny colors, like yellow and apricot, or even warm sand. Can you show me those?" Halley offered her friendliest smile.

Harvey scratched his head. "Um, Ben noted on his spec sheet the ones I gave you are it. Maybe you'd better talk to him."

Halley's hands found her hips. "Seriously? Is he not allowing me to choose my paint color? Am I stuck with these blues? This is insane."

"I'm sorry. Hey, I like yellow myself. Get with Ben and hurry on back."

"That's what I'm going to do. See you later, Harvey." Halley stomped out to her vehicle. "That annoying Ben Shaw. He's about to find out what a woman with gumption is all about." She'd skip her next stops. "Aqua, ten shades of it. Not happening—ever."

***

Shaw Construction's office was a beehive of activity. Subcontractors stood anxious in the reception area, waiting for their turn to speak with one of the brothers. Cell phones were screaming like drill sergeants. Halley nodded at no one in particular, escaping to where she heard female voices.

"Halley, what a nice surprise," Sally said with a smile. "Tulip and I said moments ago that we wanted to call you." She gave Halley a hug.

"Hi, you two." Halley tousled Tulip's pigtail. "What did you want to tell me?"

"We're invitin' you to a picnic on the beach with us." Tulip took Halley's hand. "When, Mommy?"

"As soon as Halley has time. Maybe next week, while the weather is still warm?" Sally glanced at her watch.

"I'd love to spend an afternoon with my two new friends. Call me, and we'll pick a day. Say, Tulip, do you like to eat silly apples?"

Tulip tilted her head, thinking. "What are silly apples?"

Halley grinned. "How about I bring some for us? You're going to love them." Being around Tulip and Sally had dissipated some of Halley's anger. "Listen, Sally, do you know if Ben's here? I've got a problem with the paint colors."

"He's not, but I am." Andy laid a file on his desk. "Hi, Halley. What do ya need?"

"Andy, we're going to scoot," Sally interjected. "You've got more balls in the air today than our school baseball team at tryouts. Talk soon, Halley." Sally headed out the back door.

Halley conjured a wave for Sally and Tulip. "I'm going to close this office door." She stuck her head into the reception room, where the sub-contractors waited. "Guys, I'm shutting this door because I'm about to throw a hissy fit. It'll be a fast one, and then Andy's all yours." Halley heard laughter from behind the door, and one guy muttered, "Poor Andy. Twenty bucks says Ben's the cause."

"What's happened, Halley? I'm a good problem solver." Andy motioned for Halley to sit.

Instead, Halley spread ten paint samples like a fan across Andy's desk. "Take a gander and tell me what you see?"

Andy frowned, not understanding. "I see ten chips of aqua. Why? What do you see?"

"Oh, I see the same thing, and that's the problem. You see, I don't want aqua walls, yet your brother left me these samples to pick. There's no shimmering yellow or rich apricot, the colors of a sunset, not even a warm sand shade. I like lively colors, and aqua isn't one of them. What's with him and aqua going steady?" she asked with a smirk.

Andy grinned. "If Ben's going steady with aqua, don't let Cara know."

"Funny. Andy, can you help me or not? Please pick up that cell phone and call Harvey. Tell him to take the padlock off the sample display." Halley pointed at the phone resting on the desk. "And, to make sure I've made myself crystal clear, no aqua on my walls, cabinets, counters, floors, not even a hint of it anywhere. Are you getting my drift?" Exhausted from her rant, Halley plopped down in the chair.

Andy seemed to stifle a grin.

One of the workmen cracked open the door a smidgeon. "We think the lady isn't a fan of Ben's aqua, and we vote with her. We don't like it either."

"You all are a bunch of comedians. Shut the door," Andy said. He focused on a simmering Halley. "Look, I get why you're amped. Miscommunication during construction wakes up nerves, and that's something we strive to avoid. I'm not sure what happened with this aqua business, but because the cottage is Ben's home, I can't override him." Andy gathered the paint samples and handed them back.

Halley grabbed them. "I understand your position, Andy. I'm sorry that you're taking my first smack, but trust me, I've only begun. Where is that scoundrel? That flimflammer? I've got plenty more hissy left." Halley stuffed the paint chips into her pocket.

Andy released his pent-up laugh. "I appreciate your understanding my predicament. If it was up to me, you could paint the place chartreuse if you wanted to. I don't know why Ben didn't give you real choices. It's not like we'd already bought the paint." Andy moved toward the reception door. "I'm sure you two will work this out."

"You still haven't said where I can find the cad. I'm not leaving until you tell me." Halley knew one day she'd see this scene as humorous, but that day wasn't now.

"Yeah, I was getting to that part. Ben planned to split his day. He was supposed to hang at Libby Wellington's this morning until the plumbers arrived, and then after lunch, he and Mick were going out in the boat for a quick check on the new winch."

Halley opened the door. "Okay, I'll find him. Hopefully, you parted this morning on good terms, because I'm going to either throw him to the sharks or—"

"Or drop him at Cara's place. She'll finish him off for you. I understand he's still in the doghouse from my party. Good luck to Ben." Andy chuckled and then hollered for the guys to come in.

Halley passed the waiting workers, accepting their high fives and encouragement. "Ridiculous men. All of them," she muttered, moving down the sidewalk.

Sitting in her vehicle, Halley pondered the next move. She couldn't go barging in at Libby's, though she was mad enough to do that. Halley glanced at the vehicle's clock. It was noon. Ben could have left Libby's. That meant the marina was the logical destination, and she was going to color Ben Shaw's world her way.

***

Halley hurried to the dock where Mick tied off his boat only to find an empty slot. "Great. They've left," she exclaimed. She'd wait him out. Andy said it was a brief trip to check something with a winch. Halley eyeballed the few empty seats along the dock, but they all had bird droppings. She squinted and saw the welcoming daisy bench. That worked. Ben couldn't slip by her there.

Grabbing a bottle of tea and a protein bar, a frustrated Halley parked herself on the seat, ready to eat her pathetic lunch. She popped the tea's lid and read the message. *"Find your gratitude."* Those three words conked her on the head and canceled the crossness. "Gratitude," she repeated aloud and took a sip.

"Gratitude has the power to change our very being. Are you finding that so, Halley?"

"Libby, how is it that you appear when I most need your wisdom? This bench must have some amazing juju that attracts people. It's wonderful to see you again. Please, sit with me for a bit." Halley looked up at the smiling face of the other woman.

Libby nodded and sat. "I agree that the daisy bench does possess some interesting qualities, or juju as you referred to it. Each visit, I'm gifted with something I didn't know I needed. So I try to return here daily. I'm grateful for the gifts. You said the word gratitude a moment ago. Why?"

Halley handed over the bottle cap and watched the boats bobbing in the bay. Cloud puffs were missing from the sky. Only the blueness followed her. "See what it says? Find your gratitude. I'd experienced a brief lapse and guess I needed that reminder."

"Do you make a gratitude list or merely speak of the many things you're grateful for?" Libby adjusted her sunbonnet, retying the aqua ribbon. "I'm grateful to have colored ribbons to change on my bonnet." Libby's playful expression hit the mark.

Halley covered her face with her hands rocking with laughter. Catching a breath, she spoke, "Of all the colors of ribbon you could have chosen today, it was aqua. The bane of my existence, thanks to Ben Shaw. Here, let me fix the twist in your ribbon."

"How kind you are." Libby dropped her head so that Halley could untwist the fabric. "I suspect a most entertaining story is forthcoming, or maybe there's something else more important that needs sharing?" Libby studied the younger woman. "What do you have for me?"

Halley sat dumbfounded. How could Libby know? She couldn't. Surely Libby's reference to something for her meant what? Halley gave up analyzing the impossible. She reached for the older woman's hand. "I do have something for you that was left at my door this morning, though how you know this leaves me astonished." Halley pulled the parcel from her tote.

Libby nodded. "Would you pass that to me at the end of our visit? I'd first like to chat about gratitude, and maybe your relationship with a certain color." Libby patted the seat.

A tan, non-descript box tied with string separated the two women while Halley opened up. "To answer your question, sometimes I do make a gratitude list, but mostly I think on my many blessings. And I must say since moving to Port Royal, my gratitude feels pretty boundless. I've experienced one amazing day after another."

"I'd enjoy hearing some of those blessings even if you've already told me."

Halley took in a breath, releasing most of her stress. "Moving to Port tops my list followed by finding the incredible cottage down the road. I'm counting the days until I move. Then, I found a fun part-time job at Deja Brew that's fulfilling so many needs. And, now, I'm able to answer the call I've harbored for so long. I've begun writing my novel in earnest."

Libby pulled a bottle of sparkling water from her bag. "That all sounds perfectly marvelous, young lady. Tell me, are you making friends? Perhaps catching the eye of a beau? Surely, a girl as pretty as you—"

"I appreciate the compliment. I am making a few new friends besides the ones I had, and I hope that includes you?" Halley worried she'd spoken too boldly to Libby Wellington.

"It pleases me immensely to see us sharing a friendship. And those beaus?" Libby's smile reflected an unexpected coyness.

Halley continued, "As for beaus, there's possibly one, an attorney, I had dinner with him last evening. It was a set-up double date, and we all had a great time. He's easy to be around and worthy of a second look. So, this morning I decided to score him on my evaluation sheet." Halley grinned.

Libby considered her words. "Your evaluation sheet? I admire the ambition and applaud a woman protecting her heart, but I must say this evaluation of yours has me quite intrigued. Would you care to elaborate?" She took a delicate sip of her drink and placed the bottle on the seat.

Halley reflected whether fate conjured Libby instead of Irene for guy guidance. She'd test fate's intentions. "Let me begin by reminding you of my sub-par history with romance. I'm completely deficient in the skills to attract ardor, but as a devout optimist, I hold out hope of finding love." Halley's expression turned wistful. "I want the enduring kind of love that seems so elusive nowadays. I know what my problem is, too."

Libby smiled. "Young lady, what's your problem?"

"The trouble is that I lack confidence in recognizing the right guy for me. I keep attracting ho-hum or ambition-driven corporate drones. What I needed was a foolproof system that could help spot these model guys. So, I tapped my sister last night to help develop this trusty evaluation form, which I've put to use." Halley paused, scrutinizing Libby's face and wondered how much more to reveal.

The older woman glanced at the taunting box and then focused on Halley. "I can certainly understand you wanting to approach a relationship without wearing blinders. No woman wants to play the fool. So, you believe this evaluation method will provide assurance?"

Halley took a deep breath noting Libby had engaged and continued, "If nothing else, it can keep me from wasting time on the wrong type of guy. However, today, I'm finding myself perplexed with the scoring. You see, something's not right, because the attorney I went out with scored high. Exceedingly high. And—"

"You're referring to Logan?" Libby's expression flashed a knowingness.

Halley paused, taking in the surprise of Libby's naming her attorney. "Wow. How did you deduce Logan? Does that mean besides a magic wand, you have an all-knowing crystal ball?" Halley walked the few feet and tossed her bottle in the recycle can. "Libby Wellington, you're a force that I don't want to reckon with."

"Please continue. I'm enjoying this immensely," Libby answered, amused.

Halley laughed. "As I said, Logan scored high, and that's well and good, I suppose, because I expect he's going to ask me out again soon."

A little giggle preceded Libby's next word, But…"

"But I didn't feel all happy when Logan scored well. I felt neutral inside. Like, oh, that's nice. Now I come to the confusing part. I can't believe what I'm about to share. You know Ben Shaw, and that I'm renting the bungalow behind his office?"

Libby's face lit, hearing Ben's name. "Yes, I do recall that arrangement, thus the pie delivery. And Halley, maybe it's time to realize that you can trust me."

"Oh my gosh! I forgot to thank you for that pie." Halley paused. "You know, I do find myself trusting you, and thank you, Libby." Halley twisted her ring, frowning before her next words. "Here goes the Ben part. This makes absolutely zero sense because the guy infuriates me to no end, and yet I get this teenage flutter right here when he's around." She rested her hand just above her stomach.

"Finish your telling, and we'll chat." Libby wafted the floral hand fan across her face.

Halley decided to condense the part about the paint fiasco. "So, crazy me felt compelled this morning to assess and score Ben Shaw, which I did."

"How'd Ben fare?" Libby's curiosity was evident.

"One point kept him from making my ideal list. One tiny point," Halley explained, sounding exasperated. "And, for some unfathomable reason, I felt hugely disappointed, but I shouldn't because Ben has some understanding with this girl, Cara. So, it's not like he's available or anything. Still, that blasted flutter when he's around is clouding things with my evaluating checklist. Logan is the one I need to pay attention to, and yet, I'm confused."

Libby sat deliberating a few moments. "I find confusion has always provided me with an opportunity to know myself better. Would you agree?"

"I suppose. Yes, of course, it does." Halley grew thoughtful. "Any other gems for me?"

"Why yes, since you asked. From my life's perch, I see the heart as a true barometer. You must always pay attention to the heart's leanings, for it's your mind that will lead you astray. And passion, well, let us say, passion wears many faces." Libby's voice trailed off.

A silent Halley allowed the words to put down roots. "You sure can say a lot in three sentences. I think I've grasped your meaning. It seems I'm the one who needs the evaluation."

Libby clapped her hands. "Yes, that's an excellent approach and sure to yield answers and clear up uncertainty. Now, before I leave, you must tell me about my ribbon's color, causing you such consternation with Ben." Libby pulled off her bonnet, studying the strip of aqua.

Halley shook her head. "I'll give you the short version and expect you to have a big laugh. I went to the store this morning to choose my paint color for the interior walls of the cottage. The clerk presented me with Ben Shaw's predetermined ten chips to pick from, only there was one humongous problem." Halley paused for effect.

"Pray continue." Libby smiled.

"They were each a varying shade of aqua. The only color this man gave me as options. I swear." Halley raised her left hand. "And I don't do aqua."

"I see. That presents a problem of sorts. So, what's your next step?"

"My next step is to sit here until that rat Ben Shaw returns to the marina with Mick, at which point I will visit on his person the most intense hissy fit ever thrown. Aqua walls all over my cottage. I'll feel like I'm swimming with mermaids. Ridiculous man."

Libby laughed until tears washed her cheeks. "If only I could stay and witness this dressing down." She stood. "You might like to know I see their boat coming into dock."

Halley squinted and made out Mick's fishing boat. "That's them all right."

"I must hurry now. Why not give some time to exploring how living in Port Royal is changing you? That evaluation sheet may reflect your ideal man of the past and not the one for the present." Libby squeezed the younger woman's hand. "Oh, I do so look forward to hearing what color paint wins out."

Halley smiled. "I can tell you it won't be aqua. And you're correct. I am different here, a good kind of different. Wait, take your box." Halley placed the parcel in Libby's hands.

"Is there any message?" Libby's voice faltered as she read the name written.

Halley shook her head. She watched the amazing Libby Wellington walk away, leaving her with another thing to add to the gratitude list.

Chapter 23

Halley hustled down to the dock at the moment Mick and Ben were tying off the boat. She ignored the seagulls parked on the posts anticipating a tasty sampling from the deckhands. She ignored the admiring glances of nearby fishermen. What she didn't ignore was Ben Shaw's surprised expression upon seeing her.

"Well, hello there, lass. What brings you to us this fine afternoon?" Mick coiled a rope but kept his head turned toward Halley.

"Hi, Mick. I came to—" The butterflies took over Halley's stomach as Ben helped her to board. She felt her hissy fit's energy petering out.

Ben grinned. "Step over carefully." He grabbed her other hand. "There you go. Now, what were you saying you came to do?"

Halley's sunglasses hid her fluster. Why couldn't Ben quit smiling? His dimple kept winking at her, which only made her body react more. Why couldn't she have logged the typical dating experiences in her teenage years and spared herself this awkwardness? She pinched her arm and recovered her gumption.

Mick came alongside Ben. "Lass, are things okay? You delivered my little box, right?"

"Yes, yes, that's all done. No problem." Halley turned toward Ben. "I came to talk to Ben about—paint. Aqua paint." Halley's glare fired off shots of anger. She was back in control and ready to hissy fit all over her contractor.

Mick wiped his hands on a rag hanging from his pocket. "Whoa boy, I sense troubled seas ahead. Methinks I'll jump ship and head to The Jetty for a tankard with ole Crusty. You two treat each other nice like." Mick stepped onto the dock and, with a wave, took off.

Ben pointed to a weathered wooden chair. "Take a seat and tell me about your problem with aqua."

"My problem with aqua? Seriously, it's you who has the problem with aqua. You might want to consider a twelve-step program for this obsession. Listen, Ben, I went to the paint store today and was ready to make my selections only to have the clerk present me with ten aqua paint samples. A color, I might add, that isn't what I envisioned for my cottage. *My* cottage." Halley clenched her fists.

Ben frowned. "Well, it seems to me that ten choices are generous, and surely one of them could work for the walls?"

Halley blew out a breath and brought her voice up an octave or two. "Did you hear me? Any variation of aqua does not work for me. It's fine for you, but I don't do aqua—ever. This is my cottage we're discussing here. What I do is sunny yellow or enchanting gold shades. I especially like the colors of sunrise. Apricots and lavenders. I want to feel enlightened and inspired, and not like I'm living under the sea. Mermaids creep me out."

Ben stared and rubbed his chin, seemingly considering his response.

"Are you listening?"

"Oh, I'm listening, Halley. Have you wound down yet?"

"No, and I won't be wound down until you call the paint store and tell them I can choose any color from the display board." Halley handed her cell phone to Ben. "Make the call, and I'll leave you be—for now."

"Look, Halley, I appreciate your eye for color, so many colors, but I've always seen blues as complimentary for waterfront homes. My clients always connect to my color scheme once the property gets completed. You will, too. I promise." Ben stood and reached for Halley's hand. "Come on. Let me treat you to ice cream. The dairy bar is a block away. It's the perfect thing to cool—"

Halley shook off Ben's hand. "I don't want ice cream. I want my color of choice on those walls. I'm going back to the store at four o'clock, and I expect the paint world to become my oyster. Later, Ben Shaw." She stepped off the boat, losing her footing, her legs splitting like a cheerleader's. Ben tried to pull Halley back on board only to lose the tug of war, sending them both overboard with a splash.

They surfaced together, but it was Ben who spoke first. "You should have gone for the ice cream to cool that temper, but I guess this works, too." He grinned, treading water.

Halley pushed the hair away from her cheek. The hilarity of their situation lapped over her like the water's chop. "That was a well-earned hissy fit. I don't have temper tantrums. How do we get out of this water? I shudder to think about what's swimming below."

"Follow me. We can debate your high emotional range later." Ben swam toward the nearest ladder, slowing his pace to match Halley's.

A small group of amused fishermen helped them. Ben took their teasing in stride and waved them off. He grabbed Halley's hand, escorting her toward his truck. "We're soaked. Better to get my truck wet than your SUV. I've got an appointment to make so we'd better get home and change."

Halley let him keep her hand. The return of the flutter was comforting as she left a trail of water and embarrassment behind. "Okay, that makes sense. Let me grab my tote from my vehicle. I guess this is the time where I need to apologize for pulling you into the drink." She stole a glance his way.

"Yeah, this moment feels about right. Well?" Ben met her grin with his own.

"Well, what?"

"I want my proper apology." Ben opened the truck's door for Halley.

She waited for him. "Okay fine. Mr. Shaw, I am so sorry for klutzing out and getting us both soaked. However, I'm not sorry one tiny bit for laying into you about trying to trick me to settle for aqua on my walls. I'm not having aqua inside or outside. Not a lick of it anywhere." Halley sneezed and accepted a napkin from Ben.

"Bless you. You need it. Okay, how about I consider tan as an alternative? There. You win."

"I'll take the blessing, but not your boring tan option." Halley sneezed again. "I must have sniffed in seawater. I'm tabling this discussion until I'm dry." He'd agreed to tan, and that meant Ben Shaw had lost ground. She'd have her victory in due time.

Ben didn't get a chance to respond before Halley's cell phone rang.

"Sorry, I'm going to take this call. Hi, Logan. How are you?" Halley plucked her wet shirt away from her skin while listening to the attorney and watching the scenery pass on the drive. "Sure. I'd love to see a movie. If there's a mystery, I choose that. Oh yes, that sounds like a winner. See you Saturday night." Halley tossed her cell phone in the tote.

Ben cleared his throat. "Uhm, so you decided to date Logan?" His voice sounded mildly interested, but his reddened face signaled more.

Halley took a quick look at Ben and kept her grin inside. "Seems so. Why?"

"I thought you were busy writing a novel?" Ben turned onto their street.

"I am." Halley clutched her tote, ready to jump out of the truck as Ben drove up the driveway.

"Listen, Halley, Logan's a decent guy, and from what I observe has no problem attracting Port's eligible ladies. He's got good credentials like coming from wealth, but he's not the type to flaunt it around town. He's fair in his business dealings, but how he is to date—"

"Good to know you approve of him." Halley couldn't decide how she felt about Ben talking up Logan to her.

Ben let the subject of the attorney fall away. He shut off the truck's engine and turned to Halley. "How's about I take you to get your SUV later, and we can finish the discussion on paint."

Halley hopped down from the truck making her shoes squish. "I guess so. Come over whenever but prepare yourself to embrace my paint choices." Halley noted Ben's raised eyebrows. "Anyway, I've carved out time from my active social schedule to write until the wee hours." Pleased with her saucy words, she slogged toward the bungalow.

Chapter 24

Ben tossed his wet clothes in the washer upon hearing Andy's approach.

"Did Halley find you? I only ask because you're still intact." Andy laughed. "She's pretty persnickety about the cottage wall color. That's Sally's word to describe Tulip's relationship with food. Works in this case. Anyway, your cottage buyer put on quite a performance here. Still, I do like her. Now that I think about it, bro, I like her for you. So, did you two connect?"

"Yeah, she found me on Mick's boat and managed to have us fall overboard while making her point. Don't ask and don't like her for me. She's too feisty." Ben dropped the washer's lid and pushed the buttons. He didn't need Andy's recommendation or approval for a woman. "And for your information, we're still in discussion about wall color. Later, I'm heading to the source of my travails to finish the discussion." Ben opened the door.

Andy pulled his brother back. "Hold up. Libby Wellington called and wants you to swing by for Sunday afternoon tea." Grinning, Andy curled his pinky finger and pretended to sip from a cup. "She's considering the addition of built-ins for the pool house and wants to discuss this when the workers aren't in the way. Give her a ring later. I'm covering the office today. You're free to deal with your travails."

Ben nodded. "I'll call her. If Libby wants me for tea, I'll be there. Tulip's little tea parties have prepared me well." Ben slapped his brother on the back and disappeared outside. "And forget your matchmaking, and tell Sally that, too."

***

The real estate office smelled like a fishmonger's shop. Agents clasping tissues to their noses whizzed by Ben as he tried to close the door. With a red scarf tied around her face, only the receptionist's eyes were visible. She'd activated a can of room deodorizer dousing anyone within striking distance. Before Ben could ask the source of the malodorous office's affliction, Oliver appeared.

"Ladies, don't leave. I'll get this smell out of here as quickly as I can," pleaded a flustered Oliver before turning his attention to Ben. "Whatever has you in a scowl, now isn't the time. I've got bigger fish to fry."

Ben released a laugh, taking in the comedy unfolding. "I can see that. Why does your office smell like last week's catch?" He buried his nose in the crook of his arm, letting his gaze roam the office. He watched the receptionist wave to Oliver and scurry outside.

"A payback prank is what I suspect. That crazy Logan warned me about calling him a judge in front of people. He's secretly hoping to run one day. Big deal, I slipped and said it the other night when we were double-dating with Halley. Anyway, my blabbing karma brought Dano delivering a quadrupled-topped garlic anchovy large pizza. He waved the open box around, stinking my agents out of here. Logan knows that I can't bear even to look at anchovies."

Ben tucked the double-date feelings away and focused on how to help his friend while containing his laughter. "Remind me not to cross Logan. Let's get the back and front doors open. That should clear the air quickly. Don't pardon that pun, 'cause I have another one. I've got a bone to pick with you, Oliver H. Moretti."

"Put your name on the chalkboard. I've got my agents threatening to toss me in the drink cause they had to rearrange to meet clients at Deja Brew instead of the office. And there's a good chance that I may never want to eat fish again. That means I may starve living at Port Royal, where seafood reigns supreme." Oliver walked down the corridor, waving a magazine in the air and throwing open the back door.

Ben caught up with Oliver. "Buddy, you won't waste away. You're Italian and have pasta as a fallback. Here, toss the skunk pizza in the dumpster. I'll be waiting in your office for our showdown."

Oliver returned and sat in his desk chair, pulling open the drawer. "Peanut butter crackers for lunch," he said in disgust. "So, what's your beef? Let's hear it."

Ben leaned forward. "My beef is with you, convincing me to sell to Halley Bowen. The same Halley you promised me a smooth transaction and closing with if I agreed to sell to her. The Halley who you assured me would not want to paint the cottage some frou-frou color. That's my beef."

"Got it. Does Halley want to paint the walls flamingo?" Oliver dusted crumbs from his lap and popped another cracker in his mouth.

"Close enough. She likes sunrise colors. Sunny yellow, enchanting apricot, or was it enchanting gold? Whatever." Ben waved his arms. "She wants to feel enlightened or something like that."

"I get the idea." Oliver rummaged in his drawer and pulled out a candy bar.

"No, you don't get the idea. I like aqua, and that's the color I want this cottage. The same cottage that you convinced me will be mine again when Halley realizes seaside town living isn't for her. This scenario of yours is what persuaded me to sell." Ben sat back in the chair and shook his head no to Oliver's half of the candy bar.

"You're an easy-going guy. Surely you can sell her on aqua?"

"She's not having it and told me that aqua makes her feel like she's living under the sea with mermaids."

Oliver tossed his napkin in the trash can. "You know I never thought of a room color making you feel like you're swimming in the ocean. I can see why she'd want to change—"

"Not you, too. Leave the sea life visual and join me in reality. I'm telling you this woman is from the planet of the pixies. All this shimmering, enchanting, enlivening about a paint color. I caved and offered her tan, but no, tan's boring."

Oliver's mirth was evident. "Planet of the pixies? Halley? Nah, she's a woman with taste. Besides, tan *is* boring. Ginger and I enjoy watching a sunrise on the beach. The colors are vivid. We even saw purples at the last one. You should consider her colors and maybe a sunrise or two this weekend. Break out of the aqua rut, Ben."

"What? Have the fish fumes in this office caused your brain—"

The broker stood, looking ready to dismiss Ben and his paint rant. "Here's my best advice. Pick your contractor battles. Let Halley have her walls painted golden goose or whatever her heart desires. You can always have the place re-painted. Not a big deal, Ben. Now, get back to whatever job needs you and let me try and coax my agents back to work."

A frustrated Ben stopped at the door. "Tell me. What is this spell Halley casts over all who meet her, including your pal Logan?"

Oliver shook Ben's hand. "This answer I have. The same spell she's cast over you, my friend. It's written all over your mug when you talk about her. To finish with our fish metaphors, Halley's a catch. Don't let her get away. Now, leave me to my office woes."

Ben sat in his truck in front of the burger joint, replaying Andy and Oliver's advice until his mind told him the truth. He'd traded one set of problems for new ones, and there was only one person to take them to. Ben maneuvered his truck out of the parking lot. His loaded hamburger and chili cheese fries could wait a bit longer.

***

"I was counting on finding you still here." Ben parked on the counter stool next to Mick, the closest person to a father he'd known. He pointed to the waitress. "I'll have what he's drinking and bring him another."

Mick squinted at him. "Methinks we need a table and some privacy for whatever has your face twisting like a toothache." Mick gathered his business files and moved toward the corner, as Ben followed with their ales.

Ben silenced his cell phone and took a sip. "Ginger ale, huh?" He grinned.

"Yep, I take my ale with ginger as well, you know. I'm listening." Mick hung his cap on the chair's back.

"It's Halley. She's messing with my—everything. And I don't let any woman mess with—"

"Mess with Ben Shaw's heart?" Mick quirked an amused eyebrow.

"Listen, Mick, you know I have zero interest in getting involved with any woman. I like my life as it is. Neat and tidy. That's why I take Cara out sometimes. No complications." Ben fiddled with the cardboard coaster, wondering if he'd made a mistake opening Pandora's box with Mick.

"Forget Cara. Total waste of precious time, and you know it, boy. Start by telling me what is your 'everything' Halley's messing with? We'll get you sorted out." Mick squeezed Ben's forearm.

A cornucopia of emotions played across Ben's face. "For starters, she's being hardheaded about paint colors for the cottage and making me crazy. Majorly crazy."

Mick chuckled. "Are you going to avoid the real truth here by talking about some paint conflict? Let's try this again. I'm getting right to the crux here. What's your heart saying about the lass? Get honest. When did you realize you might more than like her?"

Ben's look changed as awareness replaced confusion. He blew out the breath he'd held. "Okay, I suppose this gnawing in my gut began when I heard she's going out with Logan. It bothered me." Ben rubbed his stomach and winced.

"By George, methinks you're jealous and worried. Two lethal combinations when it comes to women. Duels have been fought over such emotion." Mick waved to a local fisherman.

"I'm not fighting any duel. I'm trying to get things figured out here."

"Look, Ben, it's basic. You don't want Halley seeing Logan because you want to be her fellow. You more than like her, and that feeling sneaked up on you fast. Has you plenty scared. I understand more than you know, as the same thing happened to me long ago." Mick's face darkened.

A surprised Ben asked, "What did you do?"

"Not enough. Not near enough. Why not begin by admitting to yourself and me that you have serious feelings for our Halley? It's time you decide whether fear or love will run your life, lad. For once, let your heart guide you toward that right answer."

Ben could only nod as he wrestled the unwelcome emotional deluge.

"Before leaving, I'm going to suggest one or two things man-to-man here. Spend time with Halley as a suitor. See how you two get on and if she's indeed your 'everything.' Mayhap get out on the water this weekend. My compass always gets righted when I'm on the boat." Mick rose and patted Ben's shoulder as he headed toward the exit.

Chapter 25

The sun's movement had gone unnoticed by Halley, so engrossed was she in the romance unfolding on her laptop's screen. Her heroine's abject denial of attraction to the hero caused Halley angst. And, she knew why. She and her character shared glaring emotional similarities around the men in their lives. Yet Halley refused her muse's demand for flutters to befall her character. One of them dealing with this annoyance was all she could handle.

Taking Libby's advice, Halley had devoted an hour earlier to evaluating herself and what qualities in a man truly mattered. She'd abandoned the impersonal approach for a heart-led one. And, surprise on her, the heart who'd been ignored for so long had plenty to tell her. She decided to apply the "have faith" advice and allow love to find her.

Halley stared at the manuscript's word count, astounded how many pages she'd managed to write by grabbing any free time. Her favorite romance publisher required only fifty thousand words, which meant she was a quarter of the way to completing her first novel.

Sam Langdale flashed in her mind. Halley shifted to her email screen and sent him a short update on her writing accomplishment. She valued the trust shown her by the attorney and, most notably, her benefactor, and she wanted to do her part to honor the relationship. Halley paused, feeling the strangest feeling come over her. For the first time in her adult life, she felt anchored to a place.

Realizing she'd eaten little all day, Halley stood and stretched. The cat mimicked her. "Such a silly kitty. Come on, Éclair, let's get you fed first." She poured kibble into the bowl. "You're lucky to have such an easy dinner." Halley opened the refrigerator and was greeted by two cups of vanilla yogurt and one lonely dried-out English muffin. A door knock interrupted the yogurt's fate.

Ben peered inside at his aqua walls. "I see you're still living with the sea creatures. I was worried you'd painted my walls sunny apricot." He waved a bag.

"That's not close to funny, and it's *sunny yellow* and *harmonious apricot*. I swear a school of dolphins was swimming on my wall moments ago. Most disconcerting. What's in the sack, Shaw?" Halley perked up, sensing food.

He waved the bag under her nose. "Guess, and I'll share half."

Halley pretended to consider her response. "Give me one more sniff." She watched Ben open the bag a smidge and waft the smell her way. "Ahh. Got it. Hamburgers with onions and fries. Bring that sack inside, and you may come with it."

"So, you haven't eaten dinner yet?" Ben unpacked the food.

"No, I ignored the clock. Writers possess that talent. Sorry, water is still what I can offer—"

Ben shook his head. "I figured as much. Here's your malt." He put the straw in the cup and moved it toward Halley's surprised lips. "Taste it."

"Oh, I—" Halley took a sip and hurried to swallow. Her puzzled expression met Ben's as he kept the straw in place. The butterflies fluttered. In what realm was this guy now orbiting? She needed to say something fast. "I love a chocolate malt."

"I'm glad. I took a chance ordering you one," Ben replied. He slowly took the straw away and moved in closer. "I'm forced to admit you're growing on me, Halley Bowen, despite our color clashing."

"Are we ever glad we found you two together," said a voice from outside. "In here, Ginger." Oliver walked through the open door with Ginger on his heels.

Ben reacted first by pulling back from Halley. "What's going on?"

An embarrassed Halley recovered. "Yeah, what's going on here?" She watched her real estate broker bustling around her table.

Oliver replied, "Hurry and scarf down whatever's in the sacks and come bowling with us." He grabbed one of the bags and started unwrapping the hamburger, laying it on Halley's table.

Ginger came inside, a knowing smile on her face. She hurried to Oliver's side. "Sit down, kids. These fries are getting cold." Ginger helped finish unwrapping the food. "You're going to the lanes with us. We need four to make bowling fun."

Halley frowned. "Geez, I don't know. I need to get my vehicle from the marina, and I'd planned to write more into the wee—"

"We can drop you both off later for the SUV. Let's all have a couple of hours of fun." Oliver handed Ben a hamburger with a nod.

Ginger grinned. "And Oliver needs the exercise. Don't you, handsome?"

"I keep saying you gotta love the package you have here." Oliver patted his stomach.

Halley and Ben gobbled down their food while Oliver and Ginger explained they had a lane reservation, which allowed eleven minutes to eat according to Ginger's watch.

***

The bowling alley was awash with colored shirts identifying the leagues in competition. Shouts of encouragement testified to serious camaraderie. Both couples voiced gratitude for getting a lane assigned away from the boisterous groups. The foursome walked past the teams and placed their belongings on the curved bench and bowling balls in the return. Ginger got tapped for scoring, so she claimed her seat.

Oliver stood facing them. "Okay, here's the lowdown. Ginger and I are a team, and Ben and Halley, you're a team. Be warned I bowled in high school and was pretty good." Oliver turned his head and pretended to straighten his collar.

"Sure, okay wise guy, you can go first. Show us what you've got." Ben grinned and motioned for Halley to sit next to him.

Ginger popped up. "Hey, you. That's my ball. Yours has an orange stripe. Geez."

Laughter rang out in their corner.

"Shut up, yous three. I gotta concentrate." Oliver released his ball. "Six pins down. Not bad."

"Ah, but you missed the kingpin, mister." Halley moved into position, wearing a bright smile.

"Kingpin? What's a kingpin, and how do you know about them?" asked an impressed Ben.

Halley released her ball and jumped in the air when a strike rewarded her. She turned to Ben. "A kingpin is the fifth pin and key to doing what I did."

"Wow, girl, you can bowl. Now, I wished we'd gone girls against the guys." Ginger studied the lane and corrected her stance.

"Watch your body, English," instructed Halley. She nodded, seeing Ginger modify her approach.

"Don't help her. Did you forget we're a team?" Ben dropped his arm around a surprised Halley's shoulder.

"Slipped out. Sorry, partner." Halley laughed, savoring their moment and his closeness. "Whoa! Ginger, you got a spare. Okay, Ben, go make me proud."

Ben nodded and went for his ball. He looked over his shoulder. "Do I need any adjustments?"

"Yeah, adjust your axis tilt," Halley hollered.

"His what?" Oliver asked. "Send that ball down the lane, will ya, Ben?"

Halley watched the ball and hung her head in mock shame to a returning Ben. "Gutter ball. Your address needs work. Next turn, I'll help you."

"I can do better," Ben offered, sounding contrite.

Halley smiled. "Yep, you can only go up from a fat zero." She didn't care if he ever knocked a pin down as long as he kept looking at her in this new way—this new confusing but heart-stopping way. She abandoned the business-only oath with a sigh. Out of the corner of her eye, Halley saw Ginger clamp her hand over Oliver's mouth, stopping some male retort directed at Ben's performance.

"Watch and learn, my man," Oliver managed to get out before releasing his ball.

Ginger threw her hands up. "Three measly pins. Quite the teacher. Is it too late to change teams? I want Halley."

The hijinks continued until the last ball rolled, resulting in a solid comeback by Team Halley and Ben.

Halley sensed something had changed between them, something that would go unnamed, but not unseen by their friends. She thought of a flower opening to the sun and wondered fancifully whether what she felt was similar—was she blossoming from the power of attraction to Ben?

She'd let the flutters guide her.

***

Halley and Ben stood in the marina parking lot, watching Oliver's car drive away.

"Those two are perfectly suited and way too much fun." Halley felt Ben take her hand from behind. A tiny quiver shot through her.

"They aren't sore losers either." He squeezed her hand. "Would you mind going down to the boat with me for a moment?"

"Sure, as long as I don't need to board. I'm not ready to tempt fate again with another klutzy overboard maneuver." Halley shivered for effect.

A laugh escaped Ben. "I agree, no walking the plank for you. Come on then." He released her hand only when they reached his boat. "Give me five minutes below. I need to leave a part I ordered for my marine mechanic."

Halley looked at her watch and nodded. "Five minutes, starting now. You drag this out, and I'll leave you, buster. Remember, I've got our ride home this time." Her teasing hit its mark.

"Aye, aye." Ben delivered a smart salute and stepped on board his boat.

The moon disappeared behind a cloud, cloaking Halley in darkness. She heard a tapping behind her and turned. Another shiver claimed her body. Only this one portended approaching unpleasantness.

Cara stood there, hand on her hip. She touched her gold chain and lifted her chin. "Well, I see once again our paths merge. I caught sight of you as I was leaving my dad's yacht. You may recall I'm the hostess tomorrow evening for the Port powerful, and I needed to make sure things were executed properly."

"I'm sure the evening will be lovely." Halley looked away, hoping to discourage more conversation.

Cara glanced at Ben's boat. Her features turned sharp. "I assume this time you're with Ben. Should I also assume our little talk at the restaurant didn't resonate?"

"Oh, you mean that Ben and Logan are off limits until you decide which guy you want? I find that particular tune tiresome and insulting to them both. So yes, I ignored your warning. I spend time with the people I choose, and those who choose me." Halley leaned against the dock's railing.

"How provincial of you. I know Ben, and your type bores him."

"Oh, I don't know about that." Ben appeared from below deck. "I find myself attracted to women who have values and principles, like Halley. You know who bores me? Shallow and self-serving types. Let's go, Halley."

"Your insinuations—your—whatever you said will cost you big. Our arrangement is over." Cara hurried past them in a huff, tossing back a stinger. "Find yourself someone else to ride on that dinghy you call a boat."

"Don't worry. I'm working on it," Ben told Cara. He smiled at Halley and grabbed her hand again. "Not the best way to end a big nothing with Cara, but long overdue. It seems she was confused about some things. Sorry you had to be on the receiving end of her forked tongue."

Halley smiled, happiness wrapping around her heart. He didn't care about Cara in a meaningful way after all. Ben Shaw cared about high-minded beliefs, something her lousy evaluation form had left out. "I kind of feel sorry for her. As someone else told me, she's like a gnat. Annoying but eventually flies elsewhere."

Ben bust out laughing. "What a visual. Cara as a gnat. I suppose it's better than a black widow."

Halley chuckled. "I believe the gnat analogy works well whenever we encounter the Caras of the world. Walk faster. I feel raindrops. One drenching a day is my limit."

Their conversation on the ride home centered around the final touches to the cottage and its completion date. They avoided any reference to the paint impasse. Halley's interest in construction seemed to delight Ben. He explained other jobs he and Andy were involved with, excited mostly with the job they were doing for Libby. Halley sensed Ben's fondness and respect for Libby Wellington, and on that subject, they found more common ground.

Ben's tone turned playful. "I'd like to change the subject for a moment while we're getting along so well. Would you consider going out Sunday, say three o'clock, on that 'dinghy' I call a boat?"

Halley stole a glance Ben's way and determined he meant the humor-laced invitation. "Hang on. I'm considering it." She paused a beat. "Why yes, I'd like to spend a couple of hours on the dinghy. And, I give you my solemn promise to remain on board and dry." Halley turned into the driveway.

"Now, that's what I call a worthy promise." Ben jumped out of the vehicle. "Give me a minute. I've got something to hand off."

Halley frowned. "Sure. Come to the bungalow." She watched Ben unlock the office door and disappear. Shrugging, Halley walked the few yards to greet a meowing Éclair. Her mind slipped into reliving their wonderful evening. Ben grabbing her hand brought them to a new place. He'd sailed them into uncharted waters.

A knock on her door interrupted further reflection.

Ben entered the living room bringing an air of comic relief. "I come bearing gifts and a paint truce." He kept one arm behind his back.

"I like the sound of that. What ya hidin' from me?" Halley attempted to steal a peek, but Ben danced away.

"We need to settle this paint war before the sun comes up and definitely before I get you near water again. Agreed?"

Halley's eyebrow went up. "Hmm, I cautiously agree. What's a truce look like to you, Ben Shaw?"

"Like this." Ben waved a paint fan. "Pick whatever color you like, my pixie."

"You called me a pixie? A pixie?" Halley snagged the fan, laughing.

"I meant pixie in the most—"

"Wait. Are you giving me the win? No, there's more to this. Spill it, mister."

Ben drew her nearer. His expression claimed hers with a sweetness she'd never known in any man. "All I ask is you agree to the white cabinets and quartz counters I've chosen, which will look great with any wall color. Will you give me this small thing, Halley?"

His closeness robbed her of air, of thought, of words. She managed a nod, wondering if Ben was going to kiss her.

Éclair shattered their moment with a loud meow.

Recovering herself, Halley snatched up the kitty, mentally chastising her for lousy timing. She watched Ben step back, shaking his head as if to break the spell.

He reached over to stroke Éclair's back. "Since we agree, let's sit down a moment, and you tell me the colors you want." Ben moved to the dining chairs.

Halley released Éclair and grabbed a paper and a pen. "Here, you can write down my selections." She spread the colors out like a peacock's feathers. "So many beautiful shades to enliven the spirit and creativity."

Ben frowned when she stopped at a bright flamingo. He cleared his throat uncomfortably. "Uhm, I thought you loved the colors of a sunset. That shade is migraine vibrant."

"It's sunrise colors I gravitate toward most. Hey, you said I could choose—" Halley bit down a laugh at her teasing. She hated the color flamingo.

"Of course I did. Shall I write down—what's it called?" Ben leaned over to read the name. "Ah, Flamingo Flight."

"Gotcha." Halley chuckled. "You passed the test. A man of your word. I sorta dig that." Halley continued studying the colors.

"I'm staring at a tease, and I fear a vixen with too many wiles."

"Sounds like you could write a romance novel yourself. These are my two shades. Withholding any comment, please write down conch shell for all the rooms except the master suite." Halley held up the sample. "You like?"

Ben stared at a neutral being shade with a hint of peach. "Where did you find that one? It's actually pretty cool."

Halley smiled. "It's marked as new. Isn't it so interesting how light plays off it?" She held the sample at different angles, admiring her choice. "I'm in love with Conch Shell for the cottage. It's perfect. Now the master area."

"Take your time choosing for the bedroom. I find that room challenging for most." A patient Ben watched Halley deliberate.

Finally, she slid the sample toward Ben. "Found it."

Ben's eyes widened. "You want aqua?" His voice went raspy like he'd enjoyed a taste of an aged brandy.

Halley took in this too-appealing version of Ben and felt the breath sucked from her. She pinched her arm since it had worked so well before. "I do want aqua. I find myself feeling quite captivated by this shade's nuances."

"It matches your eyes."

"What?" Halley looked at the sample, confused. "The shade is called—Cloud Nine." Her face colored.

Ben's hand brushed her cheek. "Your eyes. They may well be my ruin." He smiled and stood clasping the paint fan. "It's getting late, and you wanted to burn the midnight oil writing, so I'd better let you get to it."

Halley followed him to the door. The wild fluttering had taken control of both her body and mind.

"Tonight... tonight—" She swallowed, looking up at Ben. She felt hopelessly besotted by this man. Was this what love felt like? Impossible. How could she find love in a mere few days? Collected and always in control, Halley Bowen didn't succumb to such emotions until now. Embarrassed, she realized Ben was waiting on her to finish speaking. She needed to gather her wits fast. "Sorry. Momentary lapse. Tonight's been so—"

"It sure has." Ben pulled Halley gently into him and bent low, allowing his lips to find hers. He offered a first kiss of tender promise.

Chapter 26

Halley tossed and turned the night away, replaying her mystifying time with Ben. When the sun made an appearance through her bedroom window, she traded the hope of sleep for a jam-packed Friday. A shower would energize her, and after that, she'd eat one of the boring vanilla yogurts in the fridge for breakfast.

While she ate, she answered Beth's last email, where her sister had begged for dating updates on the builder and attorney. Halley confessed their evaluation system proved a flop, and she'd decided to trust as the heart dictates. She chose not to divulge the kiss she'd shared with Ben. That tidbit would surely make her cell phone ring, and she didn't want Beth reading more into whatever was happening with her new wooer. Halley grinned, thinking of Ben that way. *Wooer. I'm going to use that word in my story.* She heard a pounding sound outside and opened the door.

Grabbing her sunglasses, she headed to the source. "Hey, guys. Thanks for making me the first stop." Halley watched two jean-clad young men from the sign shop manage a post digger and shovel. Ben had also pulled up in his truck.

"Good morning." One of the young men smiled. "We'll have the bungalow's sign planted in a few minutes. Take a gander and tell us if you like it, okay?"

Halley bent over to examine the sign. "Looks great, and your graphic designer captured the color and font I wanted perfectly." She watched Ben load his truck and then walk their way. Her tummy fluttered. His expression showed little interest. Her butterfly's movement ceased. Something felt different.

"Wow, I forgot all about the sign for Sea Glass," Ben exclaimed. "I like it. Thanks, Halley, and guys."

"Of course. It's my pleasure." A perplexed Halley tried and failed to get a read on Ben. His words had been polite but lacked warmth. "Are things okay?"

Ben glanced at his watch. "Yep, things are dandy. Listen, I'm late. Catch you later. Thanks again for getting the Sea Glass sign." He jogged back to his truck and gave a slight wave as he drove off.

Halley waited for the sign to get planted before taking her snit inside the bungalow. Men were an enigma to her with their mercurial behaviors. She reflected on the last evening for the millionth time. What had the rising sun done to the fun and caring Ben she'd become so smitten with hours ago? Didn't the kiss mean their relationship had momentum? That they were feeling something more than friendship? And, P.S., didn't she witness him ending things with Cara? And, P.P.S, they had a date to go boating Sunday, unless he'd changed his mind.

A quandary settled upon her mind, with one certainty hanging over her. She lacked experience with affairs of the heart, which proved her benefactor's requirement correct. How could she write about abiding love until she experienced it? Halley's snit left her put out with Ben Shaw's aloofness and caring about a guy more than she ever had before.

She went to claim another yogurt's cooling effect only to hear footsteps on the porch. "Geez, I never lived in such a beehive of activity in Charlotte. Let's see who's about now," Halley told Éclair. The feline trotted along, bringing her curiosity.

"Morning, lass. I come bearing bear claws from the bakery. It's a thank you for couriering to Miss Libby." Mick held up a white box.

"You didn't need to do this, but a cup of yogurt is no match for bear claws. Come inside, and I'll make us a cup of tea. I remembered where I put the tea bags."

"Can we breakfast on the porch? It's too pretty of a day to be inside." Mick didn't wait for a reply. He set the rocker in motion.

"You bet. I'll join you in a minute." Halley returned with two mugs of green tea and napkins.

Mick sniffed his brew. "You do know this isn't a proper cuppa?" He took a sip. "Not even close, lass." He grinned.

Halley broke off a piece of the pastry. "Beggars can't—"

"Right you are. Speaking of begging, I left Buttercup, having failed at begging for breakfast. Irene was at sixes and sevens with a full house of guests, each having special diet needs. I took one look at her face and did a U-turn out of that kitchen. Yes ma'am, to the bakery I went. So, if you had any ideas about stopping by to see her,

I'd advise you to wait till after the weekend." Mick took a bite of the pastry, looking toward Ben and Andy's office.

"Don't ask," Halley said, reading his mind.

"Right." Mick paused, considering his next words. "I'm going to say this because it won't stay inside me. Attraction to another can be powerful and often confusing."

"Yes, I suppose," Halley replied, not willing to elaborate.

Mick shifted topics. "Why don't you tell me what your Friday looks like? Hand me another claw. We've got two more small ones in that box to finish."

Halley passed him the pastry. "Let's see. I'm working at the coffee shop a few hours, making myself go do a serious grocery shop, and spending the rest of the day writing." Halley tossed a morsel to a female cardinal who'd joined them for breakfast.

"A productive day is a good day, I always say. I'm proud to know a writer committed to her craft." Mick nodded and offered the last piece to the bird. "She's friendly and deserving like you, Halley."

"Ahh, Mick, your words are a balm to my spirit. Writing is giving me unexpected joy, and I'm grateful for the amazing opportunity to do this work. I can only hope a publisher connects to the finished manuscript."

"The right one will as long as you write from here." Mick tapped his chest. He crumbled his napkin and put it in the empty mug. "Well, time to see if those fish want breakfast."

"I bet they do," Halley answered, chuckling. She stood to bestow a kiss on Mick's bearded face. "Thank you for showing up at the perfect time. You and someone else that I'm quite fond of have a knack for knowing when I need bolstering."

"Happy to oblige, lass." Mick walked toward his vehicle, waving to Andy, who'd come out the back door.

Halley watched the other Shaw head her way. The procession to her porch continued, one person at a time. She found her smile. "Hey, Andy. To what do I owe the honor?"

"I'm the messenger bringing news that the painters are working at the cottage today. It seems they had a job cancel, so we moved you up on their schedule. Feel free to stop by this afternoon and make sure you like the color. After yesterday, I'm not assuming anything with you and paint." Andy grinned.

"That's wonderful news, and I will swing by after work. And I am sorry about my hissy fit, but it did the trick with your brother. Aqua will be found only in the master." Halley laughed.

"Yes, but your win sure left Ben crabby this morning. I sent him off to oversee the job at Miss Wellington's. I told him either go there or sit in Tulip's timeout chair until his mood improved. He made the right choice. His frame would never fit in her seat."

"No, I can't imagine that tall drink of water sitting in Tulip's chair. As for our disagreement over paint causing your brother to act ornery, I think you'd better look for another explanation. We patched things up nicely—at least I thought we did." Halley's expression changed to wistful.

"He'll work through whatever it is. Ben's even-keeled. It's not like him to act tetchy. See you, Halley." Andy trotted back to the office.

"Even keeled, is he? Debatable," Halley mumbled, going inside to get ready for work.

***

"Boy am I ever glad to see you." Ginger wiped her brow. "I was about to quit, but remembered I own this joint."

Halley took in the scene. There wasn't an empty table in the coffee shop. "Let's both quit and go to the beach. My right arm is screaming from throwing that bowling ball. I don't know how I'm going to lift those coffee trays you've lined up."

"Humor is exactly what I needed. Get that apron affixed to your body fast before there's a mutiny." Ginger nodded to the group entering the shop and winked at Halley. "Battle stations."

The two women lost count of the beverages that moved across the counter but welcomed the lull that came two hours later. Tables once again cleaned and fresh-baked cookies under the glass dome, they collapsed on the stools.

"I'm giving myself a raise after this hustle-bustle. Want one?" Ginger teased.

"I'm still waiting on the first one you promised," Halley joked.

"Yeah, Oliver tells me I'm all talk. Speaking of guys, you and Ben seem to have something brewing," Ginger quipped. "Sorry I can't help myself."

Halley shrugged. "I'm not sure. We did have a great time last night, but when I saw him earlier, he was all standoffish. I honestly don't get men."

"I'm told it's mutual. They don't get us either. I wouldn't fret too much about Ben, besides, tomorrow night you and Logan have a date. Your dance card isn't collecting dust, kiddo."

Seeing customers entering, Ginger retied her apron and scurried behind the counter.

Halley came alongside. "You're right. I'll look forward to my date with the Judge. I like him. And, besides, I've always heard we shouldn't put all our eggs in one basket." Halley waved to Sally and Tulip as they approached.

Tulip ran to grab Halley's hand. "We've come to invite you to a picnic Monday."

"You have, huh?" Halley smiled at the two.

Sally placed her order and turned to Halley. "Yes, Tulip and I are hoping you'll join us for a fun beach outing. We can pick you up around eleven if that works?"

"Hang on while I look at the work schedule hanging right here. Yep, that day works. I'm off."

Tulip tugged on Halley's apron. "Don't forget you promised we'd make funny apples."

"You mean silly apples, but they're definitely funny apples, too. And I haven't forgotten, Miss Tulip. I'm going grocery shopping later and will make sure to buy what we need. How's that sound?"

Tulip nodded. "Can we make extra ones for Daddy and Uncle Ben?"

"Sure can." Halley spied a tray of waiting drinks. "Girls, work beckons. I look forward to our play date."

"Wave bye, Tulip." Sally ushered her magpie toward the door.

Ginger came alongside. "They are such a sweet family, and you're a natural with kids. I see you with a brood."

"A what? Do you forget I don't even have a boyfriend?" Halley called over her shoulder.

"The last count you had two," Ginger hollered, laughing.

***

Having finished her shift, Halley paused outside Deja Brew and drew in a cleansing breath. Noontime always symbolized a kind of transition to her. Halley found the whole circadian rhythm thing fascinating. Maybe Ben was out of sync with his. Perhaps she should quit thinking about him. So far, fifteen minutes had passed without his face flashing before her, and not once did she see Logan's. Maybe that was because she needed to spend time with the attorney. "Too many maybes," Halley declared.

"Don't you hate maybes? They lead you nowhere." Libby stood a few feet away, dressed for gardening in her signature denim overalls and a knit shirt.

"And here's my favorite sage, bringing wisdom to me on Port Royal's sidewalk." Halley leaned in for a hug.

"You're too kind with the compliments. I'm here to bring you an invitation."

"An invitation? This makes my second one today. I feel special," Halley said with a smile.

"Young lady, you are indeed most special. I'm inviting you for Sunday tea, say one o'clock, but I confess to an ulterior motive or two. You see, I picked up on your decorating gift when we spoke, and I find myself needing your valuable input on a few selections." Libby stepped aside to allow a couple to enter Deja Brew.

"My gosh, Libby, I'm honored you'd ask me. I confess to also having an ulterior motive in accepting." Halley's expression brightened.

Libby drew closer, smiling. "And what might that be?"

"I get to see Magnolia Manor, or course," Halley whispered.

"Ah, then I shall look forward to Sunday. For now, you might like to ignore those distracting maybes that live in the future. The place where nothing can happen until it becomes the present. I hope you find pleasure in the remainder of this day."

"Thank you, Libby, for that insight and invite. I hope to give something back to you." Halley opened the coffee shop door for Libby. She agreed that maybes felt like a dead end emotionally. Seconds later, her mind recalled Libby saying she had ulterior *motives*—plural—but only declared the decorating one. Halley dismissed the pondering and focused on visiting her cottage. With any luck, the painters had covered enough walls with Conch Shell for her to experience its unique chameleon ambiance. As for the bedroom shade, Cloud Nine, she dismissed the second thoughts and blamed them on her snit. Ridiculous man and his thing for aqua.

Halley recalled what Ben said about her eyes being that same color. She sighed. *Stop this silliness. I need to go by the cottage and grocery store then immerse myself into writing. That's my plan, nice and tidy.* And, for once, the sound of nice and tidy bored her.

Chapter 27

"Figured I'd find you here once the clock struck five." Mick sat down next to a simmering Ben. He waited for a reply that didn't come. "At least I taught you to seek solace on your boat, but I'm a wonderin' what's brought you here wearing such a chapped face? Mayhap you're worried a certain lass has indeed lassoed that heart of yours?" Mick sounded a deep chuckle.

Ben came out of his trance and rewarded Mick with a glare.

"You're making this guessing too easy on me." Mick winked. "If it'll perk you up, I found Halley behaving the same way when I stopped by the bungalow earlier. All I had to do was take a gander at your house, and the lass reacted. Two peas if I ever saw them."

"Hardly. I already told you Halley's got a date with Logan for a movie tomorrow night, which means one of your peas is not in the pod." Ben held a piece of rope and retied a knot over and over. He'd awakened, at first feeling happy followed by feeling out of sorts about Halley seeing another guy. As the day wore on, that looming date ate at him. "She's with Logan come tomorrow night."

"Which also means a suitor must best his competition. I feel confident saying the lass wants you to win, but you have to compete like I told you yesterday. Now that you've determined you like her 'everything,' I'm going to remind you of another piece of sound advice I gave you. Look me in the eye, son. I want these words to sink in." Mick's expression turned serious.

Ben laid the rope aside and stared at the man who meant the world to him. The man to whom he and Andy owed a lifelong debt. The man he allowed himself to trust and who treated him like a son. "Okay, I'm listening and staring into those Scotsman baby blues, you ole salty dog." Ben released his first grin of the day.

Mick gave a solemn nod. "I say again. It's time you decide whether fear or love will run your life. Fear or love? Stay on this boat until you decide. Halley deserves a man who knows his mind and his heart. If that's Logan, so be it then. You can always continue your life with an empty dalliance like Cara. Stew on all of that."

Both men grew quiet watching charter boats enter the bay bringing home happy memories for those on board. Ben knew they both took solace on the water. The experience was unique, as if ancestors had imprinted their love for the sea on each of them. The sea bound them.

Mick sighed. "I know you'll soon power past the waters' chop and find your calm seas. There's always time to think out there." He waved at the sea. "I need to head over to the Bait Shack and order ice for my boat's coolers. Shrimp are runnin', so we're going out to try the new nets and winch tonight. It'll be an all-nighter. Normally I'd invite you to lend a hand, but—"

"But you've exiled me to my boat." Ben managed a chuckle. "A sentence you've laid on me countless times."

Captain Mick stroked his whiskers. "A whole lot less nowadays, so must mean you're learnin' something. And, so you know, I'd bet tonight's catch that our Halley stays on your arm if you but offer it." Mick slapped Ben's back and jumped nimbly to the dock.

Ben dropped his sunglasses and watched Mick saunter toward the Bait Shack, greeting folks as he went. His respect for the older man and his many accomplishments grew with each passing year. Mick continued mentoring him on any problem that Ben brought his way, and some he didn't. It seemed that tutelage now included his love life. *There*, he'd officially thought the four-letter word, but could he say it to her? And, once more, he questioned the speed at which love had clobbered him. Mick's advice made sense. Ben didn't bother telling Mick that he'd come prepared to spend a night or two on the boat—alone. He glanced up at the stars. The wind had morphed to a whisper, and the ocean became a calm, sentient being. That was the sign to release the ropes and all the fearful emotional ties that bound him. A tucked-away quote inside of him came calling. Ben liked to draw from Samuel Johnson's view on life: "Life is not long, and too much of it must not pass in idle deliberation of how it shall be spent." Ben started the boat's engine. He'd idle no more.

***

At midnight, Halley quit listening for Ben's truck to return home, but she couldn't stop wondering where he'd spent the evening, and maybe even the night. Surely not with Cara. Did he date other women? No, that image didn't fit Ben Shaw. Relationships weren't his thing, yet she and Ben had something "brewing" as Ginger called it. Only she sensed Ben had turned off the flame. Was it all because she was going out with Logan? It wasn't like she and Ben had any kind of understanding about not seeing other people. Logan was fun and she liked fun. No harm there. Why? She'd asked herself the whole livelong day. *Why?*

"Ugh, enough of this mental torment. I've beaten this dead horse as far as Pluto. Get back to your romance story where the characters all behave as you tell them," murmured Halley to the cat. She turned to the computer screen and re-entered her story. There she remained until Éclair's meow much later called her to bed.

Chapter 28

Halley's Saturday morning shift brought a grateful calm to Deja Brew. A few stragglers ambled in to order refreshing drinks. An unusual scorching September day's temperature drove most all to the beach or pool. Deja's air conditioner strained to keep the inside at seventy-eight degrees. The town's sidewalk was bereft of tourists, and the ever-present ice cream cart was missing in action. Taking advantage of the lull, Ginger and Halley mopped the vintage oak-planked floors and polished the chairs and tables. Books and games got re-positioned on shelves to invite a closer look. Ginger declared it their day for accomplishments.

The bell on the door jingled, announcing Oliver. "Morning, ladies. Are you as bored as me? I haven't seen one walk-in at my office. I made an executive decision and put the 'gone fishing' sign in the window." Oliver came over to Ginger and pecked her cheek.

"As I recall, you eat fish, but you never catch them?" Ginger grinned and offered a sip of her frozen mocha drink to Oliver.

"And may I remind you I'm still off fish thanks to Logan's pizza prank? Speaking of the rat, don't you two have a date tonight, Halley?" Oliver took Ginger's drink and sauntered over to the nearby stool.

Halley promptly snatched the glass and handed it back to her boss, grinning. "I do, and the Judge allowed me to pick the flick. Wow, pick the flick, I'm a poet, too. Who knew?"

"You're busting with talent. What kind of movie?" Ginger asked.

"A mystery—my favorite genre, because I stay engaged."

"We both hope you have a fun evening. Don't we, Oliver?" Ginger poked him in the side.

"If you say so, babe, though I'm partial to Ben, after our bowling night." Oliver looked up at the ceiling, thinking. "Still, I admit Logan's pizza prank may have colored my opinion."

Hanging her apron on the hook, Halley turned back to the two friends she knew wished her only the best. "You guys can discuss my dating future. I'm going home to write the first kissing scene."

"Excellent. That should prime you for Logan later," Ginger said.

"Or Ben," Oliver supplied, smirking.

"Enough. I'm leaving. See you," Halley laughed. She closed the shop's door and felt the heat zap her. She'd better use the tail of her shirt to touch the SUV's handle. Growing up in Miami taught her that trick at a young age.

"Here, let me help you. It's an inferno out here today." Logan carefully held open the door to her driver's seat.

"Hey there, Judge. Inferno is exactly the word." Halley tossed her handbag in the passenger seat.

"Again, with the judge thing? I may send another pizza delivery to Oliver." Logan crossed his arms beside the open door.

Halley chuckled. "Poor Oliver. He lamented to me earlier how he and fish have broken up thanks to your gift." She liked Logan's humor. "Are we still movie-bound at seven?"

"Absolutely. Bound and determined. Let's get your door closed so you can crank up the AC. Count on seeing me later." Logan waved her off.

***

Taking a break from the computer screen, Halley did a bit of reflecting. She was living the writer's life and never felt more passionate about her path, all thanks to the benefactor's generosity. She yearned to thank the woman for the gift but accepted the terms of their agreement would never afford her the chance. The one way to show sincere gratitude was to make a success of the opportunity and keep her faith in the highest and best outcome. Halley vowed to arise each day, renewing that pledge.

Devoting the entire afternoon to her novel, she stared in shock at her word count. She needed fewer than fifteen thousand words to meet the novella submission requirement. How had she and the muses managed such an accomplishment in so short of time? Yes, she'd fallen in love with her heroine and hero and loved spending copious amounts of time with them. And yes, so she'd only slept two to three hours each night, but still, this meant she could soon tell Mr. Langdale she'd completed the novel with the speed of light.

Halley jumped, hearing a sound outside. She hadn't seen Ben or his truck since he left yesterday morning. It was the weekend, so asking Andy where his brother had disappeared to wasn't an option. She opened the door to see the sprinkler system as the source of her disappointment. Glancing at the porch clock, she decided to make a chef salad for dinner and then find enthusiasm for her date night.

***

Promptly at seven, Halley sat in the rocker. She'd chosen a turquoise sundress and strappy black open-toed heels to elevate her mood. Bright coral lipstick and few gold bangles helped, but if anyone looked closely, they'd see past the façade to a woman in waiting, but not for the man due to arrive. Logan's vehicle came up the driveway.

He greeted Halley with his usual friendliness and opened the car door. "Hi there. Ready for a Sherlock Holmes extravaganza? Remember, you picked him."

"Hi yourself, and yes, I'm ready for any of Sherlock's adventures. He's one of my most beloved sleuths." Halley settled into the luxurious leather seat and waited for Logan to join her.

Minutes later, they were forced to claim seats on the front row. "I guess the heat brought half the town here tonight," Halley offered.

"Yeah, and I fear our necks will never be the same, looking at the screen from this angle. We may have to stop by the drug store for two of those neck collars when we leave, but hey, I'm a glass-half-full kind of guy. I can play for juror sympathy next week, pleading my cases." Logan cast a grin.

"You're a cunning man, Judge," Halley snickered.

"I'd like to think so," he replied, teasing. "Listen up, if you drop the Judge, I'll buy you a large buttered popcorn and a pop. Deal?"

Halley nodded, smiling. "Boy, I can tell you're from somewhere else, drinking 'pop.' I'll take your deal, but instead, I want a ginormous box of chocolate nonpareils."

"Chocolate what?" Logan frowned.

"You know the round candy disks with crunchy white sprinkles on top. Forget it. I'll go pick out my bribe."

Logan laughed only to have a woman behind shush him. "If you're sure you want to go, but I'm happy to try and find the chocolate things," he whispered loudly for effect.

"For Pete's sake, let her go get the goods. She's not Jane Austen needing your bidding," grumbled the woman.

Halley delivered a grin to the woman and stepped into the aisle.

"Fine, take this money, and would you mind doubling whatever you order?" Logan placed the money in Halley's hand.

"Do I get to keep the change as a tip for turning you onto the nonpareils?" Halley didn't wait for his reply, nor did she experience any flutters from his touch.

A familiar voice spoke to Halley in the concession line. She turned to see Sally and her mom, Liz, wearing happy faces. "How nice to run into you two. Let me guess. Girls' night out?"

"Yep, Andy and Tulip are home enjoying cartoons and popsicles. And Mom and I love a good mystery so voila, Sherlock to our rescue." Sally dug in her purse, looking for her wallet.

"Speaking of mysteries, I haven't seen Ben at home since yesterday. Anything going on with him?" Halley seized the opportunity to at least solve one mystery.

"Mom, go ahead and order while I talk to Halley." She turned to face Halley. "Andy hasn't said anything about him. I bet he's on the boat. Whenever Ben stays on the boat, it means, well, it means he's trying to get clear about something. Know what I mean?"

"I guess so," Halley answered, squeezing the money tighter in her hand to release stress.

"Sally, you're next to order." Liz turned to Halley. "Are you settling in nicely with us at Port? I do hope you'll stop by the Book Worm again soon." Liz munched her popcorn.

"I feel like Port has always been home, and yes, I promise to drop by. Thank you." Halley saw a concession employee signal her. "Excuse me. Candy time." Halley waved bye to Sally and her mom.

While Halley waited for the drinks, her mind noodled about Ben escaping to his boat for solace and answers. What had him troubled? The construction company seemed viable thanks to her purchase and Libby's job. He'd rid himself of the annoying gnat, Cara. Ben and Andy seemed to enjoy a close bond. To an outsider, Ben's world appeared blessed, much like Halley's. Out of time for further speculation, she took the two sodas and tucked the boxes of candy under each arm and made her way to the Judge, henceforth known as Logan.

"Logan, I'd like you to meet nonpareils." Halley passed him a box. "And, I warn you trying to give these up for Lent will meet with failure. Of course, assuming you practice the discipline."

A few of the chocolates disappeared into Logan's mouth before he replied. "Oh my, these are—"

"See? Didn't I tell you? Good, huh?" Halley preened for fun.

"I was going to say disgusting wax disks," Logan finished, grabbing his napkin.

"Seriously, you hate them?"

"Would you two please be quiet? The movie's about to begin. Go get yourself some popcorn and give her the candy," said the exasperated woman behind them. "Honestly, I could have stayed home and refereed my kids for free."

Halley scooted down in the seat, covering her mouth to stifle the laughter.

Logan passed her the box and took a big swig of his drink only to pucker again. "Orange pop? Who over ten drinks orange pop?" he whispered exasperatedly. "Don't give my seat away. I'm going for popcorn and a man's beverage. That is after I rinse out my mouth, Bowen."

Halley couldn't resist. She knew both she and Logan had the pranking gene. She stuck her foot out as Logan maneuvered past. He stumbled enough to cause his drink lid to fly off. Orange drops trickled down his beige shirt. He retrieved the cover. "Oh, your punishment is going to be stellar, woman," Logan said good-naturedly as he wiped his shirt.

"Go get your heart's desire. We can negotiate my sentence later, Judge. Oops, sorry. Make that Logan."

***

Logan and Halley stood under Sea Glass's porch light.

"I guess I should let you get some writing done tonight. I had a good time at the movie, despite the embarrassing debacle you visited upon me." Logan grinned and moved closer, his face mere inches from Halley's.

"I had a good time, too. This evening was the perfect distraction I needed." Halley knew Logan wanted to kiss her, and she needed him to, but not for the reasons most women wanted to be kissed. She helped by tilting her face up.

Logan smiled and bestowed a gentle kiss on Halley's waiting lips.

Nothing. She felt nothing. Halley gazed up to Logan, seeing his expression mirrored her own. She smiled. "You neither?"

Logan stepped back. "Sadly, no. How about friends?"

"For always, Logan. Count on more pranks, too."

"Speaking of pranks." Logan snagged the full box of chocolate nonpareils from the nearby chair. "Consider this your payback from trying to trip me up at the movie. I'm relieving you of eating this disgusting candle wax you call chocolate candy. You're demented to think these are a treat."

Halley knew their banter was what would build a lasting friendship. She giggled. "Give me that box." She chased Logan to his car, at which point he pivoted, holding the candy in the air.

He leaned down and kissed her cheek. "You're a good egg, Halley Bowen. You lack taste in confections, but a good egg. I'm counting on us having more laughs soon. 'Night."

"Which one of us lacks taste is debatable, counselor. Get out of here and leave me bereft without my nonpareils." Halley stood watching the sports car take her new friend home. Could she trust the answer her body gave her? More, what good did it serve when Ben had turned into a Houdini with his disappearing act?

Chapter 29

Halley gasped as Ben appeared from the shadows. "You didn't kiss Logan the way you did me. Why did you kiss him?"

"What?" Another emotion flooded Halley's being: happiness. Ben was standing next to her.

"I said you didn't kiss him the—"

"Skip it. I heard you. For starters, we're starting this conversation at a different place." Halley's indignation at Ben for challenging her on her actions welled up, mixing with happiness at seeing him looking all flustered with—was that jealousy? Great. Now her traitorous body added a low-voltage hum to Ben's proximity. She gathered her thoughts. "Where have you been, and why were you spying on me?"

Ben stroked her arm. "I've been in hell, thanks for asking. And I return home only to find you kissing Logan. Why?" The low timbre of his voice masked emotional pain.

Halley faltered, searching for words, but not too many. "He kissed me. And you act like a whiplash," she answered hotly.

"A whiplash? What the heck does that even mean?" Ben said, exasperated.

"It means I feel jerked around by your behavior. Furthermore, you're a Houdini type. Kissing me one minute and disappearing the next. Houdini. Now, I come home and find you lying in wait to grill me about having a friendship with Logan. Whiplash." Halley blew out a breath and held her ground.

Ben stepped closer. "Friendship? Ha. Since when do friends kiss like—"

"You don't have a clue what that kiss meant. You don't have a clue what it told me." What her heart and soul wanted was Ben to wrap his arms around her and do something. Any something. Instead, he stood inches from her face glowering while her heart skipped beats.

Inhaling deeply, Ben released Halley's arm and turned toward his truck.

Halley followed on his heels. "Hold up. Now, where are you going?"

Ben halted. The moon illumined the hurt on his face. "Back to hell."

"If they'll have you," Halley volleyed back and stomped toward the bungalow. She knew how she'd spend the coming wee hours—she would go for a trifecta, starting with a hissy fit, and then a snit, and ending with a fine dither. That should cover all her emotional bases. Then, she'd hang out with her characters until they sent her to bed.

` ***

Ben released the boat's mooring lines and prepared to depart. A quick radio call informed him his destination was a mile out due east. He throttled hard, hurrying his boat. As Seas the Day skimmed along, Ben observed boat lights strung like pearls ahead. The calm ocean welcomed shrimpers this night, as well as one frustrated contractor who'd discovered building a relationship with Halley was far more complicated than building a structure. His foundation was showing stress cracks, and that usually meant more steel, but this was Halley. He guessed that meant more giving more honesty and more trust, which asked a lot from him. And he wasn't sure he had all of that to give any woman.

He came alongside Mick's boat and dropped anchor. "Ahoy, captain. Permission to come aboard?" Ben tossed the rope to the first mate.

Mick hung over the rail puffing his pipe. "Come aboard, son. Coffee's hot."

"I've come to work. What's running tonight?" Ben respected Mick's philosophy of small catches and protecting other species by having proper nets.

The wise captain studied Ben's face before replying. "Yep, long hours of hard work are what you need. I've given you enough guidance on the fairer sex. Tonight, we've got greentail shrimp about to bust out of my new mongoose nets. Hear those winches groaning, lad? That means the tail bags are about to dump. Let's get you outfitted and ready to cull." Mick slapped Ben's back. "Yes sir, you came to the right place to get rid of that scowl. I need to thank our Halley for sending me another mate."

"Say any more about her, and you'll lose this mate," Ben barked, going below. He'd spent enough time shrimping with Mick to know the rigorous labor demanded concentration and not the distraction of some blond sprite who'd stolen his heart. He would down a gallon of Mick's high-octane coffee this night, but the reward was trading emotional hell for purgatory. He could do limbo for a bit longer, and come Sunday, face teatime with Libby Wellington's latest renovation ideas. He'd keep busy with work until he figured out how to fix things within himself and then go to Halley. He refused to suffer another failure to launch.

Chapter 30

Looking at her disheveled bed, which she'd left after only two hours of troubled slumber, Halley escaped to her manuscript. What better place to hide out until Ben returned from hell? She smiled, reliving their parting words. In the coming light of day, she saw the comedy of assumptions that had befallen them. Dodging the explanation for Logan kissing her had inflicted unnecessary pain on Ben. Why had she sparred with him, instead of merely telling him she and Logan had agreed to a friendship? Perhaps because she felt hurt and angry at Ben for acting detached hours after they'd enjoyed a special night together, only to emerge questioning her about Logan. He'd behaved as if he didn't approve of her kissing someone else. Whiplash described Ben Shaw's behavior to a T, and there was nothing more to do with that awareness but let it stew.

Halley opened her laptop, choosing to devote the next free hours to writing before heading to Libby's. Heavens, she'd typed a slew of pages last night. At this pace, she'd complete the first draft within days, but without fulfilling one of the benefactor's requirements—a grand romance to give her story authenticity. Things were all out of sync. Her grand romance was fizzling before it had a chance. She studied her story's outline, which lacked one critical detail—an ending.

Halley forged ahead. She'd expected the writing to stretch out over many months, allowing love the time to find her, but it seemed neither her story nor her feelings for Ben needed months to blossom. It simply needed a push from either one of them. With the romance of her characters heating up, Halley's anxiety bubbled like a simmering pot along with the story's climax in need of the happily ever after.

"I still have faith in you, Ben," she whispered and glanced out the window. She sighed at his missing white truck.

***

Excitement brought Halley to Magnolia Manor's door fifteen minutes early. She'd promised herself to leave all lingering Ben questions at the bungalow. Questions like, would they still go boating that afternoon? Maybe he'd kiss her again if she ignored her stubborn side and apologized for acting sassy? Or, she could kiss him hot on Port's sidewalk and clear things up for Cara. That image made her laugh, as she stood at Libby's massive mahogany carved front door.

"I'm lovestruck," Halley declared, throwing her arms up in exasperation as the doors opened.

"My, my, to hear such proclamation, and on a Sunday," Rupert said, amused. "Won't you come inside? You may call me Rupert. Miss Wellington's expecting you."

Halley's face flushed as red as the nearby rose bush. "Thank you, Rupert, and about what you witnessed, please don't say—"

"Well, that wouldn't be my story to tell. Would it now, Miss Halley?" Stepping aside, Rupert grinned. "Please wait here a few moments."

The octagon foyer's formal beauty showed off the owner's impeccable taste. A mosaic in the center of the grey marble floor had the letter M inlaid with gold tiles, and a grand staircase circled to the next floor and one beyond. Light shone from fixed glass rectangular panes three stories above. Halley smiled, wondering how they got cleaned. Oil paintings depicting landscapes from other parts of the world brought color into the room, but it was the large palms in antique ceramic planters that breathed life to the space. Halley considered taking a seat in one of the upholstered tapestry chairs, but Rupert hadn't invited her to sit, so her good manners kept her standing.

***

Mrs. Cookson greeted Ben as he entered the manor's kitchen from the service entrance.

"Good afternoon to you, Mr. Shaw. Let me pop around and find Rupert."

"That's fine, Mrs. Cookson. May I steal one of your scones warming on that rack?"

She blushed and simpered. "You must hurry, for I'm to serve them with tea in a few moments."

Ben laughed. "Oh, trust me, this one will be long gone before you return." Good to his word, he took an enormous bite, finishing seconds before Rupert entered.

"I see you've been sampling, Mr. Ben," Rupert chuckled. "Won't you follow me?" The houseman led Ben to the foyer, where Halley waited.

"What are you doing here?" Ben asked.

"Libby invited me, and I guess you decided to leave hell?"

Rupert cleared his throat, looking amused. "Excuse me. I'll let Miss Wellington know you are both here." He disappeared through double doors.

Halley and Ben each nodded to the houseman and eyed each other.

"I didn't know you and Libby were all that chummy, and my curiosity for why we're both here at the same time is undiminished. Should I expect Logan soon?" Ben moved closer to Halley. He was angrier at himself. He was already blowing his put-things-right plan.

"Try and stifle the Logan talk. If you must know, Libby invited me to tea so that we could chat about colors and decor options." Ben's ire relaxed a bit.

"Not you and colors again. I thought we were done with that subject once and for all. Now, I find you at my client's home and playing decorator for Miss Wellington. Why me?" Ben asked, looking upward.

"Let me answer that, young man." Libby entered the foyer. "Why you? Because you're my builder and Halley's keen eye for decorating is something I value and need at this renovation stage. Now, both of you put on congenial faces and join me in the drawing room. Mrs. Cookson has prepared the tea trolley." A high-spirited Libby walked out, trusting her guests followed.

The drawing room's design embodied an Old-World elegance, with walnut floors and molding and coffered ceiling, but the furnishings and accessories lacked a relationship with each other. Both the ivory shaded walls, and the swirled black and white marble framed the fireplace and served as the canvas for the two moss-green sofas and contemporary glass coffee table displaying nothing of interest. The muted colors of the Persian rug added little to the room's feel. And the gold-framed paintings of Revolutionary War officers left Halley wondering how the drawing room suited its owner.

Libby sat centered on one sofa, forcing Halley and Ben to share the other.

"Apologies for the tardy tea trolley," Mrs. Cookson said as she wheeled it to Libby's side. "Will there be anything else, Miss Libby?"

"I think not. Your scones and tea sandwiches look particularly delectable today." Libby waited for Mrs. Cookson to close the door. "We're having an early afternoon tea, so please help yourselves." Libby passed the Limoges plates and then focused on pouring the tea.

"This is a lovely treat that I've anticipated for days." Halley tasted a cream cheese and olive sandwich. "So good." She glanced at Ben, who'd chosen two scones to rest on his plate. She flashed to Tulip's tea party and him seated on a child-size chair.

"You two better grab those remaining scones, or I will." Ben grinned and took a sip of his tea.

"Halley, maybe we'd better do as he says," Libby encouraged, reaching for the smallest one. "Now, before we three delve into my ideas for the pool house, I'm most curious, Halley, about how you find this room's appeal? I couldn't help but notice your discerning eye taking in the space. Please be frank."

Taken by surprise, Halley bought time sipping her tea. She bet Ben relished seeing her on the decorator hot seat. "All right, I'll be frank as long as you understand my observations reflect my impressions but come with my utmost respect for Magnolia Manor."

Libby nodded. "Your disclaimer is unnecessary but appreciated. Please?"

Ben settled back on the sofa, his face awash in amusement.

Halley took in a breath. "First, I'm going to share my initial impression upon entering the room. I felt an absence of harmony among the pieces. The architectural components' neutrality, with the dark woods, coffered ceiling, and ivory walls, allow the room to become whatever you want. The overall furnishings and embellishments aren't taking advantage of this. To be honest, they serve to distract and confuse, yet your foyer is absolute perfection and representative of Magnolia's pedigree." Halley paused, realizing she'd probably said way too much. "Forgive me. I adore your home and felt protective of it the moment I entered."

"There's nothing to forgive, dear. Now, Ben, I'm interested in your impression of this room. You're a talented young man who has an eye for structure and design, though I've heard you have a proclivity for a certain color that's proving somewhat limiting." Libby's teasing nature found Ben.

He glanced toward Halley, suppressing a grin. "Someone in this room has, to borrow your word, Miss Libby, a *proclivity* for saying too much. Overlooking that for the moment, I find myself agreeing with Halley's keen assessment, but I'd add the walnut molding and floors could use refurbishing, and the ceiling needs some repair. Once that's accomplished, you will know the wood's true colors in choosing the other décor. I'd also consider revamping the fireplace mantel and hearth still in keeping with Magnolia's grand style." Ben held out his cup for a refill.

Libby spoke as she poured more tea into each cup. "I'm so pleased with your valuable input, and I find myself ready to make a proposal."

Halley leaned forward to take her cup from Libby. "A proposal? I can't imagine—"

"No, I'm sure you can't, but my idea is quite splendid. I want to offer you and Ben the opportunity to breathe fresh air into this stale drawing room that mother decorated oh so many years ago. I seldom use the room because of how it makes me feel, though I could never have explained it as well as you, Halley. The time has come for me to transition Magnolia Manor into a gracious but updated home and I need you two to help me accomplish this worthy undertaking. Be warned, other rooms want your attention, too, if you work well together. Of course, the compensation must reflect your talents, and it will. And, Halley, I know you're working part-time at the coffee shop and writing a novel, so I'm happy to work around those commitments. So, what do you say?"

Halley and Ben turned to each other as shock colored both their faces. Neither spoke.

A tick later, Ben reached over and lifted Halley's hand. "Double dog dare you."

Halley straightened her shoulders. "Please excuse him. He's humor challenged. I accept your generous offer and will gladly take on this project but without payment. To have a chance to enhance Magnolia and spend time with you, Libby, is a gift and I can't—"

"Oh, but you can, my dear. We shall have no more discussion about compensation. Ben? I'd like to hear from you. Do we need to double-dog you?" Libby asked with a smirk.

Ben broke into a laugh. "Like I ever had a say with two women such as you at my side. Of course, I say yes to you, Libby. I could never deny you anything, much like my niece. My one request is, don't involve me in paint selection."

"Trust me, Libby. You want to agree to that post-haste," Halley said.

Libby extended her hand. "Let's shake on this exciting new undertaking. Now then, I'd like us to visit the pool house and discuss my latest ideas. Shall we?" Libby rose.

"By all means. We're right behind you." Ben passed Halley and whispered, "Truce?"

"May it hold more than five minutes," Halley retorted. Her day had taken a surprising turn, thanks to Libby Wellington and a healthy helping of faith.

***

"I want to thank you both for giving up part of the afternoon. Magnolia Manor will soon experience a renaissance of no small order, and we will enjoy each moment." Libby paused in the foyer as Rupert approached.

"Excuse me, but there's a phone call. I shouldn't think it'll take but a moment." Rupert held out the phone.

"Libby, please take your call. We'll wait in the drawing room." Halley motioned for Ben to follow her.

"I'm not sure what's happened here today, but I'm willing to go along," Ben said.

"Ditto." Halley hesitated. "Umm, Ben, I need to ask you—"

"If we're still going out on *Seas the Day*?"

Halley nodded. Her throat felt tight and looking at Ben woke up the flutters.

"If I promise not to act like a jerk, do you want to spend more time in my company?" Ben seemed to hold his breath.

"I do if you do?" Halley cocked an eyebrow.

Ben chuckled. "Okay, how about you visit with Libby for a half hour while I get the boat ready for our outing?" Ben glanced at his watch. "Would you mind telling Miss Libby I said goodbye and explain why I left?"

"Go. I'll handle things here and enjoy a few private minutes with Libby." She had some suspicions around Libby's soiree today, and Ben's departure allowed Halley to go fishing. She felt confident that the other ulterior motive Libby referenced in her invitation was now transparent, but why draw her and Ben to work together?

Rupert appeared. "Miss Wellington would appreciate your joining her in the study."

Halley entered, taking in the room's coziness and masculine atmosphere. She liked it. Taking a chair next to Libby, Halley explained, "Ben asks your forgiveness. He's gone to ready his boat for our planned outing today. I hope you don't mind."

Libby beamed. "Mind? I'm thrilled to hear this."

Halley beamed back. "You're thrilled? Hmm, this leads me to a question that latched onto me upon Ben's arrival."

"I confess to expecting your question. You're a sharp cookie." Libby noticed something she'd left on her desk.

"Oh, Libby, you know I'm clueless on the subject we're about to discuss. Aside from giving me a wonderful opportunity to tap into my love of decorating, why did you put Ben and me together knowing I was struggling to understand the man?"

"Remember when I told you passion wears many faces?"

Halley nodded.

"I'd like to add to that. First, you must care, and only then does passion come alive. Think of it in another way. A safer, less emotional way. You first had to care today about the drawing room's needs, and once you did, the passion for making improvements took over. Would you agree?"

"Yes, I think so."

"You and Ben care a great deal about each other. It's evident and so is the passion. I wanted to afford you both the prospect of discovering—"

"Our love?"

"Your love, yes."

"But, Libby, we can't be in love after only a week or so? That's what I keep telling myself. Besides, I'm a novice at romance. That's where my mind has me—full of doubt. How can this qualify as forever love?" Halley sighed.

Libby's face took on an even more determined look. "Tell me something. How long does it take to fall in love with someone? Is there definitive proof that you're relying upon? Say if in ninety days you feel like you've met your mate, is it safe to proceed? What if it's seventeen days? Or maybe a year is the magic number?"

"Defining it that way does sound ridiculous." Halley nodded. "Say I agree that I might be in love with Ben Shaw, and you're validating that I'm presenting all the signs. I don't have a clue how he feels."

"Why not?" Libby nodded as Mrs. Cookson left a pitcher of lemonade.

Halley shared her latest saga riding an emotional seesaw, including Ben's exiling himself to hell twice. That part caused laughter to overtake her confidante.

Recovered, Libby turned serious. "Do you want my biased input and advice?" She passed a glass of lemonade to Halley.

"I do. We both know my guy evaluation form is a big bust. Truthfully, I don't feel led to bring my Ben problems to Ginger or Irene. My sister certainly isn't seasoned in love. So, that leaves my treasured and wise friend, Libby Wellington. You've given me amazing guidance on our daisy bench. I trust you. Please advise away."

Libby sipped her drink before placing the glass on her desk. "There's a type of energy about you and Ben. The same energy I experienced a long time ago. Dear Halley, you remind me of when I walked a similar path as you, only I stepped off that path and lost the man who had my heart. Who had my love."

Halley interrupted, "Libby, your loss makes me sad even though it's history. Sometimes pain lingers, like when my parents passed. Would you like to talk about your guy that slipped away?"

"How kind of you to offer, Halley, but no. Today asks us to devote time to your affairs of the heart. To continue, don't doubt your feelings for Ben—instead, trust them. For you see, feelings don't need time to mature like thoughts. If you're listening to your heart as I suggested before, you'll know. Trust your heart. Does it say you must do this or that to be in love?"

Halley shook her head.

"No, the heart simply asks to feel and act from that place. Those flutters of yours were the heart telling you to notice that Ben's special. Special for you."

"Yes, he is," Halley agreed, and then grinned with a recollection.

"What's funny? You must tell me."

"Oh, I remembered what I declared as Rupert opened the door a while ago." Halley's face colored again. "I was feeling so frustrated and weary of denying my heart's guidance that I threw my arms in the air and pronounced myself lovestruck. I guess I acknowledged love at your front door."

Libby clapped her hands. "See? You already knew it. My interfering wasn't needed, or rather my helpfulness." Libby's voice mirrored her merriment.

"Oh yes, that helpfulness was sorely needed and still is, Libby. I don't understand Ben's behavior. Maybe he doesn't feel the same way as me?" Frown lines appeared on Halley's forehead.

"You're right. He doesn't feel the same. What I'm about to say may stun you but say it I shall." Libby paused. "I suspect Ben's in love with you. He's confused but for different reasons than you, which means he can't feel the same way. Does that make sense?"

"Maybe, but could you elaborate more?"

"Unlike you, Ben's able to recognize love, but he's afraid to love. Somewhere along the heart's path, he experienced deep hurt from loving someone. It matters not who or when. What matters is in the present moment he's left scarred and unable to trust someone's love, in this case, yours."

"Oh my gosh! You, in this second, cleared this up for me. I get it. Is love ever complex." Halley sat, thinking. "So, when I went out with Logan—"

"Ben realized how much he cared when you seemed interested in Logan. What he felt wasn't so much jealousy, but his vulnerability." Libby gestured for Halley to continue.

"Thus, Ben's retreat—to hell?"

Libby chuckled. "Here's the summing up. How wonderful that you've found love in Port Royal so quickly. The real kind of love that carries you through a lifetime. The kind I let slip away. If you want Ben, it's time to show how he can count on your love. I leave the how to you." Libby gazed at the clock on the mantel.

"I understand so much now that had eluded me. You have this incredible way of parting a curtain so that I can see. I don't know how to begin to thank you." Halley felt tears forming.

"Thank me by always trusting your heart." Libby sat her glass on the tray. "Let us look forward to many more joy-sharing days."

"Let's." Halley's scrutiny landed on a familiar box sitting on Libby's desk. Dare she ask? She felt the nudge. "Libby, I see the unopened box from Mick over there. I'm puzzled. Maybe it's my turn to offer help?"

"Not to worry. I'll get around to opening it soon. Now, my dear, you must go. A handsome fellow is about to experience his own type of flutters."

Halley chose not to pry about the ignored box but instead offered Libby a goodbye hug. "Ben and I owe you the moon and stars."

Chapter 31

"Permission to come aboard, captain?" Halley had changed into sneakers, grateful she kept them in the SUV, but was otherwise in the same clothes she wore earlier.

Ben popped up from the hatch, wearing a carefree expression. He moved toward Halley. "Permission granted. Give me your hand. No, wait. Promise me you'll not—"

"Enough already about me pulling us overboard. Won't happen again." Halley managed to land on the deck with grace and a smile. "So, what's the plan? I've looked forward to this outing since you proposed. I mean since you invited me." Her face felt hot.

Ben tossed the tie-off rope to the side, his mood seeming to lighten. "Well, for starters, I don't know about you, but Mrs. Cookson's finger sandwiches and scones woke up my appetite. I swung by the Chicken Shak and picked up some food, so we can eat whenever you'd like. With a few hours of daylight left, there's a place I'd like to show you. Interested?"

"I am as long as I don't have to get wet. I don't have a bathing suit with me."

"Does wading count as getting wet?" asked Ben.

Halley could see budding disappointment on his face. "Nope, wading does not count. Hurry up and get this cuddy running."

"You do know that as captain, I'm supposed to give the orders," Ben teased, moving to the helm. "Come sit next to me, and that's my first order."

"Aye, aye." Halley perched on the next seat and watched Ben navigate with ease out of the marina. Let the flutters come. She'd never felt so happy.

Once on the open water, Ben shifted his focus to Halley. "I'd like to ask you a question, sort of a get-to-know-Halley-better question."

Pleased by his interest, Halley nodded. "Sure, as long as you return the favor. Shoot."

"Agreed. I'm curious about your educational background. You seemed pretty confident and knowledgeable discussing decorating with Libby, not to mention me." He added the last comment with a playful lilt to his voice. "Anyway, my keen observation skills tell me there's a reason."

"Your keen observation skills are right on, captain." Halley hesitated. She wanted to give Ben more than her standard answer. His question begged for more. "I have a double degree in commercial interior design and marketing. I guess the design component fills my hunger for creative pursuits, but so does writing. I'm passionate about both forms of expression and couldn't choose one over the other, especially now that I'm writing with intention. The marketing piece goes along with almost any endeavor, so I chose both." Her face glowed from sharing her truth and that Ben cared enough to ask. "How'd I do?"

Ben turned the boat north and lifted his sunglasses to regard Halley. "You did awesomely. I'm super impressed with your educational accomplishment and even more that you appreciate your talents."

"Much appreciated, and now it's my turn. I saw your drawings of the pool house renovation. You're a talented guy in your own right. Why didn't you pursue architecture?" Halley waved to a passing boat with a family.

"Now, that's an insightful question. The short answer is working as an architect is too confining for me. I'm better out and about with jobs and not working for a firm that asks me to fit a certain template. I'm a draftsman and a contractor, which allows my creative expression." Ben reached for Halley's hand. "I like that we share that bent."

"You do?" Halley's voice faltered, but not from the butterflies moving through her torso.

"Yep. Please don't think me a jerk, but wanna know what I don't like?" Ben throttled the engine back. He faced Halley. "I don't like that you and Logan—"

"Hold up, Ben. This is my cue to clear up some things. Okay?"

He nodded. "Okay."

"Great. First, you get my apology. I'm sorry, sincerely sorry for acting sassy last night and not setting you straight about Logan and me. Instead, I let you go back to hell." Halley's grin broke through.

Ben rallied and matched her grin. "You might like to know that I detoured hell and went to purgatory. I worked on Mick's shrimper all night. That distraction helped a little. And you and Logan?"

"Easy. We're best suited as friends. There's no chemistry between us. That kiss you witnessed proved it. You jumped to the wrong conclusion, and again I'm so sorry. I was plenty ticked at your acting all aloof earlier and confused about how you felt about us. Your behavior didn't jibe after we'd spent a fun evening bowling and—"

"Exchanged a real kiss?" Ben interjected. He killed the engine and moved closer as his lips found Halley's.

Halley pulled back for a moment, studying his face. "Yes, we real-kissed." She grinned and waited agonizing seconds, observing Ben wrestle with trusting them both. "Ben, don't you know that I'm not interested in making out with anyone but you?" There. She'd declared herself as Libby advised.

"Make out? Who says *make out* nowadays?" He wrapped his arms around her.

Halley stood on tiptoes and touched her nose to his. "I did say make out, and I'd like for us to do more of it, but maybe not here in the middle of the ocean. Assuming, of course, you've banished the 'I can't trust a woman' demon?"

Halley's last words appeared to have an impact and his arms released her. "I'm working on said banishment. It's my Achilles heel, I admit. I think more of your making out strategy will do the trick." Ben planted a brief kiss on Halley's mouth to seal his words. "I need to get us to the destination before it gets any later, but fair warning, I plan to pick up where we left off applying your strategy."

"That gives me two things to look forward to. This mysterious destination and more cuddling. Fire up that engine." Halley hopped back in her seat.

"Again, with the orders, squirt?"

"Always, you tall drink of water." Halley watched Ben's muscular forearm push the boat's gear max forward.

"Grab hold, mate," Ben hollered over the engine's throaty response.

She gave a thumbs up. Joy returned, and so did the hope their relationship was moving full speed ahead like *Seas the Day*.

***

Twenty minutes at top speed brought Ben's "something" into vision. "Look to your left, Halley." He extended his arm, pointing and changed course.

"Is that a lighthouse? I adore lighthouses." Halley jumped up to hug him.

"I'm fascinated with them, too. Take hold of the railing. We've got that other boat's wake heading our way." Ben put the cuddy's bow into the waves, sending them on a brief roller coaster ride, albeit an ocean one. He grinned at Halley's excitement.

"That felt exhilarating, and hey, I'm still upright. I think me and the cuddy are simpatico." Halley patted the gauges.

"Appears so." Ben throttled back coasting nearer the island's point. "Lighthouse up ahead. I'm going to get as close as possible so that we can wade in."

Halley stared at him in horror. "Wade in?"

Ben nodded firmly. "Yep, that's what I said, Pixie. It's time to lose the shoes." He grinned at her look of distaste then kicked his sneakers off and peered over the starboard side. "Nothing but a few small nosey fish down there. Let's go introduce you to Lighthouse Point."

Halley climbed over the side, only to promptly step in a deep sand hole. Water reached almost to her neck. He burst into laughter. "Once again, I find myself saying you sure know how to make a splash."

Halley slogged her way to shore, in her white jeans and silk top—which Ben appreciated much more now it was soaking wet—and scowled as she squeezed the water from her shirt.

"I'm *so* glad I can continue providing you comic relief. You do realize I have no dry clothes here?"

Ben stowed his laughter and came up to Halley. "I'm going to do the gentlemanly thing." He began unbuttoning his shirt. "Go behind that tree and put this on. It'll come down to your knees, so your dignity stays preserved."

"Dignity? I have no dignity left. Give me that shirt, and don't you dare peek." Halley scurried into the brush. "With any luck, I'll get poison ivy to take home as a souvenir," she mumbled. A few minutes later she reappeared and Ben bit back a smile. His shirt touched her knees. Halley rolled her jeans and shirt into a ball as she trudged back to Ben. "Thank you and can we not say any more about—"

Ben made the motion to zip his lips and started walking. "Come on. Let's say hello to the lighthouse. Did you know lighthouses are painted different colors so that mariners can recognize them during the day?"

"That makes sense. What else?"

Ben slowed down to let Halley catch up.

"Well, a lighthouse flashes a different sequence of lights for the same reason. It's like their signature. Cool, huh?"

"Too bad they're not in much use anymore. I've read the government has auctioned or even given some away. What's this one's story and the keeper's cottage attached?" Halley stood at the base of the lighthouse, craning her neck to see the top.

Ben lifted a shell at the entrance and waved a key. "Better yet, wanna see inside?"

"You bet." Halley held a dilapidated screen door while Ben unlocked the wood-planked one. "So much history here."

They toured the keeper's cottage, waving cobwebs away. A narrow door opened into the body of the lighthouse. The metal staircase wound upward, but the lighthouse's unique quality showed in the ample square footage. Evidence of squatters was strewn about the floors.

Halley surveyed the structure once more. "Who owns this? And what's its future?"

"Ahh, ever the designer, which is a good thing. An idea, actually a brilliant idea came to me a little while ago. I'll start by answering your questions. A real estate investor purchased the lighthouse and contacted me with his business plan. Andy and I accepted the project yesterday to turn this grand dame into a bed and breakfast for him." Ben leaned against the cement wall.

"Wow. What a fantastic gig. Are you excited?" Halley sauntered over to an old table and chairs.

"Yes, this job taps my creative side and shows our company's ability and openness to unique projects. We're not starting until early next year. Now on to my idea. How would you like to take charge of the interior design phase? You've got the credentials, and I feel sure the owner would agree."

Halley's face went blank. "Another gift?" she muttered dazedly. "How can this keep happening?"

Ben frowned at her reaction, confused by her words. "Of course, you may miss Charlotte and want to return?"

Halley shook her head. "What? Go back to Charlotte? Why would you think I'd want to do that?"

"Well, Oliver felt like you'd grow bored living in Port Royal." Ben wished he could pull his words back.

"Ah, I get it. Then, you'd get the cottage back. I see it now." Halley walked out of the lighthouse, shoulders stiff.

Ben followed her, rubbing his forehead. "Listen, I admit early on, I did hope the cottage might come back to me."

"And what changed?" Halley moved closer to him, an encouraging sign.

"What changed was the other night bowling. I realized that we made a winning team, even if you did have to coach me. What changed was I sent Cara on her way, which incidentally I should have done after the first date. What changed was how I felt after kissing you that night. I no longer cared what color you painted the cottage or if you lived there until you were a hundred. I wanted you happy and near me." Ben pushed her hair away from her face. "Am I asking too much? Too soon?"

"Not if you're saying what I think you are. I want the same thing. You happy and near me whatever that ends up meaning. I need you to hear—and trust—what I'm about to say."

Ben nodded, stroking Halley's cheek with his thumb.

"I'm not going anywhere. Port Royal is my forever home now and has what I want. I've never been happier, and you, Ben Shaw, are one of the major reasons for my happiness." Halley paused. "And besides, you're close to finishing my cottage. That's making me sublimely happy."

Ben moved to speak and Halley touched his lips. "Not yet. The offer to work with you on the lighthouse, that's another point in my happy column. And I accept that offer. Now you stubborn man, you may kiss me."

"Stubborn? Couldn't you have left that part out? Always a jab with you." His arms pulled her into him, letting the kiss ignite feelings he'd longed to feel again with this woman in his arms.

Halley came up breathless. "Count on more jabs if I get these results. Could we maybe do this a bit more?"

"I'm a goner," Ben mumbled as Halley leaned in for the aforementioned making out.

Chapter 32

"Pardon me, Miss Libby, but a dapper older gentleman is asking for a few minutes of your time," Rupert said.

Libby sat behind her desk, reviewing invoices for the renovations. Interest piqued, she directed her attention toward Rupert. "Can you tell me anything more about this dapper gentleman?"

Rupert gave a slight nod. "He appears to have a bit of a Scottish brogue, and when I asked his name, he said, 'Just Mick.'"

"Mick," Libby repeated, casting her focus toward the unopened box. Fluster knocked on her inner door. Mick was here at Magnolia Manor, only steps away from her. She swallowed and gathered some visage of composure. "Please escort Mr. Duffy to my study."

"Right away," Rupert replied and left.

Libby paced the room, trying to release anxiety around this unexpected visit. What did Mick want with her? The box. His presence must have something to do with it. Why had she ignored the contents? The answer lived tucked away in her heart. Her musings were interrupted as the study's door opened.

Mick entered and paused a tick. "Hello, Libby." His expression softened, seeing her face turned toward him. He approached and bestowed a light kiss on her outreached hand. "My apologies for showing up without an invite, but I needed to see you. I could wait no longer."

"After all these years, you decide it's time to see me?" Libby's tone turned frigid. "Please say whatever you came to say. I have matters to attend to."

Mick saw the sealed box resting on her desk. "May we sit? I find my words come easier—"

"I suppose," Libby answered, choosing one of the nearby upholstered chairs. She waited for Mick to settle.

"You look well. I—"

"Mick, suspend the polite conversation and explain why you're sitting here?"

"The box. I sent you the box, and I see it's unopened. Why?" Mick's expression was full of pain.

Libby straightened her carriage. Her mouth became a hard line. "I hadn't gotten around to it. I'm involved in renovation projects. Whatever are you doing?" She watched Mick retrieve the parcel and place it on her lap.

He untied the string. "Look inside, Libby." Mick returned to his chair.

"Very well." She lifted the lid. "Letters? Old letters from you? I don't understand." Libby thumbed through the box, touching a few yellowed envelopes in the stack. She held her composure. "Why don't you enlighten me?"

"Oh, I intend to do that, tardy though I may be. A friend of mine discovered my unopened letters in what was your father's office, and now the pool house. He's a carpenter working for Ben and Andy and was demoing wall shelving. He found the hidden box with my name on it. Unsure what do, he brought it to me. Once I looked inside the box, our unfinished story became clear." Mick's expression shifted. "You hold the letters I wrote to you, begging for an explanation of why you didn't show at the church."

Confusion wrapped around Libby's next words as she reflected back in time. "Am I to understand you were at the church on the day we planned to elope?"

Mick leaned over and clasped her hand. "Aye, I was there despite your father telling me you'd come to your senses about marrying a Scotsman with little money. He told me you had sailed to Europe to keep company with some earl. Your father offered me money to disappear, but as you see, I've stayed in Port Royal. The letters you hold, that your father surely confiscated and hid from you, hold my pleadings for you to trust in our love, and come back to me. Libby, you've hardly spoken to me all these years, and if you choose to continue acting like I don't exist, I will accept those are your wishes, but not before you have the truth." Mick stood. "Read the letters. And know this: nothing has changed inside of me. What I wrote then is still true today. Now, if you'll excuse me, I'll take my leave."

"Please don't go," Libby said, her voice trembling with pent-up emotion. "I fear there's been a terrible injustice done to us by my father. I can't fathom how he could think his deception was an act of love for me. However, I must suspend judgment and try to make sense of this." Libby grew silent, allowing the memories to return. "There's something I need you to hear, my side of what happened. My father came to me the day before our elopement and said you'd only pretended to love me to get my money. He showed me. Excuse me." Libby pulled a tissue from her pocket and wiped away tears. "My father showed me a photo of you holding a briefcase of cash."

Anger colored Mick's face. "He must have paid someone to snap that picture when he shoved the money at me. I swear, Libby, I walked out and left it on the floor. I didn't want your money, for I knew myself capable of success, and I thought you believed in me."

"Oh, Mick, I did. I wanted to, but the picture and my father's telling was so convincing. I was young. Naïve. I tried calling you before I left, but some unknown guy told me you'd gone to Boston to buy a fishing boat. I knew if you were in Boston, there couldn't be a wedding, which proved my father's story." Libby paused, letting the painful memories return, appreciating Mick allowed her this time. She looked his way. "I did sail to Europe, but not to see some earl. I fled, taking my shame that the man I loved had abandoned me."

"My dearest Libby, I never went to Boston, nor do I know who you spoke to that day. I suspect your father's hand was on that call. I did drive to the Queen City and find us the fanciest honeymoon suite my fifty dollars could buy. I wanted our first night as husband and wife to symbolize how much—"

Libby sobbed. "Don't say any more. I can't bear this. All these lost years."

Mick dropped to his knees, taking the tissue from her slender fingers and dabbed her cheeks. "There now, my dearest. I won't ask you not to shed tears for us. I blubbered a night away when these letters appeared and learned we'd been cheated out of what was most precious—our love for one another." Mick stood and gently pulled Libby from her chair.

Her tears continued flowing as the dam erected long ago was breeched. "So much wasted time," she cried into Mick's shirt. "How stupid we've been." She let his arms wrap tightly around her and draw out her pain.

"Listen to me, Lib." His pet name for her returned. "Spending more time in the past will rob us of this moment. Shall we bury it all now? We've suffered long enough. What matters is now we know the truth."

"Yes, you're right," Libby replied. She stepped back, feeling a sense of peace around them. She glanced at the letters, full of wondering what Mick had written to her.

Mick kissed her cheek. "You need to read those. For now, that's all I can ask. I leave us in your tender care."

Libby managed to nod as she watched Mick leave her side. The familiar emptiness rushed in.

He stopped at the door and turned back to her. "I will wait for you like I always have."

Chapter 33

High tide returned *Seas the Day* to the marina before the sun had been swallowed by the horizon. Hopeful pelicans stood as sentinels next to fishermen cleaning their catch. Boats received a wash and lines were secured before their owners returned home to face Monday's unwelcome coming. Holding hands, Ben and Halley smiled at each other like the world was their oyster, and today it was. They joined the procession toward the marina's parking lot discussing details of Halley's design work and timetable. That topic rode with them home and to the bungalow's entrance.

Halley faced Ben, knowing she must devote the remainder of the evening to her novel. "This is my most favorite day since moving to Port Royal. I'm feeling so much gratitude and happiness for the doors that keep opening."

Ben nodded in agreement. "And how do you feel about our door opening?"

Halley stood on tiptoes and kissed him. "Like that."

"And I say again, I'm a goner."

"Yes, you're a goner, all right. I need you to go so I can write," Halley chuckled.

"Okay, but you're going to miss out on my cheddar popcorn and a new release movie DVD." Ben handed her the wet ball of clothes and grinned.

"You're a big tease. Now leave me to write. I'm mission-driven to finish the first draft and send it to my editor friend in Florida before I can begin working on these cool projects with you."

Ben's cell phone rang before he could reply.

Halley smiled, waved him off, and went inside. She scooped Éclair up in her arms and danced around the bungalow. "Halley Bowen has found a grand romance—well, at least a budding grand romance—and in less than two weeks. How incredible is that?" she asked her kitty. Halley reflected on the day's twists and turns that culminated in being with Ben. Merely thinking his name woke up a flutter.

Before returning to her manuscript, Halley wanted to share her happiness. First, an email to Beth with a full accounting, and then to Mr. Langdale, a condensed version focusing on the novel's progress and the design projects she'd accepted. The surprise of finding romance she'd save for his last paragraph, hoping this news pleased her benefactor. *Irene.* She must call Irene pronto. Halley knew Buttercup's owners worried about her leaving the security of her past life. Sharing the fresh direction her talents were taking her should help extinguish that concern. *Faith was such a beautiful noun.*

***

As Halley buckled her seatbelt to leave for her morning shift at the coffee shop, Ben tapped on her SUV's window.

"Good morning lovely Pixie, I have something for you." From behind his back, he produced a hot buttered biscuit wrapped in a napkin.

"Other than calling me that loathsome name, you've started my day darn near perfect with a buttermilk biscuit." Halley took a bite. "Yum."

"Pretty good, huh? I made them," Ben said proudly. "And for the record, I think Pixie fits. Ask Oliver." He tipped her nose. "See ya." Ben jogged over to talk to an approaching electrician.

Halley shook her head and drove off with her flutters. *Ridiculous man.*

The morning had gone eleven before the steady stream of customers moved on with their day, and Halley could put tables and chairs back in order. She felt happy thinking about the beach picnic with Sally and Tulip. She'd brought the makings for silly apples with her to work and stashed them in Deja's fridge. She'd endured all manner of teasing from Ginger about being ripe to have a gaggle of kids. She did want children, but a gaggle sounded like too many.

Halley's cell phone sounded from inside her purse. She motioned to Walker to take over. Thankfully, he'd returned to work that morning, full of stories about his sister and the new baby. Seeing the caller was Langdale, she darted to the alcove and put him on speaker while she folded dish towels. "Good morning Mr. Langdale. You must have read my last email report?"

"That I did, and I'd like to say I'm astonished by the speed you're executing the terms of the agreement." Sam paused and cleared his throat. "I'm especially amazed that you've found that grand passion. As my client's attorney, I'd appreciate some form of evidence that you and this man are keeping company. By the way, may I ask his name?"

"His name is Ben Shaw. The same man I managed to purchase the cottage and rent the bungalow from, if you recall? Look, Mr. Langdale, I can fully understand why you expect proof of this required romantic relationship. To stay in compliance with our agreement and the money coming to me, please email me what verification you need. I will try to get proof." Halley thought about Ben and the terms of this agreement. There was a bit more she needed to say. A noise from the office behind distracted her and she stopped. The noise abated and all was silent. Halley gave a little shrug.

"Let me think about that verification and get back to you," Langdale replied. "I certainly don't want to cause any suspicion or hardship."

"That's fine, and I appreciate the consideration. Mr. Langdale, this doesn't qualify as tangible proof, but I feel led to say something. If you told me I had to choose between having Ben Shaw in my life, or all the perks and monetary gain of this agreement, I'd pick Ben. As crazy as this sounds even to me, I've fallen for the guy. And love means far more to me than what's been offered."

"I see. Well, Ms. Bowen, you're a most determined young woman and have earned my respect. Your Ben is lucky to enjoy your affection. We shall speak again soon."

"Thank you, and I'll wait to hear what I'm to do next." Halley disconnected, realizing the truth of her words spoken to the attorney.

***

Halley enjoyed spending the afternoon with Sally and little Tulip. A rainbow-colored quilt spread on the beach became their picnic table and seats. They watched Tulip using a paper cup to build a dry moat and fortifications, fully engrossed in her sandcastle.

"Looks like she got Andy's construction gene," Halley observed.

"And her uncle's." Sally gazed at the ocean. "I hear you and Ben are seeing each other, and I want you to know I'm thrilled. You're exactly the kind of woman to break through my brother-in-law's barriers and bring happiness into his life."

"Wow, word travels with the speed of sound around here. What you said means a lot, though I admit Ben has kept me off-kilter since day one. I've struggled to—"

Sally's expression grew solemn. "Look, I don't know how much you've heard about their past, but Andy and Ben's mom left them standing outside social services in the town where they lived." Sally cleared her throat. "Can you believe it? She left them, Halley, and never looked back. Ben was older and remembers more, hurts more, hides more, but Andy's scared, too. Mick came along and played a major role in helping them chart a course with a future. He's taught them so much about honor, integrity, and the reward of hard work. He earned their trust. I love that man. How can I not? He brought Andy to me." Sally grabbed a fresh napkin and blew her nose.

Halley nodded. "I love Mick, too. I'd probably do most anything for that salty dog. You know, Sally, I'm sitting here unable to imagine the hurt, and of course, fear that Andy and Ben experienced as young boys."

"I know. They developed a strong bond that helped see them through living in countless foster homes. Anyway, you can better understand Ben's wariness to trust women until he met you. You've found yourself a forever kind of guy." Sally's face brightened. "You better not break his heart, or I will do serious harm to your person."

"I believe that." Halley grinned. She let the sand trickle through her fingers, weighing what to share with Sally. "I don't exactly have a stellar history picking the right guy. Since moving to Port, I've come to realize that I sought the wrong qualities in a man. I'd say yes to a date if they were ambitious, bright, and financially sound. Not anymore. It's like a portal opened when I moved here, and I see things anew."

Sally nodded. "And, I'm sure you see the goodness and kindness in Ben, which are rare commodities nowadays. He's solid."

"Believe me. I'm a self-proclaimed president of the Ben Shaw fan club. He's wonderful in all the ways I'd want a man wonderful. Ask my heart." Halley's cheeks flushed.

Sally's expression changed to playful. "Let's be honest here. We don't mind those Shaw boys' handsome faces one bit."

Halley laughed. "Not one bit." She reached into her tote. "Okay, enough about Ben and me. Should we make silly apples with Tulip? I've got three Granny Smith apples needing faces. I have raisins, marshmallows, and assorted edible features." Halley waved each plastic bag in the air.

"What a super fun and creative activity. Tulip's going to love making silly apples. Thank you for doing this. I want to say I'm so happy we've become friends.

"Let's toast." Halley held up her can of fizzy water and clanked Sally's. "To the sisterhood. Long may we wave."

Chapter 34

Halley steered for home after an afternoon of pure delight with Sally and Tulip. In the middle of naming her blessings, the cell phone rang.

"Hi, Irene. I bet you read my email about Ben and me."

"Why, yes, I did, but I'm calling for another reason too, which I'll get to in a sec. First, Joe and I are thrilled. You and Ben are a perfect couple and have so much in common, you're your building and design interests. I'd say you're on one fast track to settling in with us at Port Royal, which only proves destiny is alive and well," she declared.

"Golly, but I do like the idea of that destiny part. What's the other reason for your call? Let's see if destiny and I align," teased Halley.

"Oh, you do. I'm offering an invite you can't turn down. Mick's caught one of your favorite fish and dropped a few off at Buttercup. With strings, of course."

"Guessing I'd say you're serving snapper tonight, and Mick's wangled a dinner invitation for us," Halley supplied. "How I love that man. Wait. You did say yes to him?"

Irene chuckled. "Of course. Dinner's at seven and thankfully, the three couples staying with us announced this morning they'd arranged a dinner excursion. However, I do have one request."

"You're feeding me. Name it." Halley entered the bungalow.

"Bring Éclair to dine. Chaucer is pining for her, and I'm serving them snapper, too."

"I'll check with her, but I'm sure she's free," Halley joked. "See you soon, and Irene—"

"Skip it, kiddo. I know. Remember, you've become the daughter we never had. Seven sharp, as whoever they are say." Irene disconnected, laughing.

208

Cat carrier in the back, Halley climbed in the driver's side. The passenger door opened, and Ben materialized in the seat wearing a grin.

"You're driving, and I'm starving. Roll this vehicle, Ms. Bowen."

"Hold on. I'm heading over to—"

"I'm invited, too. Seems it pays to court you. Did you know Irene's making blackened snapper with smashed potatoes? Tulip and I love smashed potatoes."

"Do tell?" Halley volleyed, backing out of the driveway.

"Yes, I do tell, and I'm going to chum some extra potatoes for us to drop off to my niece, if you're agreeable." Ben noticed the carrier. "You're bringing Éclair?"

Halley nodded, grinning. "Seems she and Chaucer have a dinner date."

"Now, that's crazy even for Port Royal hospitality." Ben shook his head. "Moving along. I hear the beach picnic was 'many funs' according to Tulip."

"Yep, I had 'many funs' with Sally and Tulip."

"Did you talk about my many, many sterling qualities?" Ben asked in amusement.

"Sure did. All three of them. Tell me about your day." Halley waited her turn at a four-way stop.

"My day? For starters, I made the drawing changes Libby wanted and thought of you. I visited two worksites and thought of you. I grabbed lunch with Oliver and talked about you. I like to mix things up."

"So I'm learning." Halley's body hummed listening to his voice.

At the next stop sign, Ben made his move, ignoring a meowing Éclair. Guiding Halley's chin in his direction, he leaned across the console to bestow a tender kiss. "Ignore her. She's jealous."

Halley grinned, adoring the "go with your feelings" Ben. "Oh my gosh. It's two minutes until seven. We can't be late or no dinner. It's the rule." She gunned the SUV, pulling up to Buttercup with seconds to spare.

"Well, I gotta say the last few blocks were a blur," Ben chided. He took Éclair's carrier in one hand and Halley's hand in his other. "Ladies, let's go eat."

***

Irene chose to serve the meal in bright yellow bowls sitting on buttercup-flowered placemats with matching cloth napkins. A crystal vase held stalks of fresh greenery and served as the centerpiece. The pitcher of raspberry iced tea made the rounds before the conversation revved up. Good spirits sat with the five people at Buttercup's dining table.

As they finished eating, Halley couldn't help feeling sadness that Mick lacked a mate. With a heart as big as the Mississippi, why was there no special lady for him? It didn't make sense. He was a catch. Halley dropped her head to hide her pun amusement. She stole a peek at her watch and felt the waiting manuscript's tug.

Ben gave her a look that said he understood her need to write. He placed his napkin next to the empty bowl. "Irene and Joe, this has been a treat for me, and dinner was great."

"Hey, buster, I brought the fish. Where's *my* thank you?" Mick teased.

Ben reached over and popped Mick on the shoulder. "I was getting to you."

The group laughed and snagged a brownie from the tray Irene passed.

Halley jumped in. "Anyway, I add my thanks to Ben's. As far as I'm concerned, the best meals and company in all of Port originate at the Buttercup table." She scooted her chair back. "Will you all forgive me if I drag Ben off with me? I vowed to write a few hours tonight."

"There's not a thing to forgive," Joe chimed in. "We're all looking forward to reading that story of yours."

Irene rolled with laughter. "Joe, it's a romance."

Mick rose to the occasion. "Well, I don't know about Joe here, but I could stand to learn some tricks on that subject."

"Oh, Joe would definitely benefit from some new moves," Irene interjected, giggling.

"With that info out of the way, I think this is a good time for me to beg a take-home container of those smashed potatoes for Tulip. They're her new favorite, after silly apples, Sally tells me."

Irene hopped up and returned with a small container. "Then you must deliver this to Tulip on your drive home. She's such a sweetie pie. Now, hurry, you two."

Halley and Ben said their goodnights and went in search of Éclair and the ever-amorous Chaucer.

***

With the delivery to Tulip accomplished, Halley turned onto the bungalow's street. Having Ben next to her felt natural. Halley sensed he was studying her and felt warm inside. She glanced Ben's way. "Stop staring. What are you thinking about?"

"Me? Right now, I'm envisioning us doing Libby's project and stealing away in the afternoons on *Seas the Day*. Like my thinking?" Ben reached over and touched Halley's hair.

"It has promise." Halley cut the engine.

"*We* have promise." Ben unfastened his seatbelt, opening the passenger door. "I know you want to write, so let's say goodnight." Standing outside, he wrapped his arms around Halley, smelling the hint of jasmine in her hair. He sighed. "I'm such a goner."

"So, you've said." Halley released her arms from around Ben's neck and stepped back, presenting a grin. "Now, please take your handsome mug to your digs so that this writer can finish the first draft of her novel." Ben headed toward his place.

When Halley reached her porch, she stole a glance and watched the office lights go off downstairs. "I'm not sure who's the bigger goner."

Éclair gave a soft meow.

"You, too?"

Chapter 35

Halley brought her cup of hibiscus tea to the porch rocker and set an early morning rhythm of slow and peaceful to mirror Port Royal's vibe. Jettisoning city life was proving her smartest move ever. Her benevolent benefactor had unlocked the door to countless blessings. If she allowed her mind free rein, she'd think the last weeks a hallucination or some dream resulting from work exhaustion. Halley pinched her arm. "Yep, I'm awake and flirting with deliriously happy." She watched the major source of her 'happy' jog to his truck while juggling a clipboard and rolled up drawings.

"Morning, Pixie. I'm already late. Call you later," Ben hollered.

She returned his wave and vowed to break him from calling her Pixie. A grin broke through. "Ridiculous man."

Halley's cell phone rang. "Morning, Ginger."

"I'm calling with glad tidings. Uncle Walker's shown me countless new photos of his niece. And, now, he's busy baking the cookies."

Halley chuckled. "Guess his niece captured his heart. That's sweet." She thought about the effect Tulip had on Ben and awarded Walker a gold star for his caring. "So, what time do you need me?"

"How about ten? That gives you a little time for writing. Get that story finished. I'm bustin' to say my best friend is a published author and point to the display of books at Deja for them to buy. How's that sound?"

"I like the sound of ten o'clock and the book promotion. See you soon." Halley took her empty mug inside. She grabbed the laptop, fretting that the story's ending kept eluding her. Novel gridlock was knocking on her creative door.

***

Ben looked up from his seat in the corner of the coffee shop. He saw Cara enter Deja Brew and approach the counter. Ginger pulled a face but appeared to summon a polite smile from somewhere.

Cara tossed her hair and awakened the fake smile Ben knew so well. "I'm so glad you're still on summer hours. To start my day without a caramel latte, well, that's simply—"

"I'm pleased we're here to save you. What size?" Ginger's hand stayed suspended over the cups while Cara fiddled with her cell phone.

"Small," Cara replied, absently typing a text.

Ben stood up and approached Cara. "Okay, I'm here. What do you have to say that warranted me canceling a meeting?"

Cara took her coffee. "You're about to find out. Order your espresso and I'll see you at your table." Cara sauntered away.

Ben turned to order another coffee. "Could I have the same again, please? A no-frills large black coffee?" Ben tossed a few dollars on the counter and headed toward the waiting Cara. He sensed trouble brewing.

"Join me. You're looking dashing as always." Cara sipped her latte.

"Look, I've got a slammed day. Can we get to why I'm here?" Ben pushed the memory of his and Cara's last encounter away and made a stab at friendliness. "I don't mean to sound rude, but I'm—"

Cara touched his hand. "I understand. I'll suspend the niceties and get to the point. I overheard a phone conversation that I believe you'll find interesting between Halley and a man. And, what I'm about to say proves what I thought of her all along. She's an imposter, a put-on, a fake, a pretender—"

Ben blew out a breath. "Enough of the adjectives. What are you talking about? What conversation?"

"I'm talking about Halley telling this man something about she'd fulfilled their agreement by finding a man to engage in a romance. She even gave him your name. Your full name. Ben Shaw. There was talk of payment and other compensation. The whole conversation sounded sketchy, and clearly, Halley is involved in something improper."

Ben rubbed his chin, trying to absorb Cara's words. "Halley's great. She—"

"You don't know anything about her. She all of a sudden moves here and pretends to be all whatever. Oh, Ben, I hate to say this, but you've been duped." Cara reached over and stroked Ben's forearm and conjured tears.

Ben pulled his arm away and gulped coffee. His mind felt frazzled. None of what Cara said lined up with the Halley he knew. Still, there had to be something to the story.

"Look, no doubt this news is upsetting, but I'm here for you," Cara said encouragingly. "We've known each other for a long time, and I'm simply telling you what I heard." Cara's expression brightened. "I have a wonderful idea. Why don't we go out in the boat later? Get your mind off things."

Ben ignored the invitation. "This doesn't make any sense. Why would Halley need to find a chump to get involved in a relationship with? And get paid? What's the motive? Cara, you must have misunderstood."

"I don't know the particulars of this deception, but I didn't misunderstand. English is, after all, my first language." She softened her tone. "Listen to me, Ben. Because I care so much, I brought this information to you. I don't want to see you hurt. My advice is cut things off now, and for goodness sakes get her out of the bungalow. Who knows what someone like Halley Bowen is capable of doing— assuming that's even her name?" She stood and deposited a kiss on his cheek. "I've got to dash. Go remedy your problem. Call me in a bit, and we'll go out on the boat. I'm willing to forgive you. Let's get back to where we were before that scheming Halley showed up."

***

Cara, wearing a Cheshire Cat grin, flounced past Ginger, who was waiting on the next table. Ben followed Cara, looking stricken to the core. Ginger frowned, sensing trouble. "Walker, please take the helm. I need to make a call." Ginger headed toward the kitchen. She dialed her boyfriend.

"Oliver here. How can I help you?"

"It's Ginger, you dope. I fear we've got trouble in Cupidville. Cara just exited the shop looking all smug, and Ben flew out of here with his tail feathers on fire."

Oliver chuckled. "Maybe Cara and Ben disagreed?"

"No, didn't you hear me? Cara looked all self-righteous. Like she swallowed a canary," Ginger explained. "That woman lives to create drama."

"Man, you've got a thing for birds this morning. Tail feathers. Canaries." Oliver laughed again.

"Will you please get serious? I'm telling you that Cara has stirred some hornet's nest, and I bet it stings Halley." Ginger noticed Walker hadn't washed the cookie sheet but tossed it in the sink.

"Now you're onto hornets and their behaviors. Who can keep up?" Oliver teased. "Honeypie, I've got well-heeled buyers walking in the door. Relax. Ben knows his mind. Let this situation, if there is even a situation, play out. It may be nothing."

"Okay, I guess, but my instincts tell me something is afoot. Go sell the Taj."

***

Ben spotted Halley in the street, trying to park. *If I wasn't so upset, I'd be laughing. It's déjà vu all over again*, he thought, in the voice of his favorite baseball legend, Yogi Berra. He crossed the street and bent down to her open SUV's window.

"Hop out."

"No. We're not doing this again." Halley grinned, recalling their first meeting. "I've only attempted to park once so far. I get another chance. I feel lucky this time."

Ben ignored the words. He couldn't ignore how looking at her melted him each time. Right now, his hurt trumped all other emotions. He opened the door. "Let me park the blasted vehicle. We need to talk."

His tone clued Halley in that something had changed between them again. She nodded and stepped out, waiting on the sidewalk. Ben parked the car expertly and got out, tossing her the keys.

"Let's walk over to the gazebo where we can sit down." Ben took a few steps and stopped. "Are you coming?"

"No. You didn't ask me, and I have to get to work. And, P.S., I don't like your mood."

"You want me to say what I have to say on the sidewalk? Fine. Here goes. Someone overheard you talking to a man on the phone yesterday about some agreement you entered into that involved duping me into having a romantic relationship with you and who knows what else. And, all for money. Money, Halley. I don't understand what you're about here, and I don't want to. I trusted you. I thought we had a future, and you deceived me." Ben felt like his heart was going to explode in his chest.

"Ben, I can explain—"

"Did you or did you not enter into some kind of agreement that's now involved me? Yes or no." Ben's eyes sparked with anger.

"Yes, but I can explain," Halley pleaded.

"No, you can't, because I'm not going to stand here and give you the chance to pretend you care. The cottage is yours, but not my bungalow. Be out by tonight." Ben took one more look at the woman who was his everything and walked away.

Chapter 36

Libby sat at her desk, pondering whether to call Sam Langdale. Making a decision, she punched in the numbers. Her happiness increased with each ring.

"Hello to my favorite client," Sam said.

"And a warm hello to my favorite attorney. Do you have a moment? I've made a decision that requires your attendance, and I hope you'll agree." Libby jotted a few notes as reminders.

Sam left the firm's coffee maker and returned to his office. "All right, I'm in a confidential mode ready to do your latest bidding."

Libby chuckled, appreciating Sam's long devotion. "Let's release Halley from her side of the agreement. After seeing her with Ben, I know they are well suited. I will, of course, honor my part by continuing to pay her expenses for the rest of the year. I do want the cottage's deed put in her name at the closing. We both know she's met the requirements, though I confess to marveling at the girl's speed of delivery, especially finding romance."

"I'm in agreement with your wishes. And the funny part is I've come to understand, thanks to our Halley, that a grand romance doesn't always require a long time to germinate." Sam tapped his pen on a legal pad.

Mick's face came into Libby's mind. "No, it doesn't, but to use your planting analogy, time has the power to blight that grand romance. Anyway, I've enjoyed getting to know Halley, and as a result, we've developed a friendship and a soon-to-be working relationship. I've grown quite fond of her, Sam."

"You've never allowed yourself to get involved personally in the past. I grant you Miss Halley is a most special young woman. I knew that truth at our first meeting. She'll be hard to top going forward, but that's not for today's discussion. I'll prepare the release and refresh the agreement reflecting your wishes and email it to Halley within the hour. She can execute the documents with her bank's notary. Simple enough. I've no doubt she'll ask again if there's any way she might thank you? Since you've developed this friendship, do you want to make an exception this time as a benefactor and reveal yourself to Halley?"

"No, Sam, and for the reason you stated. Friendship. I treasure my budding relationship with Halley, and if she knew I was her benefactor, it would surely change things. I don't want her feeling beholden. I want to leave things as they are. We shall keep the benefactor's 'secret gift' door closed as we always do."

"Your assessment makes sense. Is there anything else you'd like me to do?" Sam waved his paralegal to enter.

Libby smiled. "Not until another quester is revealed to me."

She rang off. Mrs. Cookson appeared with the tea tray. "Miss Libby, would you like me to pour a cup? I picked fresh spearmint from the garden and brewed with the green tea."

"How lovely. Thank you." Libby knew Mrs. Cookson would stand in front of her until next Christmas, waiting for a compliment. Taking a sip, Libby rewarded her with, "Mmm."

"As you wish, ma'am. Ring if you'd like another pot." Mrs. Cookson paused at the door.

"Yes? Is there something else?" Libby removed her reading glasses.

"Well, Andy and those nice boys of his wanted to know if they'd ever get any more of my scones?" Mrs. Cookson simpered. Her ordinarily, rosy cheeks grew deeper in color.

Libby hid her amusement. "I'm leaving that decision up to you. If you want to bake them scones daily, I take no issue with that. The kitchen is your domain. I'm sure any of your confections would get a welcome from those hungry men. I fear you've spoiled them horribly."

"I fear so too, ma'am. They're a nice lot." Mrs. Cookson closed the study door.

Mick's box of letters stared at Libby. She'd read all but one. The white sealed envelope contrasted the yellowed ones, cluing her the contents were scribed recently. She touched the envelope with a gentleness of spirit and blamed her hesitation on fear, but fear of what? That answer hid deep within her heart. Did she feel brave in this present moment? Time had proven her enemy. Her recent words to Sam returned. Time had blighted her grand romance with Mick.

Libby slit the envelope open and feeling a renewed sense of empowerment as she read Mick's words.

Chapter 37

Halley surveyed the bungalow. Any vestige of her presence now removed, she scooped up Éclair. "Well, at least you're getting a happy ending. Chaucer is waiting, and Irene and Joe have our old rooms ready." Tears had streamed with a steadiness since Ben walked out of her life less than two hours ago. A lifetime. An ache that could only be felt and not described had taken up residence where the flutters once lived.

Numb and confused, she'd scarcely recalled going to Ginger and asking for the day off. Ginger had explained what she'd seen when Ben and Cara chatted then hugged her and whispered something about things working out. Somehow, Halley had managed through her weeping to call Irene and beg a room. More lucid now, she hoped Irene hadn't moved a guest out. Fresh sobs broke through as Halley and Éclair closed the door on what she had come so close to experiencing—her one and only grand romance.

***

Irene and Joe insisted on helping Halley settle back into her rooms at Buttercup. Neither one asked any questions. They didn't need to. Halley knew her sad story was written across her face.

"There now. You're all settled back with us." Irene closed the dresser drawer and leaned against it. "Éclair's having lunch. What about you, Halley? Let me make you something. Name it."

Halley dabbed at her tears yet again. Her eyes felt like someone had sprinkled salt in them. She must look a fright, but what did it matter? "I'm not hungry. What would I do without you two?" Halley sniffed. "You and Joe are my haven. I'm so sorry to cause you so much trouble." She felt the waterworks returning.

Irene wrapped her arms around Halley. "I keep telling you that you're the daughter we never had, so hush that trouble talk.

Whatever is going on, time will take care of it. Wait and see. Now, missy, what you feel next is to enjoy one of my world-famous BLTs."

"World famous, huh?" Halley rallied for Irene.

"Well, maybe Buttercup famous?"

Halley stared out the window. "You know, Irene. I'm going to take my laptop and hang out with nature and the bay. I'm discovering that spending time amongst the trees and fauna has a way of healing. Looking at the bay calms my spirit. I need both right now and know where to find it."

"That's an excellent plan. We all need a place to find peace within. Stop by the kitchen on your way out. I'll have that sandwich wrapped and ready. You may not be hungry now, but that'll change."

***

What did the afternoon have to say to her? Halley paused in the marina's parking lot, waiting for the answer. She gazed up at the blue sky, wondering why a dark cloud hadn't formed over her yet. Why were the birds so chirpy? She grabbed her tote and trekked to the daisy bench, whose color managed to contribute to the conspiring happy theme surrounding her. "Not working," Halley proclaimed, looking skyward. Sighing, she pulled the laptop from her bag.

"I felt this inexplicable pull to visit our bench, and now I see why. Hello, Halley." Libby sat down, her face awash with emotion.

Lost in her inner turmoil, Halley attempted a smile of welcome. "Hi, Miss Libby. Yes, it seems our enchanted bench has brought us together again. However, I should come with a warning today. I'm lousy company so you might want to rethink conversing with me." Halley grabbed a clean tissue from her pocket. She felt the next deluge gearing up.

"Seems we share an emotional plight visited upon each of us this day." Libby waved a pale blue polka dot handkerchief. She took a long glance at Halley. "I declare you the winner of the most puffed eyes, which means you share first. Worry not, I have another handkerchief should your tissue supply run out."

Halley caught a glimpse of *Seas the Day* tied at the dock. Three tissues later, she managed to blurt out what happened earlier with Ben, including the starring role she suspected Cara played by twisting the conversation she'd eavesdropped on with Sam and Halley. "I trust you with my secret, Libby. I'd trust you with anything, and I'm so grateful you're in my life, a mess though it is right now." Halley leaned over and hugged her surprised seatmate.

"Ditto on all you said, including our lives seeming a mess," Libby replied, her voice warm with compassion. "So, here you sit feeling in tatters, but I sense this is but a temporary—"

"Libby, he walked away with my heart. Now I have this emptiness, this hole. I don't have a clue about what I should do." Halley touched her chest.

"I understand too well how you feel. Please take these earnest words inside. Ben may have walked away with your heart, but not your faith that things can still work out. Your faith belongs only to you. Draw on it now, Halley."

"I know you're right, but what chokes me is that Ben didn't trust my feelings for him, or give me a chance to tell him my side of the story. He didn't trust us and what we've found in each other." Halley stared off, allowing anger to enter her emotional pool. "Boy, he's blown it."

Libby grinned. "Somehow, I doubt that." Her expression changed to a resoluteness. "You're all aflutter about trust. Ben's mishandling of things reflects the degree of his feelings for you. Now, I'm going to ask you an important question. Do you trust in Ben and how you both feel for each other?" Libby paused, allowing the message to penetrate. "Solid relationships travel a two-way street."

"I did until he pulled this stunt and whiplashed me again."

"And, now, after this misunderstanding, you no longer trust Ben or the love that's found you?"

Halley stood and walked a few yards, releasing the anger to find her truth. The question's irony wasn't lost on her. She returned to sit. "Libby Wellington, you are without a doubt a sage extraordinaire. You are making me realize I was letting my mind dictate yet again, and I have my answer for you: I do trust Ben and what we feel for each other. I've never felt this way about another man. Ever. I do trust us, though I can't see how this gets fixed." Halley stuffed the tissues in her tote. She didn't need them or her tears.

"And, that, my dear, proves your love is the enduring kind and worth pledging. What's your next step? Think about taking only one step. What is it?" Libby's relief was evident in her face.

"Hmm, my next step? A wise woman, I like to call my fairy godmother, has told me when you don't know what to do, wait for a next step to be revealed. I'm going to take that advice and stay surrounded by these daisies until I get a nudge or something. That I can do."

Libby patted Halley's hand. "That you can most certainly do."

Halley took a few deep, cleansing breaths. She repositioned herself and sat cross-legged facing her fairy godmother. "I'm temporarily collected, thanks to you. Now, I believe it's your turn to share what's brought you to our daisy bench. I don't have your wisdom, but I care for you. You're a treasure. Share with me."

"You're such a beautiful young woman inside and out. I'm going to tell you my long-held secret. You see, I find myself trusting you implicitly as well." Libby touched Halley's shoulder. "In a past chat, I alluded to someone who was my first and only love."

"Yes, I remember and confess to wondering about this mysterious man."

"That man was Mick Duffy." Libby nodded more to herself than Halley.

"Our Captain Mick? No," Halley said, trying to process this bombshell.

Libby nodded. "Yes, the same Mick. Many, many years ago, he and I fell in love, and tried and failed to keep it from my father. You see, he didn't approve of Mick's lack of social standing. We'd planned to marry in secret on a certain day. Mick had arranged things with a minister he knew, only my father somehow learned of this and sabotaged the plan by telling us each lies about the other. He was most clever in his ruse."

Halley sat speechless, not wanting to interrupt with questions.

"The short version of our saga is in that box you passed to me. It had letters from Mick. My father had hidden them away, and I never read them until now." Libby swallowed back her tears. "They proved Mick's love and more. He'd shown up at church that day trusting I'd be there. I wasn't. I took my shame of falling for a man who I'd been convinced betrayed me, and I fled to Europe. Now I discover that Mick never betrayed me. That failure belonged to my deceptive, overbearing father." Tears trickled down Libby's cheeks. "You see what's happened? Mick and I wasted all these years believing the lies told to us. We didn't trust our love enough. Do you understand why I asked you to find your inner truth about Ben?"

Halley's mouth hung open as she attempted to absorb this newest version of a tale of star-crossed lovers. She nodded her head. "I understand. My gosh, what an incredible story. Tell me, how did Mick come to find these letters?"

A smile graced Libby's face. "A workman of Ben and Andy's discovered the hidden box while tearing out old shelving and gave them to Mick."

"Wow. Is there more?" Halley reached for Libby's hand.

"Goodness, yes. You see, that box has brought Mick and me to this place of realization. We have all those lost years we can't get back." Libby looked away.

"No." Halley sighed, feeling the heaviness of their loss.

"When I told you that I understood what having a man walk away with your heart felt like, you know now that I do."

Halley nodded. "I sense there's more to say about the letters."

"Yes, which brings me to why I seek your counsel. There was an additional letter tucked at the bottom of the stack. A letter Mick wrote to me a few days ago and added to the batch." Libby held the letter with trembling hands. "He wants me to meet him at the church in three days and take our marriage vows. The vows we never made to another, but instead remained tucked away with our love for each other." Libby burst into tears.

Halley scooted closer and held her friend. "Am I right these are tears of happiness? 'Cause they need to be. Mick is beyond wonderful, like you. I swear I adore you both to distraction. Tears of happiness, yes?"

"Yes happiness, but I'm worried it's too late for—"

"Hold on. Too late for love? Libby, you know that this type of enduring love doesn't mark time. You and Mick belong together. You deserve to grab every moment of happiness out there. Don't waste another minute." Halley hesitated and then smiled. "My final words on this subject are get thee to the church on time."

Libby chuckled and then sat quietly. After a few moments ticked by, her face lit up. "Yes, I think I will get me to the church this time, on time." Libby gave a determined nod. "But first, I need to tell him how I feel."

"Excellent." Halley's expression grew wistful. "You know Port Royal folks may grow hoarse from shouting congratulations to their most beloved two residents. And to think, I know the secret before the announcement hits the paper." Halley tossed her head in mock flaunting.

Libby's laugh sounded giddy as a young girl's. "Thanks for taking me to the humorous side."

Halley squinted. "Well, well, I see Mick's boat is pulling into the marina." She gave Libby a gentle shove. "Get off this bench. He's waited long enough for your love."

Libby rose and gave a tentative nod.

She watched Libby walk toward Mick, taking her future *I do* with her.

Halley's melancholy washed back in, but she wasn't budging even if all the cows in the Carolinas came home at once.

She'd sit right where she was and wait for—something.

Chapter 38

The needle on Ben's emotional compass had spun him in circles since leaving Halley distraught and standing on the sidewalk. He'd walked block after block trying to make sense of Cara's words only to return to the coffee shop's door where his world had imploded. He'd reached for the door handle three times, then released it and stood back. He had believed his true north pointed toward Halley Bowen until this morning. Now, he knew nothing.

"Are you going in or simply using the door as a workout?" Walker asked, arms laden with supplies. "If it's in, would you mind holding the door for me?"

"Sure. I've got it," Ben said, and with a heavy sigh, followed Walker inside to the coffee bar.

Ginger glanced up. "My gosh, you look worse than the stray mutt I saw Sally and Tulip loading into their vehicle this morning." Ginger shoved a coffee toward Ben. "Let me guess. Trouble in Cupidville, and you've come to ask for my exceptionally fine advice?"

Ben glared at her.

Ginger took a read on Ben. "So okay, I'm going with that look means sort of a yes." She tapped her forehead. "I've got it. The poisoned-tongued Cara told you something about Halley that lit your tail feathers. At least that's the image I had earlier seeing you leave. I told Oliver—"

"Who speaketh my name?" Oliver approached, putting his arm around Ginger. "Man, he looks rough. Not talking, huh?"

"Not yet, unless you count a groan when I said Halley's name."

"You were right. Cupidville woes." Oliver poured himself an iced tea and parked on the stool next to Ben.

"Will you both shut up about Cupidville? I came seeking peace and understanding, and what do I get?"

Ginger jumped in. "You get sound advice once you tell us what's happened. Either spill it or go sit in the corner and mope."

Oliver grinned. "She's good at that tough love stuff."

"Okay fine. Cara told me she overheard a conversation between Halley and a man discussing some monetary arrangement if she got me interested in her. There's more to it, but right now, I can't think straight. Cara said I'd been duped. I'm an idiot to have fallen for Halley."

"Hold on, mister. Are you telling me that you'd believe that conniving Cara over Halley, who I might add, is the most wonderful person I know?" Ginger huffed.

"Well, explain this. How come Halley didn't bother to correct me when I told her what Cara said?" Ben rubbed his neck.

"Man, oh man, this sounds pretty—" Oliver felt Ginger's hands cover his mouth.

"Not now, Oliver. You're not helping." Ginger turned to Ben, her freckles popping out. "You've been duped all right, but by Cara. It so happens, you big dope, I heard that same conversation. Halley was in the hall talking on her cell with the speaker on."

"Well?" Ben and Oliver said in unison.

"What Cara neglected to tell you is Halley told the guy that given a choice of having you in her life or whatever this windfall requires of her, she'd choose you, Ben Shaw, current moron of Port Royal. I heard Halley say as proof of her feelings for you, she'd gladly give it all back. Whatever 'it' encompasses, and that 'it' is none of our business, buster," Ginger said emphatically.

"Wow. The woman has never called *me* that many names in so few sentences. Mister, dope, moron, and buster." Oliver hugged a fired-up Ginger. "I like you feisty. Goes with the hair and freckles."

Ginger's expression changed to amusement. "I've got a customer. Why don't you wrestle with what I told you, Ben? See if you can get a stray neuron to fire in that—"

"Enough. I get the picture." Ben took his coffee and went to stare out the window. He'd made a mess of things with Halley for the umpteenth time and this time because he listened to Cara. He'd managed to turn his fear of being hurt on an undeserving Halley. The same Halley who'd been willing to take a chance on his flawed self. This was why he'd always avoided emotional attachments. She'd been willing to give up something significant to share her life with him. He deserved the censure Ginger laid on him unless he made a move.

Ben knew what he needed to do.

"He's back and looking better," Oliver announced.

"Where's Halley?" Ben asked.

Ginger puffed up. "I'm not telling. You don't deserve her, and she doesn't deserve you, for obvious reasons." Ginger motioned for Walker to deliver a tray of drinks.

Ben turned to Oliver with a raised eyebrow. "You two share everything. You tell me where Halley has gone."

"Sorry, man, I guess I gotta act mad at you, too." Oliver shrugged and disappeared down the hallway.

Torment chased Ben. Halley must hate him. *He* hated him. What if she'd returned to Charlotte? How would he ever find her there? His chest ached, and his throat felt like it was in a vise. This is what a pint-size Pixie had done to him. Oliver came back from the hallway and plopped down next to him on the barstool.

When Ginger turned her back, Oliver winked and slipped a piece of paper to Ben and whispered, "Go make things right. You and Halley are meant for each other. Do whatever it takes to convince her you're worth the risk."

Ben read the folded paper and slapped Oliver on the back. "I owe you."

Chapter 39

Buttercup's flower gardens presented a "many splendored thing" as Ben turned onto the driveway weaving around guest's parked vehicles. He'd always admired the property and its owners' friendly style of hospitality. He walked toward the kitchen's side entrance. At least Halley hadn't moved back to Charlotte. Yet. Irene and Joe had provided her a haven once again, thanks to his imbecilic actions.

Joe caught sight of Ben. He wore a somber expression. "Word is you're in the doghouse." He opened the door. "Come on inside."

"Thanks, Joe. I guess by sundown, every person in Port will know what an idiot I am."

"I think that depends on what you plan to do next. How can I help?" Joe asked.

Ben glanced around. "Oliver told me Halley is staying here. I came to try to fix things between us. Is she around?"

"She's here, but not here now if that makes sense?"

Ben nodded. "Do you know where she went? Did she say anything?"

Joe scratched his head. "Seems like I heard her tell Irene something about taking her laptop to write at a peaceful place. Sorry, that's all I've got for you."

"Thanks. I think I might know where she went. Wish me luck. I've got a lot of crow to eat."

Joe chuckled. "You're a big enough fellow to handle that bowl. *Bon appetit.*"

***

Halley sat deep in thought on the bench, watching the boats go chugging by. *Around me the world continues*, she mused sadly. *No one knows my heart is broken and yet—I still have hope. Hope that things can still be the way they were supposed to be.*

A beloved voice interrupted her reverie.

"I'm looking for a pixie, but not just any pixie. My Pixie is pint-sized with the most amazing aqua eyes. I'm told from reliable sources that she has a forgiving heart. Do you by any chance know her?"

Halley glanced up, joy leaping wildly in her heart. "She's been here waiting."

Ben's face lit up with hope. "Yeah? May I?" he asked, pointing to the daisy bench. "I'm counting on its charms."

Halley gave a slight nod and stared out into the distance. Ben sat quietly, gazing across the sea. When he spoke again, his tone was wistful. "I bet you didn't know that I built this bench. I didn't know at the time it was destined to get painted this glowing yellow and would be festooned with daisies." The tenseness in his face relaxed.

"That I believe," Halley said with a small smile. Deep inside, she loved the fact Ben had been responsible for this enchanted bench and all the people with dreams who sat upon it.

"Right. Well, here's something I bet you don't know. The idea for the bench came from Port Royal's benefactor, Libby Wellington, who donates to any cause she deems worthy. I'm told sometimes her gifts come anonymously. Anyway, I learned Libby felt the daisy bench invited the unexpected, but in a good way. I'm counting on her being right about that." Ben grew quiet.

Halley's throat tightened. "That makes sense. I wonder—" Her voice trailed off, and she turned to face Ben, her heart lightening. "Oh, the benefactor is right about this bench. The benefactor's right about a lot of things."

Ben frowned, looking puzzled by Halley's cryptic words and response. "I'm not sure I understand—"

"That's okay. Do you have anything else riveting to discuss? I need to work on my novel," Halley murmured.

Please Ben, tell me we're still together. Bench, make it come true.

"Look, I made a mess of things this morning. I've made a mess of a lot of things with us. I acted like an idiot. I am an idiot," Ben blurted. "I'm sorry. Sorry that I listened to Cara and didn't give you a chance to set me straight. I'm sorry that I needed to get set straight. Ginger did a stellar job of straightening me out. She spared me no kindness, and I have Oliver as a witness. I think my ego is permanently deflated." Ben paused.

"Remind me to thank Ginger," Halley said as her spirit soared and took flight.

Thank you, bench. Thank you.

Ben expression turned solemn. "I should have trusted in you—the woman who stole my heart the day I took over her SUV. You're beautiful, and you're honest. I know how much you care about others and how easy it is for others to care about you. I'm not going to ask anything about this 'agreement.' I trust it's something good like you. You'll tell me if and when you're ready, and I'm cool with that. I swear, Halley."

"The trust is appreciated. I can tell you the confidential agreement, and its secret gifts are indeed 'good and high-minded' by the giver. My gratitude will live forever." Halley took Ben's hand. "One day soon I'll tell you all about how I wound up here, but not today. That story needs seasoning, like our relationship." She squeezed his hand. "Back to us. That's what matters most."

Ben reached forward and tilted Halley's chin with two fingers. "You're amazing in all the ways that matter to me. I can't undo what's happened, but I can promise you I'll never doubt you again, or what I feel for you."

"What do you feel for me, Ben?" She held her breath.

Ben reached for Halley's hand. "The kind of love I never expected to find. The forever kind. And I'm wondering what you feel? I mean, could you—do you want forever with me?"

"Hang on a sec." Halley laughed softly and reached for her laptop to begin typing.

Ben stared at her in disbelief. "Are you kidding me? I declared my undying love, I'm waiting to hear if you feel the same, and you want to type? You're killing me here. What are you writing?"

Halley grinned and closed the laptop as she turned to him. "I typed the happily ever after ending to my story...our story. You ridiculous man, don't you know that I love you, too?"

"I know now." Ben pulled her closer. "By the way, your story ending still needs something."

Halley felt the flutters return. "Oh yeah? What?"

"The kissing scene."

"You're right." She wrapped her arms around Ben and their lips came together in a forever kiss.

Sometimes, Halley thought with a contented sigh, reality *was* better than fiction.

ABOUT THE AUTHOR

Tonya is moved by humor and narratives that have an effect on readers. She's enthusiastic about crafting stories with beguiling characters, adding dashes of snappy humor, and engaging dialogue that leaves her fingerprint on each page.

From Tonya's favorite porch chair gazing at a tranquil mountain lake, came the nudge to write her first novel, and from her beach chair she got the idea for a cozy series. She confesses a newfound respect for a chair's ability to motivate a writer. She now chases her writing joy from the mountains to the seashore.

Her fiction and non-fiction stories are published in numerous anthologies, e-magazines, local press, and literary magazines. She is a member of Poets and Writers.

Connect with Tonya:
Webstite: www.tonyawrites.com
goodreads.com/author/show/18266687.Tonya_Penrose
Twitter: @TonyaWrites

www.BOROUGHSPUBLISHINGGROUP.com

If you enjoyed this book, please write a review. Our authors appreciate the feedback, and it helps future readers find books they love. We welcome your comments and invite you to send them to info@boroughspublishinggroup.com. Follow us on Facebook, Twitter and Instagram, and be sure to sign up for our newsletter for surprises and new releases from your favorite authors.

Are you an aspiring writer? Check out www.boroughspublishinggroup.com/submit and see if we can help you make your dreams come true.